D0869189

Bittersweet

True North #1

By Sarina Bowen

Part One

July

A fruit is a vegetable with looks and money. Plus, if you let fruit rot, it turns into wine, something Brussels sprouts never do.

–P.J. O'Rourke

Chapter One

Tuxbury Vermont

Griffin

"Griffin?"

My mother sat down across from me at the big farmhouse table as I chewed the last bite of her home-smoked applewood bacon. My farmhand and I had already finished Vermont-cheddar omelets and homemade bread with butter from our own cows.

Breakfast had been great, but what Mom said next was even better. "I found you some more seasonal help."

My coffee mug paused on its way to my mouth. "Seriously?"

"I did. And he starts today."

"You'd better not be teasing." We were always short-staffed at this time of year, when the grass grew so fast you could practically watch it lengthen, and the bugs waged a full-scale war against my apple trees.

It wasn't even nine o'clock in the morning, and my farmhand and I had already worked for hours. At dawn we'd milked several dozen cows in two different barns. We always came in for a nice breakfast after the milking, but then it was back to work. For the next eight hours we'd tackle a to-do list of projects and repairs as long as a country mile.

Mom's promise of a new employee was music to my ears. I lowered the mug to our dining table and met her gaze. But when I spotted her uncharacteristically tentative expression, I felt the first prickle of worry. Maybe I wasn't going to like the sound of her new hire.

"Angelo called last night," she said.

Oh, hell. Now I knew where this was going. Angelo was a lovely man who attended our Catholic church a couple towns away in Colebury. He was also a parole officer.

"He's dropping off a young man today. Just released. He spent three years in jail for manslaughter. It was a car accident, Griff. He crashed his car into a tree."

The familiar flash of stress that came from running a struggling business bolted through my chest. That second cup of coffee might have been a mistake. "Crashing into a tree isn't illegal, Ma. There must be more to it."

"Well." Her face went soft. "He killed the sheriff's son, who was a passenger in his car. And he was high on opiates at the time."

"Ah." The truth comes out. "So you hired a drug addict?"

She frowned at me. "A *recovering* addict. He got out of jail a month ago, and he's been in rehab since then. Angelo said this kid can make it, but he just really needs a job. He'll stay in the bunkhouse. Unless there's something you're not telling me, our property is a drug-free zone."

Zachariah, our farmhand, gave a snort of laughter. "Coffee is our drug, Mrs. Shipley. But we're in pretty deep."

She reached over and gave Zach's wrist an

affectionate squeeze. My mother was good at taking in strays, and Zachariah was her most successful acquisition. But they couldn't all be Zachariahs. I felt my blood pressure notch higher at the idea of adding a drug addiction to our long list of difficulties. Like I needed one more complication.

Since my father passed away three years ago, my mother and I ran the farm together. I made all the farming decisions—what to produce and where to sell it. But make no mistake—Mom kept the place running. She did the books. She fed me and our farmhand Zach, my three younger siblings, my grandfather and whichever seasonal employees were around. And when apple-picking season began five weeks from now, she'd run our busy pick-your-own business while somehow feeding an army as our workforce quadrupled.

So my very capable mother had every right to make a quick hiring decision, and we both knew it. Still, her choice of hires made me nervous.

"He's twenty-two, Griff." She crossed her arms, waiting me out. "The young man is clean, as they say. He's off drugs. But nobody else is going to take a chance on him. And we'd only take him on for the growing season and through the harvest. Sixteen weeks, tops."

Right. *The sixteen most crucial weeks of my year.*

A smart man knows when to back down to his mother. She'd obviously made up her mind already, and the day was getting on. "Okay," I capitulated. "We'll set him up in the bunkhouse when he shows up. Call me and I'll give him a tour. Let's go, Zach." I stood, grabbing my baseball cap, and Zach did the same.

Carrying our dirty plates, we exited through the kitchen where my sister May was tidying up. She was on summer break from law school. "Did the twins move the chickens?" I asked by way of a greeting.

5

"Yes, captain," my sister snarked. "They're outside already."

"Thanks." I gave her elbow a squeeze as I passed by to make up for my lack of manners. At times I could be an overbearing grouch, especially during the growing season. And my sisters were quick to call me on it.

"Hey, Griff?" May called after me as I opened the door. "Do you still plan to send Tauntaun off to freezer camp today? I'll need a heads up."

I paused in the doorway. "Good question." Butchering the pig would be a lot of work, and I didn't really have the time. Then again, next week would be the same story, if not worse. "Yeah. We should get it done, unless the day gets crazy. I'll give you some warning, so you can heat the water." May gave me a salute, and Zach and I went outside.

Scanning the property, I spotted the twins in the back meadow, beyond the bunkhouse. They were moving the portable electric fence we used to keep our chickens safe from predators, and probably squabbling over something. At seventeen, they were a decade younger than I was.

A year from now I'd be paying both their college tuitions, and not a day went by when I didn't worry about it. I gave my property the usual critical glance. The big, aging farmhouse where I'd grown up was in good shape for now. We'd redone the roof and the paint last year. But on a farm, there was always something going awry. If there wasn't a problem with the farmhouse, it would be the stone bunkhouse or one of the dairy barns. Or the cider house or the tractor.

And even if nothing broke down today, there were business decisions in my near future. I needed to reinvest in the farm, yet we also needed cash. Somehow I needed to guide the farm toward greater profitability without borrowing a pile of money.

If only I knew how to do that.

With a sigh, I turned to Zach. "You want the fences or the mowing?" I asked him. There was plenty of work for both of us, so I was happy to let him choose.

"You pick," he said immediately. Zach was a dream employee. He worked like an ox from sunup until supper, and he never complained—I didn't know if he even knew how.

"I'll mow," I said. "But maybe we'll swap after lunch. The new guy'll be here..." *Shit.* "Walk with me a minute?"

"Sure."

I headed across the circular meadow toward the tractor shed.

"We're going to have to keep an eye on this kid. I never asked you to spy on anyone before. But this is a little weird."

He grinned. "It is...colorful. But Angelo's no fool."

This was true. "Now, is there anything I need to know about the Kubota?" Not only was Zach a model employee, he was a skilled mechanic.

"She's running fine. I'm more worried about the milking rig in the big barn."

I swore under my breath. Most of our dairy cattle lived across the street on a neighbor's property. The bulk of our milk went to an ordinary dairy. On our own property, we raised a dozen organic cows, and that milk was sold to friends down the street who made fancy cheese from it.

"Did the pump give you trouble again?" Every farm had aging equipment, because no farmer could afford to upgrade his tools like the rest of the world upgraded their cell phones every year. I was a chemist by training, not a mechanic. So Zachariah was the one who coaxed all our most difficult equipment into performing. And the milking rig was about the most important machine on the whole property.

"It's not going to last much longer. Some of the gears are stripped, and I can't find those parts anymore. Odds are we'll have to taker 'er out back and shoot 'er before New Years."

I groaned. "Never tell me the odds."

"Right, Han."

"Thank you, Chewie."

"Don't mention it."

Chuckling, I walked off through the July morning toward the tractor barn, my head full of worry. I tried to imagine walking a hundred cows across the road to be milked in the smaller of the two dairy barns twice a day. Investing in new equipment on land I didn't own sounded like a bad idea.

I'd figure it out somehow. I'd have to.

Chapter Two

Boston, Massachusetts

Audrey

I wore a halter top to be fired.

If that sounds inappropriate, I should point out that I couldn't afford to be jobless, even for one day. The bigwigs at Boston Premier Group had asked me to appear in their corporate headquarters first thing in the morning. So I wore a halter top because I was ninety percent sure I'd be pounding the pavement in search of employment before nine-thirty.

I was a trained chef, and a damn good one. But, sadly, cleavage was more interesting than knife skills to most of the restaurateurs of Boston. I'd already learned this the hard way.

These were my thoughts as I rode the elevator up to the Boston Premier Group corporate headquarters.

If anyone should know what to wear to be fired, it was me. I'd been kicked out of two colleges before I turned twenty. Disgusted by my lack of academic achievement, my mother fired me next. She took away my car and withdrew all financial support.

Things seemed to turn around then. I put myself through culinary school, which I really enjoyed. But now my first job had proven to be a disaster, and I really didn't know what came next.

When the doors parted on the fifteenth floor I looked at my watch. At least I was five minutes early. My mother, wherever she was, would be thrilled that I was prompt to face the firing squad.

Go me!

"Mr. Burton will be right with you," the receptionist said from behind a beautiful desk outside several C-suite offices.

"Thank you." Nervous, I slipped into one of the deep leather chairs in the waiting area. I picked up a copy of *Boston Magazine* from the selection of periodicals on the table and hid behind it.

The corporate waiting area was not a safe place for me. By now, the details of my latest failure would have made it into every manager's office. Not only had I ruined an entire night's worth of business at their top-rated restaurant, my fuck-up had made the gossip pages of the newspaper.

My hands began to sweat on the magazine. If I lost this job, I'd need to find another one immediately. There would be no drowning my sorrows and licking my wounds, because I needed cash.

The problem wasn't my cooking, of course. I was a good chef. A *natural*, as one of my teachers had said. It had taken me twenty-two years, but I'd finally found something I was good at. I'd needed this job on my résumé, damn it.

"Audrey!" a voice barked.

Startled, I dropped the magazine and scrambled to stand. "G-g-good morning," I stammered, shaking the hand that Bill Burton offered me.

"Come with me," he said, leading the way into his plush office.

My mouth dry, I followed him. He waited for me to sit down in the chair facing his big desk, and then he shut the door with an ominous click.

Shit!

I sat up straight in my chair. I was going to go down fighting.

He sat in his chair and measured me with his eyes. There was a deep silence before he finally said, "Why don't you tell me what happened?"

Right. Okay. That was a better opener than "*Get the fuck out of our office building.*" But where to start? "Well, sir..." I hesitated, hating the tentative sound of my voice. *C'mon, Audrey! This is for all the marbles.* "I'm an excellent chef, sir. Top of my class. But BPG keeps giving me assignments outside the kitchen."

He raised an eyebrow. "Your job title is intern, sweetie. Nobody becomes a great chef without learning the business."

Sweetie? I had to bite down on my tongue to keep myself from screaming. But now was not the time for a rant. *Deep breaths, Audrey.* "I do want to learn the business," I said carefully. "But when you toss an intern into a job unprepared, you shouldn't be astonished when things go badly."

Flipping open a folder on his desk, he frowned down at its contents. "Six weeks ago your first assignment was tracking seafood deliveries at the fish market. You lasted one day."

"True." I'd reported for work at four-thirty in the morning, where a computer system I'd never seen before had greeted me.

"You were supposed to order two hundred lobsters for our flagship seafood restaurant. But you ordered two hundred *gross*. That's more than twenty-eight thousand lobsters."

I kept the cringe off my face, but just barely. "Nobody taught me the software," I insisted.

Bill Burton sighed. "Fine, but software wasn't the problem last night, was it?"

"Yes it *was*," I insisted again. "Indirectly."

He sat back in his chair. "Explain."

"My latest position has been at l'Etre Suprême." It was Boston's only Michelin-starred restaurant, and I'd felt lucky just walking in there every night. Chef Jacques was one of my culinary heroes.

But they hadn't put me in the kitchen where I could be useful. Or course not. They had me up front, working on the restaurant's reservations.

I cleared my throat. "The other night, the software hid a special reservation for thirty demanding CFOs." The men had turned up unexpectedly at seven o'clock. "When the CFOs realized we weren't prepared to seat them in our private alcove, they began abusing the staff and they never really stopped. And while I scrambled to solve the problem, the rest of the seating and dining schedule went haywire. Orders were lost and meals were delivered out of synch..."

I started sweating just remembering this disaster. Chef Jacques had nearly had a coronary. His screaming could be heard all the way out to the beaten copper bar, where bartenders in elegant vests had poured free drinks to soothe irritated customers.

Jacques did not know my name and was therefore unable to scream it. But that was no blessing, since it takes longer to screech: "Zee fucking wench who makes zee reservations."

That would be me.

"Go on," Burton prompted.

"I was mortified that I'd caused trouble in the kitchen." I folded my damp hands in my lap and looked him in the eye. "My roommate is a pastry chef." A slovenly one, I could add. I rented a room in his apartment because it was all I could afford. "I wanted to make amends, so I took a big pan of brownies he'd baked, and I brought them to work with me last night. It was a peace offering." I'd deposited my chocolaty gift in the middle of the kitchen. The staff fell on them like seagulls. "Then I'd gone out to the front of the house to spend the evening working on reservations."

That wasn't exactly true, but Burton didn't need to know that. In between tasks I always headed back to the kitchen. Some women might have trouble staying away from designer shoes or hot actors. My weakness was a star chef in action. I'd rather watch Jacques whisk a balsamic reduction than watch Channing Tatum strip for the camera. So I had a front row seat on the evening's unfolding disasters. When I'd snuck back to watch, I'd found Chef screaming at the grill cook.

"Zat is not how we treat zeh fish!" he had yelled at Enrique. "You must respect zeh filet!"

I'd cringed as Chef Jacques smacked Enrique on the back of the head. Jacques was an asshole on his best day, but last night he seemed to be wound even tighter than usual.

On the other hand, Enrique *had* been acting awfully sluggish. Normally a hard worker, last night he'd seemed off his game. If Enrique didn't treat the fish like the governor of Massachusetts, I'd known it wouldn't bode well for him.

Now, if there were any justice in the world, *I* would've been the one wielding the fish spatula. I would have respected the *hell* out of that filet, if they'd only given me a chance. I knew I could cook circles around many of the people in that kitchen.

But no. It had been back to the reservations system for me.

The next I'd seen Jacques he was chewing his salad

boy a new one. "Leaves should make pretty *hill*," he'd said, holding a plate in the air for the entire kitchen's inspection. "Zhis is alps after earthquake. Feex it!" He'd tossed the plate onto the steel work table, where it broke in two.

Haute cuisine may be the only industry where the boss is encouraged to behave like a cranky toddler. They pay extra for that, especially if you're a man and from France.

Strangely, the salad guy hadn't looked as put out by his ass-ripping as I'd expected. Instead of leaping to clean up the mess, he pinched a salad leaf off the pile and shoved it in his mouth. Then he did it a second time.

I'd thought it was weird. But I still hadn't guessed why.

"It was a busy night," I told Burton now. "I took a call from the concierge at Hotel Mandarin. He said he had a couple of A-listers who wanted a reservation."

Across the desk from me, Burton's eyes closed wearily. "Go on."

"I knew Jacques would *love* to have a movie star in his dining room. So I told the concierge to send them over, even if he wouldn't say who it was." Burton should know that I did have a good head for business. I knew that a restaurant's magic depended on its reputation. If Page Six got a photo of luminaries in Chef's dining room, it might've been just the stroke of luck I'd needed.

But when I'd stopped by the kitchen again, I could hardly believe my eyes. The salad boy had been slumped over his station, which was freaky enough. But Jacques hadn't even noticed. He'd been busy screaming at the fish cook again, while the mega-horsepower exhaust system tried in vain to remove fish-scented smoke from the kitchen.

Jacques's rant had been unintelligible. When he got angry, his accent thickened. I couldn't make out a word of it.

I'd stood there with my mouth hanging open when the dishwasher stopped beside me, laying a hand on my shoulder. "Awesome revenge, Audrey. Seriously. You're my fucking hero."

Um, what? I'd almost missed what he was saying. As I'd watched, another line cook shoved hand-cut polenta medallions into his mouth. It was as if the whole kitchen lost fifty IQ points and then got the munchies.

"Doesn't affect me, because I've built up a real tolerance. Looks like the salad boy can't handle his weed, though. You should get out now, girl," the dishwasher was saying. "Any second now Jacques is going to figure out who brought in the spiked brownies."

"The spiked—" I'd bitten off the sentence as horror crept up my spine. "Oh my God."

"I'm *definitely* inviting you to my next party. Those were killer." Chuckling, the dishwasher had wandered off to have a cigarette.

And to think that I hadn't even needed a lighter to burn my own career to the ground.

"So..." Burton sighed. "You're saying you didn't know the brownies were spiked?"

"I had *no idea*," I whispered. "There are always baked goods in my apartment. I don't, uh, usually steal them. And I really wish I hadn't this time."

He pushed the file folder away from him on the desk. "I could fire you for this."

"I know that, sir," I said quickly. "But I know I can do better if you give me a second chance." *Or a fifth chance.*

He folded his hands onto the desk blotter and seemed to think it over.

I held my breath. Bill tapped his fingers on the expensive-looking leather blotter and sighed once again. "All right, Audrey. You're heading to Vermont."

"I'm...really? Did you say Vermont?" Did that mean I wasn't fired? Did BPG own a restaurant in Vermont? I didn't think so.

"We can't put you in another front-of-house job. And we can't send you back to the fish market."

"I understand, sir," I said in my most humble voice.

"But we're going to give you one more chance, as a favor to your mother."

"My...*what?*" My mother and I hadn't spoken in over two years, since she cut me off financially. I'd put myself through culinary school, renting rooms in dives all over Boston. "What does *she* have to do with it?"

"She owns fifteen percent of the *company*," Burton said in a voice that made sure I knew how stupid I was. "We can still fire you next week. But we'll give you one more chance at bat as a courtesy to her."

I didn't even hear that last bit, because I was still stuck on the bomb he'd just dropped. *My mother owned a stake in BPG?* I'd had no idea. I guess it shouldn't be a complete surprise. My mother had her hands in moneymaking ventures all over Boston. And since she dined out with business associates four or five nights a week, she knew her restaurants. In fact, when I'd worked the reservation system at l'Etre, I'd wondered if she'd come in for dinner some night.

But an owner? Ugh. I could see how she and the company were a good fit. BPG was ruthless, and so was she.

"Audrey?" Burton prompted.

"Look," I said, hating the desperate sound in my voice. "I need this job. But keep me because I'm a good chef. Not because my mother has deep pockets. She doesn't even know I work here." We weren't on speaking terms at the moment.

He shrugged, as if it made no difference. "Are you going to go to Vermont for a few days or not?"

"I'll go," I said quickly, "as long as you don't throw out my application for the Green Light Project." I was in no position to make demands. But if he wasn't going to let me compete for my own kitchen, I might as well cut my losses and find another job.

Burton startled me by laughing. He actually *laughed* at my dream. "Audrey, it takes a hell of a lot of savvy to win the Green Light. There are guys who have been trying for *years.*"

I knew that. But I didn't have years. I needed to win BPG's annual new restaurant competition on the first try. "I know it's hard to win." It had to be. A company like BPG didn't just fund every idea that walked through their door. But I was going to bring them a great idea, and I was going to take top honors. "But promise me you'll let me try."

"Go ahead and give it a shot." He spread his hands magnanimously. He was humoring me, I was sure of it. "You never know. Now, let's talk about this assignment in Vermont." He picked up another file folder and opened it. "I'm sending you to talk to some farmers for me. I want you to help our supplier fill some late-summer, farm-to-table acquisitions. You'll be negotiating prices on two dozen agricultural goods."

Oh, brother. Here we go again. I was a trained chef. A good one. And yet BPG kept giving me tasks that weren't aligned with my skills, and then yelling at me when I failed.

"Sir, I don't know anything about negotiating." He could have sent my mom, though. The woman could make a deal with a field mouse and come out ahead.

"Doesn't matter." Burton grabbed a printout from the folder and tucked it into a BPG envelope. Then he handed it to me. "The goods and the prices are listed right on these pages. All you have to do is stop by each farm and offer to purchase the items on the list. Just fill out the sheet with who's supplying what. These guys will be eager to sell their organic produce to upscale Boston restaurants. It's good exposure for them. Here."

I took the sheet of paper from him and scanned it. It was a list of farms and addresses. They all had cute, scenic names. Muscle In Arm Farm. Misty Hollow. The Lazy Turkey Farm.

The task sounded easy enough. But I'd worked here long enough to be suspicious. Nothing was ever simple when it came to BPG. "Why aren't we doing this over the phone?" I asked. It had to be cheaper than sending me off to Vermont in a rental car to go door to door. And a hotel, too? BPG hated spending money. Something about this whole idea was just weird.

"Farmers don't answer their phones," Burton said. "They're too busy growing things. So off you go. Pack a bag and get on the road already. It's a two-hour drive."

I stood up, clutching the envelope, hoping for the best.

"Do a good job, Audrey," he said as I turned toward the door. "If this doesn't work out, I don't know if we can give you another chance."

"I will, sir."

***

Two and a half hours was a long time to ponder one's failings, even if the scenery was beautiful. I wound the rental car higher and higher along a country road on a pretty Vermont hillside. Out the driver's side window I caught glimpses of the Green Mountains in the distance.

I was still a bit stunned that Bill Burton hadn't fired me. But the more I thought about it, the more convinced I became that my mother's stake in the company wasn't the reason. Premier Group was famous for chewing up and spitting out culinary grads. Having their corporate name on your resume was like a badge of honor. It was the Purple Heart of the foodie world. There was even a Facebook group called *I Survived BPG.*

Their business model seemed to *depend* on slaves like me. As an intern, I was expected to work seventy hours a week for very low pay. They called the paycheck a "stipend" only because it sounded better than "slave wages." If they fired one of us every time something went wrong, there would be nobody left to do the shitty jobs and fetch the coffee.

That's what I was going to keep telling myself, anyway. Because I was sick of letting my mother influence my life. I'd thought that moving away from Beacon Hill would be enough to shake her off. Turns out I should have left the Commonwealth of Massachusetts.

Maybe Vermont was far enough to avoid Mom's bad juju. I hoped so, anyway. Outside my car windows, everything was green. Meadows lined the hillside, and the tree branches that framed the country road created a leafy tunnel. I didn't have the first clue where in the hell I was. But it was very beautiful.

Thank God for GPS, because navigation wasn't my strong suit. Again—put me in the kitchen with a knife and I'm a happy girl. But if you want me to run your business or negotiate your multi-farmer purchase agreement in the wilds of Vermont in a rental car? *Dicey, people.*

According to the dashboard indicator, I was just a half mile from the first grower on my list—the Shipley

Farm. I'd known a Griffin Shipley during my first unsuccessful year of college. He was a football stud and party boy, and we'd hooked up a couple of times. I remembered those nights with perfect clarity. Every thrilling moment.

But I hadn't known Griff very well, except in the biblical sense. And I couldn't remember whether he was from Vermont or not. Maybe Shipley was a common name. The man I'd been sent to find today was someone else, anyway. My instruction sheet listed *August Shipley: Apples and Artisanal Ciders.*

I'd picked the Shipley Farm as my starting place not because of the name, but because of the artisanal ciders. Perhaps Mr. August Shipley would let me taste them. If you were drinking for business purposes, it didn't matter that it wasn't quite noon yet, right?

The ciders were the most interesting product on my shopping list, with a few gourmet cheese products tying for second place. Before driving out of Boston, I'd put in a call to Bill Burton's son, Bob. He was the buyer who'd made up the list. "We're a bulk buyer, so we need the bulk price," Bob had said. "The rates on this list ought to do the trick. Call me if you need to wiggle some numbers around, but we can't negotiate much."

That was no surprise. I was already familiar with BPG's take-no-prisoners approach. But I was determined to make the whole thing work. I needed this job. My arrogant mother had made sure of it when she took away my car and my tuition money. Yet she still emailed me all the time and demanded updates on my progress at adulting. She left voicemail messages, too.

I responded only occasionally—just frequently enough to let her know I was still alive. But I thought about her more than I liked to admit. I often fantasized about the day a restaurant critic would give me a favorable review in the *Globe*. I wanted her to read it. Though I'd probably blacklist her on my reservations list, just because I could.

The dashboard GPS spoke up. "In two hundred yards, the destination is on your right." I sped up. It had been a long two-and-a-half hours in the car.

A moment later, the road turned suddenly from pavement to dirt, taking me by surprise. The little rental car bounced on the rough surface, and I felt a sudden loss of traction. So I slammed on the brakes.

Big mistake.

I skidded, the back of the car swinging its ass over to the right. I experienced a moment of terror as the earth shifted in an unpredictable way. Two seconds later, the car came to a dramatic stop. My teeth knocked together and my seatbelt bit into my shoulder. But I was still clutching the wheel, still vertical. Mostly. The passenger side had dipped into a gully at the side of the road.

Okay. I'm still on one piece. Thank you, baby Jesus.

With shaky hands, I unlatched my seatbelt, opened the door and struggled to climb out of the tilting car. My heart was whirring like a KitchenAid mixer on the highest setting. I had a rush of adrenaline from the loss of control. "Shit!" I swore, standing on wobbly knees on the dirt road.

Trying to get my breathing under control, I eyed the Prius. It wasn't at *that* weird of an angle. Maybe I could just drive it out of the ditch.

But when I circled the rear bumper, my heart sank. The back tire was as flat as a fallen soufflé.

Damn it!

And now where was my phone? I opened the car door again to look for my purse. But naturally everything had shifted toward the passenger side and then slid onto the floor. The angle was a bear, so I resorted to lying on the driver's seat and sort of diving for my bag on the passenger-side floor. I got my hands on it, but of course the bag had been open. So I spent the next couple of minutes grabbing stuff and shoving it back in the bag. Lipsticks. House keys. My phone.

Only when I thought I had everything did I finally heave myself up and out of the car again, ass first. When I spun around, my heart nearly failed. A giant, bearded man was standing in the road behind me, muscular arms crossed over his chest, frowning. "Audrey Kidder?" he growled.

The growly monster knew my name. Wait. I *knew* that growly monster. "Griffin?" I squeaked. He looked so different. Five years had elapsed since my freshman year at BU, so it hadn't been *that* long. He'd been an upperclassman and a football star. I was used to seeing him clean-shaven in football pads or holding a red cup at a frat party.

The man standing in front of me was still just as tall and muscular as the football player I'd once known (biblically). But there the resemblance stopped. *This* Griff Shipley was tanned and ripped in a different way. He wore a tight T-shirt reading FARM-WAY and a baseball cap with a tractor on it. His work pants were paint-spattered and worn in a way that did not resemble the faux-aging of an Abercrombie pair, but rather seemed weathered from actual work.

And my God did he fill them out beautifully.

I had a flicker of a memory of the last time I'd seen Griff Shipley. We were in his room at the frat house, and he had me up against his bedroom door. My legs were wrapped around his waist while he fu—

"What are you doing on my farm?" he demanded. "Aside from driving into my ditch."

"Your...farm?" I squeaked, feeling hot all over. "I'm,

uh, here to see your father. I work for Boston Premier Group. They want to talk about buying produce. And cider. The yummy alcoholic kind." I was babbling now.

He lifted his chin thoughtfully. "Do they now?"

Get it together, Kidder. I stood up straighter. "I'm the representative. Is your father home?"

Griff lifted an eyebrow. "You're too late."

"Really? I can come back tomorrow." That was a great idea, actually. I needed to compose myself.

"You're too late, because my father passed away a couple years ago."

"He..." Griff's words finally sunk into my addled brain. "Jesus, I'm sorry."

"Thank you." He waited, staring me down.

"So..." I dug into my purse for the list of farmers. "BPG gave me his name. August Shipley. I'm sorry they got it wrong. Are, uh, you the one I should speak to?"

He grinned, and I saw just a flash of the old Griff. "That piece of paper is right. My full name is August Griffin Shipley the third. And yeah—I'm the farmer and the cidermaker."

My brain struggled to wrap itself around this idea. Football jock Griff Shipley in charge of a business? I hoped his family had other means of income. Griff Shipley in charge of a tailgate party—maybe I could see that. But a farm and beverage operation?

Nope. Not possible.

"Okay," I said slowly. "Can we talk? Do you have some time?"

Griff lifted his big, bearded chin toward the sky and sighed, as if I had just asked for the moon. Then he pinned me with a big, ornery stare. "Time is pretty scarce, seeing as I gotta pull your car out of that ditch, too. And your tire is probably toast. I have to mow, inspect the fences, milk the cows and slaughter a pig. I have to interview a drug addict and check my apples. But then, maybe. After that."

"All right..." I shifted my weight, noticing that my cute little strappy sandals had allowed little bits of the gravel road to sneak under my feet. "My thing might only take a few minutes, though. It's a couple of lines on a page."

He lifted one giant hand to stroke his beard. "You might have called first. Did you think of that?"

"Good point," I said gamely. "The BPG buyer told me that it was better to just drive up. He said farmers don't answer their phones."

Griff tipped his scruffy face toward the sky and made an unexpected sound which I eventually identified as laughter.

"What's so funny?"

He crossed his bulky, lickable arms. "Look," he said. "I have a feeling I know why your man at BPG doesn't have *his* calls answered too often. His prices are probably bullshit, right? So his new plan is to send a hot sorority girl in a halter top and short skirt to dazzle the poor hicks who grow his food. Your guy thinks I'm a big enough idiot that a nice rack and a bright smile will blind me for long enough to agree to sell apples for a buck a pound."

Later I would remember this moment as important. Standing there on Griff's road, I'd gleaned the first prickle of understanding that a flat tire was just the *start* of my buzz kill. A brand new sinking feeling kicked in, because I had a hunch that Griff Shipley knew what he was talking about for once. I opened the price list in my hand to see that the first item on the list was, indeed, *Apples: $0.99 / lb.*

Fuck. "So you're saying that a dollar a pound is not the market rate for wholesale apples?" I said it as sweetly as possible, but Griff's face began to darken like a stormy sky.

"Listen, princess," he growled. "You can buy shitty, mealy apples for that price from a giant orchard out west or from a farmer that got swindled into growing only Red Delicious during the eighties and can't afford to re-graft his trees. But your guy wants organic apples, probably heirloom varietals. He wants bragging rights on the menu—apples grown locally in New England with no pesticides and blessed by virgins in the moonlight. That's what he wants hand-lettered on the menu, right?"

"Right," I agreed reluctantly. That was exactly how it worked.

"That does *not* come at a buck a pound. Not from me and not from any of my neighbors."

Uh-oh. My heart sank a little further into the dirt, just like my rental car.

I wasn't a stupid girl. Maybe business wasn't exactly my forte, but I'd always been a good listener. And after listening to Griff rant for a minute, I already knew that when I visited the other farms in this county, every price on my page would be too low by half. And yet my job depended on sealing these deals.

I was so screwed.

"Now let's get your shiny new car out of the ditch, shall we?" Griff was glowering at me. For real. Before today I'd never seen anyone actually glower. It was an expression found only in books, and on Griff Shipley's ridiculously handsome yet grumpy face.

"It's a rental," I said in my own defense. "I can call for roadside service."

Glowering Griff gave a weary sigh. "I'll be rid of you sooner if I do it myself." He raised two fingers to his mouth and blew an ear-piercing whistle. Then he waited while I tried not to think of those fingers and the things they'd once done to me...

"Got a problem, Han?" a voice called from the meadow beyond the trees lining the road. A few seconds later an attractive blond dude slipped between the trees to join us. He was big, too. But where Griff was dark, this man was fair with pretty blue eyes.

Apparently all the people who grew pristine organic food were beautiful themselves.

"Yeah, we do have a problem," Griff told him. "We have to pull the princess here out of the ditch and change her tire. Then warp speed her ass back to the Death Star so she can report that the rebels are mutinying."

"Jesus, I'd forgotten about your *Star Wars* obsession." That just slipped out of my mouth. But as soon as I said it, the other guy's eyes opened wide, and the look on Griff's face made it clear that any further references to our tiny sliver of a past together weren't going to be tolerated.

Though *tiny sliver* wasn't good terminology for the boinking we'd done, because nothing on that man's body was tiny.

Moving on.

"How can I help?" I asked. "I'm happy to get going just as soon as I'm able. After we have a brief discussion about cider and apples."

"A brief discussion." He stared me down.

"Yes. You repeat things very well. Good job." I crossed my arms to match his posture. Maybe I'd been sent to Vermont on a fool's errand, but I wasn't going to cash in my chips just yet. If this errand could be saved, I'd save it. My future at BPG was at stake, and one grumpy farmer wasn't going to have the last word.

"Follow me," he grunted before turning and

marching away.

"Yes sir." I saluted the back of his head.

The blond kid chuckled to himself and went to look at the deflated wheel of my rental car.

Chapter Three

Griffin

I'm a nice guy. Swear to God. But today it was pretty hard to tell.

Blame it on the stress of running a farm, or the shock of seeing Audrey Kidder there on our road, her legs longer than the drive to town, her fiery eyes staring up at me. Blame it on a sudden spike in the summer day's temperature.

Whatever the cause, I started acting like an asshole at the moment I discovered Audrey's perfect ass sticking out of that car on my dirt road.

Trying to clear my head, I walked her up our half-mile gravel driveway at a death-march pace. But she had on those little strappy shoes, damn it. So I slowed my pace and tried to find my manners. "How've you been for five years?" I barked.

Maybe I hadn't quite remembered how to be civilized yet, though, because she looked shocked by the question. "Um, fine, thank you. I, uh, flunked out of BU. Then my mother sent me to Mount Holyoke where I repeated the performance."

I shouldn't have asked, I guess, because her story made me ragey. I'd busted my ass for four years to keep a football scholarship at BU because I knew it would leave more money in the college fund for my three younger siblings.

But Audrey had been a party girl. Always with her sorority sisters. Always looking for a drunken good time. Good-time party guy was the part I'd *tried* to play in college, but, meanwhile, I'd slept an average of five hours a night for four years so I could get everything done. Just like I did now.

"—so after I proved to everyone that a college degree was not for me, I went to cooking school where I graduated as the valedictorian. Go figure."

"Nice," I said. But Audrey Kidder in a kitchen? That was something I had a real hard time visualizing. She might chip a nail.

"I took the job at Boston Premier Group because I want to start my own restaurant. That's really hard to do—you need backers. If I kiss the ring for a while, they can help me get started."

Interesting. But now she was just buttering me up in order to get what she needed from me. She worked for a bunch of corporate slimeballs who took advantage of everyone they could. And she wanted my approval? Not happening.

"Why don't you ask your parents for the startup money?" I asked. Audrey was a rich girl. That's why the sorority types had liked her so much. "Can't they help?"

"No, Griff." Her voice dipped. "As a matter of fact they can't." And a flash of something dark crossed her face.

Whoops. I'd stuck my foot in my mouth again. "Well," I grunted. "Let's talk about my ciders while Zach fixes your car."

"Cool! Can I see where you make them?" Her face lit up like a kid's on Christmas, and I felt a twinge of unfamiliar kinship in my chest. Cider was my passion, and whenever anyone expressed interest, it made me happy.

Then again, the girl really had enjoyed getting drunk back in the day.

"Yeah. Of course. This way." We passed the farmhouse on our right, then I steered Audrey between the bunkhouse and the dairy barn toward my pride and joy—the cider house. My father had always made artisanal cider, but he made it for himself. Every year he'd sold a few gallons just for fun.

But I'd grown Dad's tiny operation into something much bigger. Pushing open the door to the barn-like building, I flipped on the old soda lamps overhead.

"Whoa," Audrey said, her voice hushed. "Those tanks are serious."

"They are," I agreed, fighting off the rush of pleasure I felt whenever someone admired my babies. "My cider wins awards." Okay, *one* award. But I was just getting started. "Any yokel can brew a decent beer in his garage, but it's difficult to create a cider with any complexity. And there's a lot that can go wrong, chemically speaking."

"Uh-huh," Audrey said, wandering over to my bottling machine and picking up an empty bottle. "Nice label."

The label was the least interesting thing in the room. "Thanks," I said tightly. "My brother designed it."

She looked up quickly, a grin on her face. "I know you don't give a fuck about the label, Grouchy Griff," she said, putting it down again. "But marketing matters to buyers. People need to feel good about plunking down a lot of cash for premium goods. They want a *story*, because the story lasts longer than it takes to swallow something."

"Uh-huh." This was the kind of mumbo jumbo that made me crazy, because people should be willing to pay for organic quality simply because *it's the right thing to do.* "So you're saying the pretty picture means more to your customers than the fact that my orchard isn't poisoning Vermont's groundwater with chemicals and petroleum-based fertilizers? And that I pay my employees a living wage?"

She tossed her hair. "Does it matter how I respond? I wouldn't want to interrupt your sermon." She came closer, her big blue eyes looking up at me, a challenge gleaming in them. "And don't tell me you've never tried to gussy up your cider house to appeal to the masses. If you don't believe in marketing, what's that?"

She pointed at a framed photograph on the wall. It was the first part of an informative display explaining how cider was made. We held tastings here during our busy apple-picking season. "My sister took that last fall. That's our fruit in the wheelbarrow. So what?"

Audrey grinned like she'd caught me with my hand in the cash drawer. "The apples in that picture did *not* go into your big, manly cider tanks. These—" She jabbed one pink fingernail at the photo. "—are fancy grade, flawless fruit. You sold those apples to tourists. And in there"—she pointed at my tanks, and raised her voice— "you put apples that look like they got their asses kicked in an alleyway! So don't even *try* to pretend you have no fucks to give when it comes to marketing!"

Christ on a cracker. The way her shapely mouth looked when she said *fuck* was ridiculously distracting. And I'd just been schooled by a girl who must have paid attention at least once in a while in culinary school.

Weirdly, I didn't care that much. I just wanted her to say *fuck* again, preferably while riding my dick in the hayloft.

"What?" she snapped. "You're staring at me."

"Did you call me Grouchy Griff a minute ago?"

She rolled her eyes. "Maybe. Does it make you want

32

to sell me cider at a competitive price?"

The truth was that I wanted very much to sell cider to the Big Corporate Assholes Group of where-the-fuck-ever. Unlike my fruit, the cider could become a brand name, and it needed to find its special market. If fancy restaurants carried my cider, I'd have an easier time convincing Boston wine shops to stock it.

Taking a small loss on the cider was probably a good business decision. If I could stomach it. "Dare I ask?" I walked closer to Audrey where she stood by the bottler. "What price does your employer expect to pay for a bottle of Vermont's finest hard cider?"

For a moment she blinked up at me, then licked her lips.

Do not look at her lips. Do not think about them. Do not remember what she once did with... Fuck.

"My pricing sheet says three dollars for a seven-hundred-fifty-milliliter bottle."

Well, that was a libido killer. "*Three bucks?* So they can mark it up to twenty? You're shitting me. The bottle and the cork alone cost a buck fifty."

Her shoulders sagged, and when she spoke again, it was in a soft voice. "I will tell my boss he's insane, okay? But if you want me to change his mind, you need to give me something to go on. I need information, not another rant."

Hell, the girl had a point. "All right. First, let's taste."

Audrey clasped her hands together. "I thought you'd never ask."

Right.

I fetched a bottle from the cooler, untwisted its wire clasp and then slowly removed the cork. To preserve the natural effervescence of my product, I used a champagne cork in every bottle. It cost more than a twist-off top, but the product had a better shelf life.

I grabbed a couple of glasses from the tasting counter and poured us each a half portion. Audrey took hers and smiled at me. "Cheers."

"Cheers," I grunted. It was hard to remember the last time I had a drink with an attractive female. A couple months ago I'd broken things off with my fuck buddy, and since then I'd been living like a monk. Tasting cider before lunch in the hopes of making a sale wasn't exactly a social occasion. But it was as close as I'd come in a while.

Pathetic much?

Audrey held her glass up to the dusty beam of light filtering down through the skylight. "A nice amber color." She swirled the class under her nose like a pro. "Pleasant, musky odor. More tannic than fruity." She sipped, her gaze drifting off to the side as she concentrated on the tart, complicated flavors of my product. I saw her delicate throat pulse as she swallowed. "Wow. That's some fine apple juice you've got there, Griff."

"What?" I yelped. "Apple j—"

She grinned. "*Joking!* It's magnificent. I get notes of oak and apricot. Nice finish. I can see why you're proud of it."

For a second, my chest swelled from the praise. But then I remembered she was trying to buy the stuff for peanuts. Obviously, she was just buttering me up. "It tastes like eight dollars a bottle at wholesale, fifteen at retail."

Audrey took another dainty sip while I tried not to find her ridiculously attractive. "I think it's delicious, and I'd pay your price any day. But the guys I work for are going to fire me if I come back with a number that's more than double theirs."

The truth was that I could do a little better than eight bucks. I just wasn't ready to admit it. "BPG will do really well with this bottle. It's still cheaper than ninety percent of the wines on their list. And we're not exactly in Napa Valley. If they want to impress the Beacon Hill set, this is the way to go. The Massachusetts Bay colonists had too little grain to make the beer they'd drunk in England, so they made hard cider instead. This right here is our history." I held up the bottle.

She took it out of my hand and put it back on the counter. "I may have flunked out of BU, but I did finish the fifth grade, where they taught us that John Adams drank hard cider with breakfast. I get it, okay? You've got the perfect regional beverage for my corporate overlords. I shall report back to the Death Star, where Darth Vader will express his disappointment and then strangle me for quoting eight bucks a bottle."

Damn this girl. Not only did she know her stuff, she was smiling at me now over the rim of her glass. The other two times we'd been this close together, our clothes had come off in a big fucking hurry.

Focus, Griffin.

"I could show you seven dollars. Why don't you just see what their limit really is?"

"Well..."

Behind me, the door opened suddenly. "Griff?" my sister called. "Angelo just drove up with the new guy."

"Be right there," I said, taking a step back from Audrey. I felt oddly guilty, as if my sister had caught us doing something more furtive than discussing the price of cider.

You wish.

"Hi!" May said, catching a glimpse of Audrey. "Are you going to introduce me to your friend?" My sister's voice was oddly bright. It was her snooping voice. I'd been hearing it her whole life.

"I thought we had a drug addict to meet," I grumbled, setting down my glass and heading for the door. Nudging May and her big mouth out of the way, I watched the back door of Angelo's old sedan open. "Excuse me a minute, Audrey."

"Audrey?" My sister's curiosity was in full swing. "I'm May, Griffin's sister..."

I had no choice but to leave the two of them to chat. I hoped Audrey wouldn't divulge our former entanglement, because everyone on the farm would be talking about it by dinnertime, even the dairy cattle. But in the grand scheme of things I had bigger problems.

One of them was climbing out of Angelo's car.

What does an addict look like, anyway? To me he looked like any kid in his twenties. He had a serious face and a lot of tattoos, but so did half the men in Vermont. He was a little thin for farm work. But that was really the worst I could say about my first impression. He pulled a small duffel bag out of the trunk, then lifted his chin to look around.

"Hi," I said, greeting our friend Angelo. Now here was a guy with a tough job. The next time I found myself grumbling about an invasion of apple maggot fly, I would try to remember that I could be hunting down ex-cons instead.

His dark skin crinkled at the corners of his eyes when he smiled at me. "Haven't seen you at church lately," he said, shaking my hand.

"What, now you're moonlighting as Father Pat's truant officer?"

He laughed. "Sorry. Occupational hazard."

"I'll bet." I turned my attention to the newcomer, offering my hand. "I'm Griffin Shipley."

"Jude Nickel." He had a surprisingly firm handshake. "Thank you for giving me a try. I need the job."

"You're welcome," I said. *Translation: we're desperate.* "If you don't mind the outdoors, it's not bad work."

"Just spent three years in jail and rehab. I could use a little outdoors."

His candor took me by surprise. "Well okay then. We pay twelve bucks an hour if you're living on site, or fourteen if you're a day worker. Lunch is free for everyone, but those who live with us get docked ten bucks a day total for breakfast and supper. The food is great, though, and we provide a lot of it. Like Guinness World Record quantities."

"Damn," said a chirpy voice behind me. "Got any more openings? You pay better than my corporate overlords."

Audrey was listening in on my little HR speech, and I didn't know quite how to feel about that. I paid my employees as well as I possibly could, though nobody was getting rich working here. Least of all me.

"That's fine. All of it," my newest employee said. He looked older than his twenty-two years. He had tired eyes. "Where should I put this?" He patted his gym bag.

"That's all you've got with you?" I asked, eyeing it.

"That's all I've got, period." He lifted his chin, challenging me to say anything else on the matter.

"No problem. Let me show you the bunkhouse."

But first my mother wanted a word. I saw her come out of the back door, her apron on, crossing the yard purposefully to where we all stood around Angelo's car. I waited while she fussed over Angelo and greeted Jude. "Honey," she said to this ex-con whom she'd never met before, "I checked every corner of our house and didn't find any medication stronger than aspirin. Angelo asked me to do that for you. He said it was easier if you didn't have to wonder."

"Uh, thanks," he said, studying at his shoes. "Appreciate it."

I glanced toward the bunkhouse. God only knew what somebody might have left in that bathroom. "I should check the..."

"Already did it," my mother said quickly. "You might want to *clean* that shower more often. There are scarier things than narcotics in there."

Audrey giggled while I cringed.

"I'm Ruth Shipley," my mother said to our uninvited corporate raider. "And you're..."

"Audrey Kidder. I swung by to ask Griff about buying apples and cider for a group of restaurants in Boston."

"Oh!" Mom clasped her hands as if the queen herself had just dropped by. "Will you stay for lunch?" She ignored the look of menace that I aimed in her direction.

"I would love to!" Audrey enthused. "Especially since my car is in a ditch at the bottom of your road."

"Not true," I said quickly. Even as we spoke, I could see the Prius turning slowly up the drive. Zach had already swapped out the tire—although it was likely the spare was a donut, so Princess Perky's troubles weren't exactly solved.

"Wow," she said, her voice awed. "He's a miracle worker."

"He is," I admitted, even if it was just a tire change. "Shoulda been working miracles on my fence instead of your car, though."

"August Griffin Shipley," my mother demanded. "Where are your manners? Since when do you not go to the aid of a stranger?"

I would have preferred that Audrey *was* a stranger. Not that I'd say so out loud.

May socked me in the shoulder. "Grumpy much? Take Jude to the bunkhouse already, because lunch will be ready soon. Brisket sandwiches and potato salad. Come with us, Audrey," my sister the traitor said. "We'll pour you some iced tea."

After saying goodbye to Angelo, who couldn't stay for lunch, the women went inside, leaving Jude and I alone. I headed toward the outbuilding where we needed to stash his things, and he followed me. "The bunkhouse is pretty comfortable for what it is," I said. "It's been here a hundred years. My great-grandfather built it with the rocks he cleared from the meadow."

Jude studied the stone building as we approached. "Pretty cool," he said. "You must not use it in the winter. Too expensive to heat."

"Not true. It has a hundred-year-old masonry heater. Every two days we build a fire in there, then seal that sucker up. It heats the place into the low sixties even on a sub-zero day. There's electric baseboard heat to fill in around the edges. We make all our own electricity, too."

Sustainable architecture was one of my numerous causes. I wanted this farm to be around for a long time. The solar panels had cost a lot, though. I invested right after dad died, before I realized how tight cash really was. Then I invested in my first round of cider equipment, and now I was out on a proverbial limb all the time. One lost harvest and we'd be looking at bankruptcy.

Holding open the front door, I let Jude enter first. "That room on the right is mine. Bathroom's on the left." I kicked off my boots and pointedly set them on the rubber shoe mat by the door. "After you've been working in the dairy barn, you'll want to leave your shoes at the door."

"Makes sense," Jude said, toeing out of his Chuck T's. I was happy to see him following instructions. That boded well for both of us. "You sleep out here in the bunkhouse all the time?" he asked. "To keep an eye on the help, I guess."

"No." Studying this very jaded young man, I shook my head. "That's not why. I gave up my bedroom in the farmhouse because Mom is trying to convince my grandpa to move in. He's about a half mile down the road, all alone since my grandmother died. Every day she asks him if he'll move today, and each time he says, 'Not today!'"

Jude laughed, and it made him look five years younger.

"Anyway, I moved out here a couple months ago, because we thought maybe it would motivate him to give in. But no luck. And anyway—I don't mind it out here with Zach. He's easy company. You'll see. Head straight back. End of the hall."

I followed Jude into the wide bunkroom with high, beamed ceilings. I watched him take in the two sets of bunk beds—one on each side—and a single bed under the back windows. "That's Zachariah's," I said, pointing at the center bed with the *Star Wars* pillowcase—a gag gift from me. "He gets the best spot, because he lives in here year round. During the harvest my cousins will sleep in here, too."

I went over to our one big closet and pulled open the double louvered doors. "Storage space is our biggest hurdle out here. You can have a couple feet of this hanging bar if you need it, and you get one big drawer." I pointed at the built-ins at either end of Zach's bed.

"One drawer is plenty for me," he pointed out as I poked around in the closet for a set of sheets and a blanket.

"True." The guy would need more clothes if he was going to do farm work, though. We got plenty dirty. "Here." I offered him the bedding I'd found. Then I sat down on Zach's bed. "Now tell me what else I need to know about working with you. Is there anything special you need? Any work that you can't do?" I'd never known anyone who was trying to get off drugs, so I couldn't guess his limitations.

Jude turned his back to me and shook out a sheet before answering. But when he spoke, he eyed me over his shoulder. "Angelo brought me here because I'm trying not to move back to Colebury until I have a few more months where I'm clean. Eventually I'll have to go home, but I need to rack up some more time off the junk. He said your place would be like a halfway house, because I'd be stranded out here. So I'd rather not be sent into Colebury on errands, if you don't mind. There's drugs everywhere, and I just don't want to think about it. Don't want to run into any of my so-called friends."

Yikes. "Okay. Sure. What else?"

"I'm a decent mechanic. Started working in a body shop when I was fourteen. If you need any maintenance work on your vehicles, just ask."

"Thanks. Zach is an engine whiz, too. He's saved me a mint already."

"Well, that's lucky," Jude said. But I swear he looked a little deflated at this news.

"What else?"

He tucked the corners of the sheet over the mattress. "I don't sleep too well. Drugs really fuck up your REM cycles."

"So if I hear you walking around at night, I shouldn't call the police?" I meant this as a joke, but when the words came out of my mouth, I realized they were a poor choice for talking to someone who'd been arrested at least once.

He sighed. "You might find me sitting outside on the porch at two in the morning. I'll try to be quiet."

"No big." I cleared my throat. "Now, don't take this the wrong way, but I say this to every man who ever stays here."

He looked up at me, amusement in his eyes. "Yeah? Hit me."

"My little sister is off limits. I have to say it. She's seventeen going on thirty."

"Aw, man. Don't feel you have to say another word. I get it." He chuckled. "Hey kids, stay the hell away from the junkie in bunk number three."

I was relieved that he didn't get pissed off by my little speech. I gave it to everyone. And this guy had that dark-eyed, brooding look working. Plenty of girls had probably flung themselves at him back in the day.

Hopefully my little sister wouldn't cast aside her adoration for Zach and shift it to Jude. Zach I trusted. This guy I'd just met. "You know, I used to include both of my sisters in this little warning, but May got wind of it. She hates it when I treat her like a kid. And she has a good right hook, which she's not afraid to use on me."

"Good to know. But hitting on your sisters is not my style. Maybe you wouldn't believe it from a guy who just got out of jail, but I'm a hard worker. Toward the end there I was mostly working hard to feed my habit. But I know how to put in a long day."

"Good. We start at six and end at five, but we take two hours off during the day for meals and breaks."

His nod was stoic. "Got it. Maybe I'll sleep better after a long day, anyway."

"You'd almost have to." I stood up. "I'm heading in for lunch. It won't start for another fifteen minutes, but be on time, okay? Lunch is at one o'clock every day and mom busts her ass to get it onto the table like clockwork, so she wants you to show up on time."

"Yessir."

I paused on my way out of the room. "And don't call me sir. My siblings do it sometimes, but they're just fucking with me."

Jude laughed as I left the bunkhouse.

Chapter Four

Audrey

Maybe Griff Shipley was a grumpy asshole. But his family was *lovely*. Their bustling kitchen was controlled chaos of the very best kind. Griff's mom was busy slicing up a slab of braised brisket large enough to feed several developing nations, while everyone else pitched in to get food on the table.

Or didn't, in the case of Griff's younger brother, Dylan. Best as I could tell, he was minding a big sterilizer full of jam jars on the stove. He had the tongs in one hand, but mostly he busied himself singing Technotronic's "Pump Up the Jam," and dancing around.

"You are killing me with that song," his twin sister Daphne complained. The two of them looked to be high school aged.

"This is what I sing when we make jam."

She rolled her eyes, her arms braced around a tall stack of plates. She nudged her brother and indicated an open drawer full of linen napkins. "Can you put those on top here?"

He reached into the drawer and piled a handful of napkins on top of the plates.

"We're ten people today," she said. "Put some more on."

"Stop calling me a moron."

She groaned all the way out of the kitchen, and Dylan went back to singing "Pump Up the Jam," changing the line about "booty" to "fruity." And all the while his mother and sisters moved like ninjas around one another.

The lunchtime bustle in the Shipley family kitchen rivaled a busy night on the cook line at l'Etre Suprême, but it was a hell of a lot cheerier.

The kitchen in the house where I'd grown up could not have been more different—it had been like a large, sparkling tomb. I'd never been allowed to cook anything in it, or disrupt its perfect order. Since my mother had been busy climbing the corporate ladder, she'd played host to guests all the time. But she didn't cook. We'd had a full-time personal chef who made me feel like an intruder if I wandered in there looking for a snack.

I hadn't started cooking until college, when I finally got free of that stifling place. My freshman year I had a rented house with a couple of girls I knew from high school. One of them was a great cook already, and I learned a lot at her elbow. In fact, I'd liked everything about that first year at BU except for the schoolwork. I'd liked our house, my friends, the sorority I rushed, and partying. If I'd spent fewer hours learning to make dumplings from scratch and more hours doing homework, I might have gotten B's instead of D's.

But I hadn't.

Water under the bridge.

Drifting into the dining room, I watched Daphne speed-set the table for ten people. "During picking season we hold lunch outdoors, because we're twenty people then," she told me.

May Shipley rushed by with a tray of coffee cups and a water carafe.

"How can I help?" I asked her for the third time, following her back into the kitchen. "There must be something."

"You are so sweet, but we've got this down to a science. We serve a whole lot of food in this kitchen."

"I can see that." It seemed categorically impossible that there wasn't something I could do to help, but if she didn't want to assign me a task, that left me free to admire the farmhouse kitchen. The house had to be over a hundred years old, but it had been lovingly handled. The giant butcher's block table in the center of the kitchen looked as if it had been there since the dawn of time—there were scars and scratches in its oiled surface. But that only made it more beautiful to me.

What I'd wished for as a child was exactly this—a storybook family on a farm somewhere, crammed around the table, a rope swing on an old tree, lacy curtains blowing in the breeze...

Someone had abandoned a small bowl of cherries in the center of the table, half of them pitted. They gleamed like perfect red jewels. "Hey—these are gorgeous. Are they sour cherries?" I lifted the bowl up to my nose for a sniff—occupational hazard of being a chef. *Wow.* Nothing else had the same rich scent as a cherry.

"Yes they are, and they're terrific in pies," Mrs. Shipley said, lifting slice after slice of brisket onto a platter. "But we won't get enough for a pie until next week. I never know what to do with the first few—it's not enough to make anything. I tossed them into a batch of strawberry jam last year."

"Can I eat one?" I laughed. "Is that rude? You can never find sour cherries at the store."

"Go ahead, honey," Ruth Shipley said.

I popped one in my mouth, and it burst forth with a wonderful sour fruitiness. "Fantastic." The flavor filled me with ideas. I wanted to make chutney from these cherries. Or a gin cocktail. Or a tart. "Damn. I always wanted to live somewhere where there were fruit trees."

May Shipley laughed. "All we've got are fruit trees. Twenty thousand of them."

"Twenty...thousand?"

"That's right. And that's not counting Griff's experimental crops."

It was hard to even form a mental picture of twenty-thousand trees. Humming to myself, I picked up the paring knife and began to pit the rest of the cherries in the bowl. Knife work was soothing to me. Some people knitted. Some did yoga. I liked to cut things.

A few minutes later I had a tidy pile of pitted fruit. "I suppose you have a compost can for the pits and stems?"

Ruth Shipley looked up from her own work. "That didn't take you but a minute."

"Cooking is the only thing I'm good at."

"I'm sure that's not true. The compost can is there beside the coffee maker."

I dumped the pits and then washed my blood-red fingers.

"May!" Ruth called to her older daughter. "Can you find the barbecue sauce in the refrigerator? We need to heat it up. Then we can eat."

"Sure!"

"Um..." Dylan mumbled in that sullen teenage way. "Didn't know you still needed that."

"Dylan Gerard Shipley! Did you finish my sauce and not tell me? Now lunch is going to be late! I can't serve brisket without barbecue sauce!"

Aw. The younger Shipley brother hung his head. He was a thinner, gawkier Griffin.

I felt bad that he'd been shamed in front of

strangers. "I'll whip up another batch if you need it," I offered.

Ruth was still staring at her son with a laser gaze, and I was pretty sure the teenager would have been incinerated if looks could kill. "Thank you, honey," she said to me. "I'd love that. There's an onion there"—she indicated a bowl on the prep table—"and you can use the same cutting board."

Yay, a task! When you've been told all your life that you're quite useless, whipping up a little barbecue sauce is a good time. I grabbed the onion and went to town. "Ooh, garlic scapes," I said, reaching for the green shoots. "I never find these, either." A quick mince had them falling into tiny discs on the cutting board.

"Yikes," Daphne gasped, watching my knife move so fast it blurred. "How are you not missing a finger?"

"Still have all ten, and none have had to be surgically reattached. But the day ain't over yet."

As she giggled, the kitchen door opened and Griff Shipley filled the opening with his NFL-sized body. I'm ashamed to say that the rhythm of my knife faltered for just a moment. That chest beneath that tight T-shirt just did things to me.

My traitorous brain was saved from further embarrassment by the look on his face when he spotted me. First a bushy eyebrow quirked, as if he couldn't believe I was still here. And then he gave me his now-familiar frown.

Ah, well. All that hotness wasted on a grouch.

I dragged my attention off Griff as Ruth Shipley scraped my minced aromatics into a saucepan. "Let's see," she said. "A little ketchup, because we're in a hurry. Some vinegar..."

"You know what would be great in here?" I couldn't stop myself from suggesting. "Those." I pointed at the cherries.

"Interesting pick, miss." She handed me the pan. "Go for it. I need to run upstairs for a minute."

"Go on. I've got this." I shooed her away and she smiled. At least one of the Shipleys liked me.

Turning my back on Griff, I put the pan on the stove on a low temperature. Then, still feeling his eyes on me, I went to his giant family refrigerator and opened the door. The ketchup was in a huge bottle. It would have to be if they served ten or twelve people for lunch every day. Before adding some to the onions, garlic and butter already in the pan, I sautéed the veggies for a minute to bring out the onions' natural sweetness.

"What are you doing?" Griff said suddenly from *right* behind me.

"Barbecue sauce. You're familiar with it, right?" The heat of his body was somehow hotter than the Wolf stove in front of me. I tried to elbow him out of the way, but that was like trying to nudge a Humvee. So I went the long way around two-hundred-odd pounds of muscle to collect the cherries.

"Strange combo," he muttered.

"You don't have to eat it," I returned. There was a nice sizzle happening in my saucepan now and I grabbed a wooden spoon to stir everything together. "Be a dear and find me some brown sugar, would you?" I asked. "And some vinegar."

Across the room, his sister May laughed. "He'd need a map and a compass. I'll grab them. White wine vinegar? Or balsamic."

"Balsamic, I think."

The kitchen door opened slowly, and Griff's newest employee eased tentatively into the room. "That smells really good," he said softly.

"Thank you!" I chirped, giving Griff a pointed look.

Griff ignored me. He escorted his new employee in the direction of the pantry. "Having the sink over here keeps us out of the way," he said. "And keeps the cooks from getting cranky."

"What keeps *you* from getting cranky?" I called after him. "Whatever it is, have some of it."

All the Shipleys laughed except for Griff.

Chapter Five

Griffin

The sight of Audrey Kidder invading my family kitchen had a strange effect on me. Watching her at our stove was like getting a glimpse of an alternate universe where I had time for a woman in my life.

Fat chance.

All the stress must have been getting to me, because there was really no reason that Audrey should make me feel wistful. Hell, we hadn't even been friends in college. She'd been dating Bryce, a younger football teammate of mine. For months, whenever he brought her by the house, I was tortured by her smile and her easy laugh.

Then they broke up, and it was ugly. I didn't think I'd see her again. But a couple of weeks later she turned up at a party my fraternity was throwing. As a smart man, I saw my chance and I took it.

Two of the best nights of my life were the ones I spent with her. Inside her.

But frivolous college hookups were no longer a part of my life, and I accepted it. Tell that to my body, though. Audrey's appearance in my home had the same effect on my libido that springtime had on the deer living on our hilltop. *Hello, pheromones.* For the first time in a long while my senses woke up and shook themselves. The curvy girl making a wacko sauce in my kitchen had once felt spectacular beneath me. And in front of me. And straddling me...

"Griff?"

"Hmm?" Shit, I was actually staring at her. "Is there something on my ass that shouldn't be there?" she asked.

"Uh." I was so busted. "Just a bit of hay."

"Get it off, would you?"

Ruh-roh. Trapped in my own stupid lie, I took a quick swipe at her skirt near her hip, where it was relatively safe.

"Thanks," she chirped, stirring.

May gave me a strange look as she dropped off a bag of brown sugar and some other seasonings on the counter beside Audrey. "Everything okay over here?"

"Of course," I grumbled. "Just hungry."

Her eyes twinkled. "Are you now?"

Aiming my grumpiest face at May, I stepped around her. Maybe if I just put a little distance between Audrey and me, the weirdness would pass.

I headed for the dining room, and Jude followed me like a shadow. "We eat most meals in here," I told him. "And after supper you can feel free to watch TV with us in the living room." I pointed. "Zach always does. I've had to train him up. He didn't see a television until he was almost twenty."

The new guy's eyes widened. "Why?"

"He grew up on a religious commune in Texas. Never left the property until he hitchhiked to Vermont. So we watch a lot of movies. Lately we're all about *The Lord of the Rings.*"

Since you can't farm after dark, movies were my respite. The nearest bar was twenty minutes away, and I didn't have a lot of cash to blow on beer, anyway. Or anything else for that matter. Last winter Zach and I watched a lifetime's worth of movies between December and March. During the growing season, we didn't have as much time to dedicate to Hollywood blockbusters.

My mother bustled into the room with an armful of clothes. "These are for you," she said to Jude, handing him the pile before he could even respond. "I'm going to get lunch on the table now."

Jude stared down at the pile in his hands. There were a couple pairs of jeans, old ones of mine. Mom had probably been saving those for Dylan, but it was just as useful to give them to Jude. There were shirts, too. Those had probably belonged to my father.

Mom was a true New England spendthrift. She mended everything until it was no longer practical. She got every drop of jam out of the bottom of the jar, then re-used the jar for the following century. It didn't surprise me one bit that she'd been able to produce these clothes with only a few minutes' warning. I'd bet cash money the things she'd found would fit him, too.

"Thank you," Jude said to the air where Mom used to be. "She didn't have to do that."

"It's nothing," I said. "She probably has a collection up there sorted by size and alphabetized by color. Now find a seat, because here they come."

My sisters brought in fat slices of homemade bread and a giant bowl of potato salad. These were deposited on the sideboard. "We'll make our plates," Mom announced, following with her platter of brisket. "Grab one and queue up."

Zach stepped into the room, grabbed a plate off the table and made it over to the food first.

"How does he do that?" May asked, laughing. "Zach has, like, a sixth sense for when food is served."

"You'd have it too if you expended as many calories in a day as he does," I said. Plucking a plate off the table, I handed it to Jude. Then I grabbed one for myself.

Our new employee did not put very much food on his plate. Just a slice of bread, the smallest piece of brisket and a dab of potato salad. Maybe he'd already had lunch, or maybe he didn't want to pig out before he'd lifted a finger on our farm. I wasn't gonna bother him about it. He'd learn soon enough. For a long day of farm work, calories were pretty crucial.

We all began to take seats around the table. I put my napkin in my lap and sat back in my chair, and Jude took this cue, copying me.

My grandfather walked in then, wiping his brow with the back of his hand. "Hot out there," he muttered, heading for the buffet.

"If you'd just move into the farmhouse, I'd put an air conditioner in your room," my mother promised.

"Not moving. Stop asking." Although he refused to sleep here, Grandpa didn't miss many meals in our dining room. He began to fix his plate.

I'd managed to put Audrey Kidder out of my mind for a good, solid five minutes, so it was kind of a surprise when she came barreling into the room with a gravy boat and a spoon. She put it down in front of my mother, who smiled and began to spoon some of the weird sauce onto her open-face sandwich.

We all waited while Audrey dashed over to the sideboard and made herself a little sandwich. When she and Grandpa took their seats across the table from me, my mother said, "Griff, why don't you say grace?"

"All right." Nothing like exchanging a few words with God while your ex-hookup watched from across the table. "Dear Lord, we thank you for these blessings we're about to receive. Thank you for the Red Sox victory last night and for the minimal amount of rose chafer beetles that the twins will have to pinch off the plum trees after lunch..."

"Griff," my mother warned. She hated it when I used grace as a means of nagging my family. Two birds, one stone, though.

"...please ease the way of our new friend Jude as he joins us here on the farm," I added, hoping the dude wouldn't die of embarrassment. But it's something my mother would want me to say. "And please help Miss Kidder find a tire shop with the right-sized tire so she can make a speedy trip back to Boston today. Amen."

May snorted beside me. And when I looked up at Audrey, she gave me a squinty-eyed look of disapproval.

"Well," my mother said in the extra-gracious voice she used whenever her children discredited her, "let's try Audrey's special barbecue sauce."

I was the last one to receive the gravy boat, and I put a truly modest amount of sauce on my food, mostly just to make it perfectly clear to anyone who might be paying attention that I had no particular interest in Audrey Kidder. Then I tucked into my mother's excellent cooking.

It was quiet for a moment, as lunchtime often is. We take our food seriously. But then May gave an unladylike moan. "Omigod," she gasped. "This sauce. So *good*!"

"It's...wow," my brother agreed. "You could, like, bottle this and sell it. It's foodgasmic."

Across from me, Audrey grinned like she'd just won an award.

"The cherries are perfect," my mother gushed. "So tart, and with the balsamic vinegar. Incredible!"

"Impressive," Zach said, and I gave my most loyal employee a glare. *Et tu, Zachariah?*

"You don't have much food, new guy," May said to Jude. "Did you try the sauce?"

"I did, and I'm speechless," he said, and I almost

gave him a kick under the table. "Then again," he hedged. "This is the first food I've eaten in three years that didn't come from a prison or a hospital. So I'm easy to impress."

A couple people snickered, but both Audrey and my mother sat forward in their chairs. Mom's eyes got misty. Audrey gasped. "Are you serious? I sauced your *first* meal out of prison?"

Jude dropped his chin. He looked sorry he'd spoken up. Getting attention didn't seem to agree with Jude.

"I think he needs another helping," my mother declared. She pushed back from the table and went over to the sideboard to fetch another sandwich for Jude. The woman just couldn't help herself. "Does anyone need anything while I'm over here?"

"Just more of that sauce," my little sister said.

Bunch of traitors. The whole lot of them.

I bit into the center of my sandwich and chewed. And—holy hell. Smoky sweet cherries with a hint of heat. I resisted the groans of pleasure the rest of my family was making. But goddamn it, the girl could really cook. She was still irritating as hell and worked for a bunch of crooks. But she had one talent.

Okay, two. Food and sex...

"Griff, you okay?" my mother asked. "You look a little flushed."

"Hot day," I grunted. And it was.

"I thought Vermont didn't get hot," Audrey said. "Where are the cool mountain breezes?"

"They'll be back at sunset," I said, speaking up for the best state in the union. "That's the thing about Vermont, it always cools off at night."

"Good to know," Audrey said, taking a dainty bite of potato salad.

"Where do you two know each other from, anyway?"

Zach asked, heading over to the sideboard for another helping.

My mother looked up. "You two met before?"

Well, damn it, Zach. Now I'd have to kill him after lunch. Shame, too. Such a great employee.

"Let's see," Audrey said, dabbing the corner of her kissable mouth with the napkin. She didn't meet my eyes and so I braced myself. "We overlapped at BU." She gave me a sidelong glance from across the table as if to say, *see what I did there?*

Oh, we overlapped all right.

"We had a few mutual friends," Audrey added. "I was dating his loathsome fraternity brother." She raised an eyebrow at me. "Do you know whatever happened to him?"

I shook my big guilty head. Bryce hadn't been my kind of guy. He ran with the rich kids.

"You know." May leaned forward. "I *thought* you looked a little familiar. What year did you graduate?"

"Ah." Audrey chased a chunk of potato around her plate. "I didn't. Failed out my freshman year. Then I went to Mount Holyoke until they asked me not to return. Eventually I found my way to culinary school. Third time's a charm."

Everybody chuckled, which was ridiculous. If either of the twins failed out of college, I'd kill 'em with my bare hands. Their upcoming tuition bills kept me awake nights.

"Culinary school was the right choice," my little sister chimed in. "This sauce is amazing."

"Thank you."

Everyone leapt in with another round of praise, as if Audrey had cured a rare variety of cancer.

I finished my sandwich in silence, feeling unsettled. And trying not to moan every time I got a taste of the weird wonderfulness that was sour cherries in a barbecue sauce.

* * *

Audrey Kidder left after lunch, so the day went back to normal.

Or rather—it should have. But I was unsettled and even shorter tempered than usual. I made some calls and did some office work, but it only made me feel crazy. So I took a jug of mom's ginger lemonade and a half-dozen cookies outside and went to find Zach, Jude and my brother Dylan where they were working in the orchard. There was always something to do out there— mowing, picking up dropped apples, setting traps for the bugs we didn't want or cultivating plants to attract the bugs we *did* want.

Organic farming is all about coaxing harmony to flourish where you need it. But I was not in a harmonious mood as I approached the guys. "How's it going?" I asked them. "See any pests I need to worry about?"

Zach shook his head. "Looking good over here, though we could use some rain."

"All right. Break time?"

"I'm free for that," Dylan said. He flopped down on the grass and I passed him the tote bag with the snacks in it. He dug in and began pouring lemonade into plastic cups. "Here," he said, passing one up to Jude.

My new employee looked sweaty but relaxed. He took the cup and gulped it down. I grabbed a jug of water out of the bag and passed it to Jude. "Here. Your face looks red."

"Thanks," he said. "I'm probably going to burn, but I don't mind. I haven't been outside all day in years."

Jesus. I couldn't even imagine. Not a day went by that I wasn't outside for hours. If you put me in a cell I'd die. "What was rehab like?"

Jude laughed. "Nicer than jail, but I couldn't appreciate it because I was too busy throwing up. The last ten days were better. There's a courtyard where you can sit outside and play cards or whatever. And three times a day you have to talk about your feelings. That's torture enough, but you have to listen to everyone else's story, too. I mean—it's motivating, but depressing. I thought I had a shitty childhood but some of these people are hardcore. The doctors asked everyone, 'Where did you get your *first* hit? Who gave it to you?' This girl—maybe she's twenty now. She got her first lines of coke at twelve. It was a birthday present from her mother."

"Hell," Zach said, shoving a cookie in his mouth.

"I know, right?" Jude took a cookie, too. "Some of the people I met in there are so fucked. They can't even remember being clean, because they were in sixth grade the last time they didn't have drugs in their bodies." He wiped the sweat off his forehead with his arm, and then lay back in the grass.

With the weather so warm, the bugs were at their most active. Grasshoppers dove past me like small aircraft, their wings buzzing as they went. Bees stopped to inspect the clover growing in the long grass.

Dylan gave my foot a gentle kick. "Where you been while we sweat out here?"

"Business crap. Had to make my market calls." I was the president of the board for the Norwich farmers' market. "Starting next month we're taking food stamps as payment. Most everybody's on board, but there are a few people holding out on me."

"Dicks," Dylan said. "Who wouldn't want to expand

their market and give decent food to people who need it?"

"Exactly. But there's paperwork. And farmers hate that shit. But I'll win 'em over."

Nobody said anything for a few minutes. The freedom to doze in the sunshine always felt pretty spectacular after a couple hours of hard labor. If I'd spent the afternoon outside, too, I wouldn't be so agitated. Today my brain just wouldn't shut up. "Hey, bro?" I nudged Dylan's shoe. "Smithy sent over new lease terms for the next couple years. I need to discuss it with you." Dylan was only seventeen, and a year away from high school graduation. But this was his farm, too. "I'm not sure it's in our best interest to keep going with the South Hill half of our dairy."

The look of shock on my brother's face when he sat up was greater than I'd anticipated. "That's ridiculous," he said. "Why would we cut off most of our wintertime income?"

"Well..." I sat so I could see him more clearly. "The price of milk is down thirty percent in the last two years, but costs are going up. Dairy isn't always a good business. A lot of guys went bankrupt during the '90s. Dad had a good run, but I don't like our chances."

"But..." My brother fretted. "Dad loved those cows. And we're diversified with the dairy. We have bad years in the orchard sometimes. What if that was our whole paycheck? We can't just cut our operation in half."

"I hear you," I said as soothingly as possible. And honestly I was happy that Dylan understood these things. It was hard to say whether he'd be farming beside me after he got a college education and a better look at the world. But I liked knowing he was paying attention. "The dairy cows across the street are worth some money. If we sell them, we'll earn a nice profit that we could reinvest in something else. I want to grow the cider operation because it's an added-value business, not just a commodity. If it catches on, we'd have a brand name. And it would be something special that's just ours."

"Or just *yours*," Dylan argued. "Nobody else knows how to make cider. What are the rest of us supposed to run?"

Ah. Maybe my little brother wanted to farm after all. Or at least keep his options open. "We'd keep the organic part of the dairy, the part that's on our own land. I'd only sell off the other side. All the organic milk would still go to the Abrahams." They were our neighbors down the road who made fancy cheese.

Dylan didn't say anything for a couple minutes. Maybe this conversation should have taken place in private. I didn't know if he was comfortable arguing about it in front of Zach and Jude. "Mom is gonna flip," he said eventually. "Those cows were Dad's babies."

"We're not selling *you*, Dyl." I chuckled. He'd been Dad's baby. I was worried about what my mother would say when I showed her the new lease terms. That's why I was telling Dylan first. "I'm not doing this because I don't like the dairy. All I want is to keep us on the right track."

Dylan snorted. "Is that *all* you want?"

"What?"

"I think you want to get into Audrey Kidder's pants."

Hell, was I that obvious?

Another voice weighed in from the grass. "I think he's already been there," Jude mumbled.

I choked on my last swallow of lemonade. "Shit. You're psychic? What's the price of milk going to do over the next five years?"

Zach and Jude laughed.

"Omigod, really?" Dylan yelped. He flopped onto an elbow. "When you said you knew her in college, I didn't know you meant *biblically*."

"Who knows who biblically?" May's voice came from the next orchard row. Then her face appeared between two Golden Delicious trees. "Wait, you dated *Audrey*?"

A moment ago I'd been celebrating Dylan's intelligence. But my family's sharp minds were frequently an inconvenience.

"How come I don't remember Audrey's name?" May asked, sitting down beside me.

"Well..." I chuckled again. "Couldn't really call it dating. Cover your ears, Dylan."

My little brother kicked me again. "I'm not twelve."

"I know." I sighed. But I didn't want my little brother to behave the way I had—not at any age. It wasn't the sex that I regretted. It was the way it all went down.

I'd always wanted Audrey. From the first moment she showed up with my teammate Bryce, I'd been jealous. And not just because she was hot. I'd been drawn to her silly spirit, and the carefree way that she seemed to enjoy life without trying too hard. Everything in my own life was a struggle. But she and Bryce were part of the effortless, rich kid crew. I wanted what they had, and I felt like an ass for caring about it so much.

But then Bryce began bringing other girls around, too. The first time I saw him with his tongue down the throat of another girl, I assumed that he and Audrey had broken up. I was bummed, because it meant I wouldn't see her anymore. But the next night, there she was on his arm, smiling and getting us all to do the best imitation we could of a...chicken. I didn't even remember why. College jokes were like that—brilliantly funny and apropos of nothing. Those were the good old days.

Later, I'd asked Bryce what he'd been doing with the other girl. "Audrey is my girlfriend," he'd said. "But she was my high school girl, you know? And her mother owns half of Boston." He'd chuckled like a comic book villain. "We'll probably get married. But I can't do four years of college without a few extra-curricular activities. That would just be wrong."

That got my blood boiling. I'd already thought Bryce was a mindless playboy. But I wanted to punch that fucker for cheating on his girl.

After that, whenever Audrey showed up at the frat house with Bryce, I always left. Couldn't stand to watch. I didn't really know her, but she turned me on like nobody's business, which was even more confusing for me. I kept wondering whether I should tell her about Bryce's extracurricular activities. And then I'd wonder whether telling her was just something I wanted to do for my own jealous reasons.

When Bryce would turn up with a different girl, I always made a point of asking him out loud how Audrey was doing. "Great," he'd always say with a grin or a wink. The fucker had no shame at all. His dates—and there were many of them—didn't seem bothered by the question, either.

The whole thing drove me insane, until one night the inevitable happened. It was a weeknight and quiet at the house. I'd seen Bryce go upstairs with some leggy girl I didn't know. They were probably in the little TV den where the freshmen pledges hung out. And probably making out on the couch.

I'd been parked on an uncomfortable sofa off the kitchen, an undesirable spot where I could do my homework in peace. When someone knocked on the kitchen door, it had been me who'd answered.

"Hi, Griffin," Audrey had said as she bounced through the door. "Is Bryce around, by chance?"

I hadn't even hesitated. "Check the TV room upstairs. Pretty sure I saw him up there."

"Thanks." She'd scampered toward the stairs.

Immediately I'd felt like an absolute shit. I couldn't sit there and wait to know what happened. Slamming my textbook closed, I'd jumped up and felt for my keys in my pocket. But I couldn't get away fast enough—someone had parked me in. So I was outside in the driveway, contemplating the sight of Bryce's fucking Mercedes behind my heap of a car when Audrey came storming back out the kitchen door, her face red. Tears running down her cheeks.

She hadn't even seen me. She'd just speed-walked down the driveway and disappeared.

I was sure I'd never see her again. And why would I deserve to, anyway? But two weeks later she came back to the house with some of her sorority sisters. Maybe Audrey had revenge on the mind because she was dressed to kill. She hadn't ever looked twice at me before, but that night when I asked her to dance, she said it was the best idea she'd heard in a long time.

The rest of the night will play forever on my fantasy reel. I came on strong and she took every hint. When I kissed her, she gave as good as she got. And when we went upstairs I thought I'd die from happiness.

A week later we repeated the same performance. I was a goner after that, and thinking about her all the time—

"Griff? Can you even hear me?"

My sister's voice snatched me out of my reverie. "What?"

"I said, I think Audrey's great." May punched me in the arm. "You should call her."

Call her. That's the thing—I *had* called her after our tryst. Even the younger, stupider version of me hadn't missed the fact that she and I had amazing chemistry. So I'd called to invite her out to dinner.

But apparently she decided I wasn't worth the effort. My call went unreturned.

Before long the year was over, and all I could do was kick myself for handling her so clumsily. I could have taken it slower. I could have apologized for sending her upstairs to see her boyfriend getting blown by his date for the evening. (Bryce was none too happy about this unfortunate incident.)

But I'd taken her to bed instead. Two different nights. I'd felt like a user, and didn't really blame her for blowing me off. And now I'd been frosty toward Audrey today. Rejection—even five years past—had turned me into a bigger grouch than usual.

Tossing my empty cup into the tote, I stood up. "Break time's over."

My brother stood up, too. "You're just gonna drop that bomb and go back to work?"

It took me a second to realize he was referring to my idea to sell off a lot of our milkers. "We'll talk a lot more, first," I said gently. "A lot more. Don't worry, okay?"

But Dylan gave me a dark, grumpy look that reminded me of me. Then he stomped off toward the wheelbarrow.

"What bomb?" May asked.

"Ask me tomorrow," I grumbled. "Gotta go check on the peach trees."

Once again, Audrey had come and gone. I was left with only regrets and a whole lot of farm work.

Chapter Six

Audrey

When I left the Shipley Farm after lunch, Griff surprised me by pressing two bottles of his cider into my hands. "I know your boss doesn't want to pay the market rate," he said. "But I'm not an idiot. I know it would be good to get into those restaurants—at least if I don't lose my shirt.

I thought Griff losing his shirt was a fine idea. But not the way he meant. I wanted another look at that spectacular chest...

"So do your best," he said with more humility than I'd expected from him. "Let the man taste it, and tell me the best he can do."

"I'll try," I promised him. Hell, I wanted to succeed, if only to see the stunned expression on his too-handsome face. "I'll call you to let you know."

"I'll answer my phone just like a city slicker."

"Right." My face burned from the shame of having listened to Burton. That man was just using me to further his agenda.

Men had done that to me many times, actually. You'd think I'd stop falling for it.

"And get that donut replaced with a real tire," Griff told me. "You shouldn't drive on that thing any farther than you have to. The tire place in Montpelier should get you done. If you're heading south, it's trickier. You might have to go all the way to Lebanon, New

Hampshire."

Yikes. I'd passed that place an hour before I got here. "Thanks. I'll take care of it."

As I got into my car, I gave the Shipley farmhouse one last look. Its proud white clapboards glinted in the June sunshine, and, as the wind shifted, I caught the faint scent of cow manure on the breeze. There were wicker chairs on the porch, the kind that weren't just for show, but for sinking into at the end of a summer day.

Nice place, this.

I drove off toward Bradford hoping to find the tire place without too much trouble. But when I got there, I hit a snag. The rental car company didn't have the place on its approved list of repair shops. The guy behind the desk explained, "You need to go to Rutland or Burlington. If you don't use an approved shop, the rental company will charge you a ninety-nine dollar out-of-policy repair fee."

Grrr. I didn't have any extra money to spend, and I could bet that it was exactly the sort of expense BPG would hassle me over. "Um," I said, my geography of Vermont a little shaky. "I'm not heading up there. What's south of here?" Maybe I could just get my meetings done and head back the way I came.

"White River Junction or Lebanon, New Hampshire," came the answer.

"Thank you," I grumbled before leaving.

The donut would have to do. People drove for weeks on those things, right?

I stayed the night in a roadside motel, where I mapped out the other farms' locations, one by one. I tried to plot a route that would keep the mileage to a minimum. But it wasn't easy. While all the farms were on the eastern side of the state, each one was down a different country road off a different minor highway.

Although one of them—Apostate Farm was its name—was almost adjacent to Griff Shipley's place. If I'd noticed that earlier, I would have stopped there already. Now I'd have to backtrack to Tuxbury on my way home.

I got on the road early the next morning. The northernmost farm was Misty Hollow, and luckily it wasn't far off the highway.

When I pulled into the driveway, chickens scattered in every direction. I stepped out of the car gingerly, hoping to avoid getting chicken poop in my open-toed shoes.

The screen door to the farmhouse in front of me banged open, and a sheepdog came charging out. Having little experience with dogs, I stiffened, hoping it wouldn't think I was an intruder. The chickens had the same fears, scattering once again. But the dog didn't run at me. Instead, he stuck his nose under a shrub and then turned around with a rather disgusting tennis ball in his mouth. Trotting over to me, he dropped it at my feet where it rolled against my bare toe.

Ew.

The dog sat on its fuzzy black and white butt and then smiled up at me, tail wagging hopefully. It was hard to say no in the face of all that longing. So I bent over and picked up the ball with as little contact as possible, then flung it to the side, away from the poor chickens, who'd already gone back to scratching and pecking at in the grass beside the gravel drive.

The dog tore off in search of its ball, and the screen door banged once more, this time behind an older woman. "We don't want any," she said from her porch.

"Hi!" I called as if she'd said something more friendly. I walked toward her in order to be heard. "I'm not selling anything. I want to buy—" I peeked at the list in my hand. "—turkey. Free-range turkey."

She still gave me the stink eye. "You want to order a Thanksgiving bird?"

"No ma'am. I'm here for the Boston Premier Group. It's a restaurant company. They're looking to buy four hundred birds."

The toothpick in her mouth traveled from one side to the other in a tidy line. "My price is five bucks a pound."

"Well..." With a prickle of dread, I glanced down at the sheet again. *$2.50.* "BPG would like to pay two-fifty. But they'll take a lot of them."

She shrugged. "I bred as many poults as I knew I could sell to the people nearby. If I sell to you, I lose money and I have no product at Thanksgiving. Looks like we don't have anything more to say to one another."

At that, she turned and went inside the house.

This same scenario repeated itself a few miles further on at a beekeeping outfit. BPG's price for honey was too low by half, of course. And then it happened again when I visited a big vegetable farm. Since the farmer's products were so numerous, I handed over my pricing sheet for his perusal.

After about thirty seconds, the bearded farmer handed it back with a shake of his head. "Griff Shipley told me to look out for you. Said you're trying to bend us all over with slave's wages. We're not falling for that."

"He... *what?*"

The guy winced. "Sorry, miss. You're working for a company that doesn't respect what we do. There must be a couple hundred farms closer to Boston, anyway."

I got back in my car, seething. If Griff had warned away every farmer in the county, then I was wasting my time. This job was hard enough without his help.

And why couldn't BPG get what they needed in Massachusetts, anyway? That question tickled my worried brain. But I shoved it aside in favor of throwing imaginary darts at Griff's picture. He'd be easy enough to hit with a dart. Those broad shoulders. All that muscle...

Focus, Audrey!

I reapplied my lipstick and visited three more farms. One farmer offered to meet my price on potatoes, but only if he could pass me scabby ones. "I'm always looking for somewhere to go with the uglies. They're perfectly good, but they get passed over at the farmers' market."

"I'll see what I can do." I sighed, making a note. I could already hear Burton's voice in my head telling me that he expected perfection.

Nobody mentioned the Shipley Farm again, and most everyone was polite. But nobody could help me, nor did they seem willing to chat about it.

Fricking Griff. If only I hadn't stopped there first.

I'd driven sixty miles on country roads and had absolutely *nothing* to show for it. Not one item had been contracted, unless my boss had a liberal view of scabby potatoes.

The last farm on my list was right down the road from Griff Shipley. I gave his farm's sign the finger as I passed by. The sign for Apostate Farm was just a tiny shingle, but I found it. Turning in, I bumped up their pitted gravel drive, which was in serious need of some attention. The car jostled me until my teeth were practically chattering. Could Vermont be any less welcoming?

I bounced to a stop outside a barn. Two men emerged from just inside, but I looked down at my phone because I wasn't quite ready to deal with them yet. I needed a deep breath. And a glass of wine, and a day at a spa and a new job.

The deep breath was the only thing on the list I

could reasonably expect to get.

I pushed open the car door, hoping to wax on my smile. But the first words I heard were, "Looks like you got a flat tire there, miss."

"Fuck!" I swore, leaping out to inspect the tire. Sure enough, the culprit was the donut, of course. No wonder the driveway had felt like a minefield.

Someone chuckled, and the sound curdled my insides. Because I knew that laugh. My head snapped up to find my nemesis watching me. "August Griffin Shipley!" I shrieked. "Did you tell every farmer in the county to give me the stiff arm? That was a dick move." I slammed my car door and wheeled around to face him.

He actually had the decency to look sheepish. He crossed his brawny arms across that impressive chest and bowed his head. "I thought my neighbors needed to know who was about to come knocking. BPG are a bunch of corporate assholes, Audrey."

"Am I a corporate asshole? You might as well come out and say it." I crossed my arms, too, mirroring his stance. If the move just happened to accentuate my cleavage, then oh well.

His gaze drifted over my body and ended up on the sky. "You're not, honey. But that doesn't fix the problem."

Honey. I hated myself a little bit for enjoying the way the word rolled off his full lips.

"Shoulda had the new tire put on already," he added, which helped to kick my righteous anger back to the forefront.

"Like I don't know that," I snapped. His neighbor's eyebrows flew upward in surprise. Damn it all. He was the guy I'd come here to find. But what were the odds he'd sell his artisanal cheeses to me now? Vermont had chewed me up and spit me out in the space of twenty-four hours. There was no reason for me to stay here. "This was a mistake," I muttered, grabbing the car door again. I tossed my purse onto the passenger seat and then climbed in.

"Hey, Audrey," Griff started to say as I turned the key. "You can't drive that thing..."

Listening to him wouldn't get me where I needed to go. So I put the car in reverse and backed up a few feet. It was rough going, but I made it. I put 'er in gear and pulled hard on the wheel, circling the nose of the car in front of Griff and his neighbor. The two men backed up quickly, as if I were a bomb about to go off.

The Prius took me ten or twenty yards down the gravel drive before the bouncing became more of a pronounced list to the right.

"Fuck!" I shouted at the top of my lungs. I wasn't even going to be able to make a dignity-preserving getaway. Sagging onto its wheel frame, the car ground to a sad halt. I threw it in park and then head-butted the steering wheel in anger, which only served to draw a ridiculous beep from the horn. The car was out to get me.

Was there no task on earth I could complete without fucking it up? No job I could keep without disgrace?

I heard the telltale crunch of gravel under someone's footsteps. There was no point in wondering whose. If I had to look like a complete idiot, did it have to be in front of the world's hottest farmer? Apparently it did, because the car door opened and his gruff voice said, "Hop on out, honey. I'll get Zach to find you another spare."

"Thank you," I said through gritted teeth.

"Since you're here, we can finish our conversation about produce prices."

"If you're just going to yell at me, save it." I grabbed

my purse off the seat and stood up.

Griffin frowned down at me. God, the man was tall. Like Paul Bunyan. "I wouldn't yell at a woman."

"Technicality," I said under my breath. "You grumble and growl."

He grunted in a way that neither agreed nor disagreed. "Come on. If you want to talk about apples, it has to be while I'm working. I have a pig to kill. You can watch."

"Are you sure?" I snapped. "I mean—*meow*. There must be a whole lot of girls in line ahead of me to watch that."

To my enduring surprise, he threw back his head and laughed. "Come on, sassypants. My truck is over here."

"I was supposed to inquire here about cheeses." Turning from side to side, I couldn't spot the farmer I'd seen before. "Where'd he go?"

"He's got a situation today. Found some wilt on his tomatoes, and it has to be taken care of fast. He called me to take a look at it and I offered to send him some help. And now Zach is gonna be working on your tire..." He ran a hand through his thick, brown hair and sighed.

"I'll ask about the cheeses later," I said tightly.

Griff crossed to a big pickup truck and opened the passenger door. "Come on, now."

He offered me his hand to help me into the truck, and I hesitated. I was sick of playing the part of the incompetent little woman. On the other hand, it was a big step up into the truck, and I was wearing a skirt. A stumble and fall—another avoidable fuck-up—wasn't going to do anything for my ego.

His big hand waited, outstretched. So I pressed mine into that wide palm, and his roughened fingers closed around mine. *Sweet baby Jesus.* His touch shouldn't feel familiar. I shouldn't have gotten a jolt of longing just from gripping his fingers. But that big hand had once touched me *everywhere.*

A *long, long time ago,* I reminded myself. *You were a different person then, and so was he.* Thinking about those times wasn't helping anyone. I blamed the warm weather or the fact that I was so tense. It's not like I'd thought about Griff Shipley at all during the past couple of years.

As soon as my butt hit the truck's seat, I yanked my hand out of his. Wordlessly, he shut the door and walked around to the other side, climbing in beside me. He made a three-point turn, and, as we rolled down the drive past my stupid rental, I spotted the farmer on the other side of his barn, bent over a row of pretty green tomato plants. "Is it serious?" I asked. "The tomato problem?" A couple of years ago most of New England's crop had been wiped out by a blight. There had been no gazpacho on Boston's restaurant menus that summer.

"Maybe," Griff said after a beat. "But he'll burn a few plants and hope for the best. Organic farming always feels like a game of high-stakes poker. That's why we're all diversified. He's got sheep, cheeses and vegetables. I've got apples, ciders and dairy. Not everything can go wrong at once, unless we're reenacting the Book of Job."

"I see," I said quietly. "His cheeses sound amazing. I looked at his website."

"They are," he agreed. "The dude built his own cheese cave to age them. It's really cool. They're pricey, though. A lot of love goes into that cheese."

I let out a sigh. "I *know* that, okay? I've made cheese. I'm not stupid. Artisanal cheese is something my company knows how to pay up for, right? The stuff they're importing from France doesn't come cheap."

Another awkward silence hung over the cab of Griff's truck, and I tried not to ogle the muscles in his arms as he drove. I looked out the window instead, at row upon row of apple trees. Little green fruits the size of tennis balls hung from branches everywhere. "Looks like a good year for apples."

"It does," he agreed with me. "We didn't have a late freeze this spring, which helps. And we didn't have any hail at just the wrong moment. Hail leaves dark spots on the skin, and people don't like blemishes." He shook his head. "The public doesn't understand that a bushel of apples with no blemishes anywhere is scary as fuck. That means the farmer sprayed poison all over the tree. You couldn't pay me to eat those apples."

"So you're saying Snow White's poison apple was from a factory farm?"

He chuckled. "Sure. People say they want to eat clean food and buy organic. But they also want it to look perfect. Before every big weekend during U-pick season we get out there and pluck all the uglies off the trees. Apples sell better when people think they're all perfect."

"You can always make cider from the uglies."

"And we do."

I pointed at Zach, Jude and the twins—they stood between two orchard rows, a red wagon between them. "What are they doing?"

"Painting sticky traps to catch bugs. During the summer we fight off borers and moths. We can never let down our guard, because we can't use toxic sprays to fight off whatever we didn't catch before it was too late."

When he swung into the driveway, the others began to walk over to meet him. "Wait here a moment," he said, killing the engine. "I'll give Zachariah the truck to take back to Abraham's place."

I hopped down from the truck without help from Mr.

Big Hands, then waited sheepishly while he went to instruct his minions.

"Hey," Daphne greeted me, wiping her hands on her jeans. "My brother ate the rest of your sauce in the dark of night, before the rest of us could have any. *Again.*"

"I'm a growing boy," Dylan said. "You want to burn tomato plants or kill a pig?" he asked his sister.

She rolled her eyes. "Why are you even pretending that I have a choice? You're going to end up killing tomato plants because you can't handle skinning Tauntaun."

Dylan's face colored. "I've handled the abattoir before."

"You fainted."

"It was *hot*," he argued, his face contorting in anger.

"Go to Abraham's." She gave him a shove. "I like gore."

He gave her an angry glare and then climbed in the truck, slamming the door. Note to self—the Shipley men did not take kindly to having their masculinity questioned. Daphne picked at a cuticle, bored. I couldn't imagine what it was like to have a twin—someone you knew so well you could effortlessly push each other's buttons. As an only child, it fascinated me.

"Okay," Griff said, appearing around the nose of the truck. He beckoned to Daphne and me, and Jude behind him. "Let's go make some bacon while Zach tries to find Audrey a tire. Did May scald the water?"

"She did," Daphne said, trotting to keep up with her brother's long-legged stride. "Is the tomato thing bad?"

"We'll see." Griff put one of his big paws on his sister's shoulder. They were a tall family.

Jude, the new guy, fell into step with me. "How was your first day?" I asked him.

"Great," he said quickly, shoving his hands in his

pockets. "I've never farmed, but I like working with my hands."

"Me too. It wasn't until I went to cooking school that I really figured that out."

He looked up with a wry grin. "Would you believe that my prison job was in the kitchen? I'll bet you've never used knives that are tethered to the work surface."

I laughed. "Wow, is that how they do it? How can you move around?" It was hard to picture. But how else could they have all those knives in a prison?

"There's a retractable cord pierced through the butt of each knife so that nobody will steal 'em. Once in a while I'd forget about the damn thing and, like, choke myself if I turned around to hear what someone was saying. Good times. I'm pretty fast at prep work, though. Three years of practice."

"Can you get the skin off a clove of garlic in three seconds or less?" I teased.

"Hell, yeah. Garlic is my bitch."

"Then you're hired! Some day when I'm a famous chef, you can be my prep guy," I promised. "But you'll have to move to Boston."

He chuckled. "Okay. Sure."

Our walk took us past the cider house. Beyond that was an old stone fire pit where a cauldron of water steamed. It looked like something out of medieval times. Beside it was a little pen where a giant pig sunbathed, his eyes closed, his ears flopped forward. As we arrived, he opened his eyes and got to his feet, then approached the fence hopefully. His expression reminded me of a dog looking for a treat.

Griffin walked up to the fence and reached down, scratching the pig between his ears. "Hey, Tauntaun," he dropped his voice to a near whisper. "Hey, guy.

You've been a good boy. Thank you."

My throat got inexplicably tight. I worked with meat all the time, but I'd never seen it killed before. This really shouldn't be any weirder than hacking up a chicken in the kitchen. I was a meat-eater by choice, right?

Right?

Out of the corner of my eye I saw Mrs. Shipley approach with May. The matriarch was the one carrying the shotgun. She handed it to Griff.

He turned around to survey the small group of people gathered there. "Anyone want to do the honors? I think Zach did the last one."

Griff's gaze came to rest on Jude, who shook his head. "Your neighborhood felon has never touched a gun before."

"Good to know," Griff muttered.

"I'll do it," Daphne said, stepping forward.

Griff chuckled and handed the gun over, barrel pointed toward the sky. "That's my girl."

His teenage sister took the gun in hand as if she'd been born to it. Taking care to position herself away from any bystanders, she raised it calmly, feet braced apart like she'd done this a million times before. I heard the click of the safety being released.

"Right between the eyes," Griff whispered.

"I know," she scoffed.

Tauntaun blinked up at her through the fence rails, unconcerned. The next second there was an ear-splitting blast that made me jump. But not as hard as the pig jumped. He fell over like a brick chimney in an earthquake and began to twitch violently.

My stomach gave an involuntary lurch. *Steady*, I cautioned myself. Like it or not, there would be no bacon in the world without this. And any pig who'd lived out his days on the grassy hills of Griff Shipley's farm probably had a more comfortable life than half the residents of the Boston metro area.

I studied my shoes and waited for the sad part to end.

Chapter Seven

Griffin

Yeah, it was official. I was going to be single for the rest of my fucking life. The guy who'd kill a pig in front of a pretty girl is the guy who will die lonely.

It's not like I had a choice. I'd put off this task for two days already, and since May had done the work of bringing a full cauldron of water to a scalding temperature, I had to follow through.

But something about having Audrey nearby made me take a look at my life from a woman's point of view. And I didn't like what I saw. The girl paled when the pig went down, and I felt like a heel for making her watch.

Zach trotted up then. "Hey," he said. "Bad news."

Oh joy. "What's that?"

"Can't get a tire this evening. They don't have the right model, and we can't sub a different one onto the same axle. So she either needs *two* tires, or they can pull the right one from the shop in White River tomorrow."

"Damn it," Audrey said. "How much are tires? If I do this wrong, the rental company will stick me with the bill."

"A hundred and twenty," Zach said. "Each."

Audrey's eyes shut and she shook her pretty head. "Figures."

"Tomorrow," I said, gesturing to Zach to call the

shop. To Audrey I said, "You can stay here tonight. It's almost six already, anyway. They'll get you set up tomorrow. White River is only twenty miles away. The shop there would be closed by the time we got there, or else I'd send someone to get it for you."

"Thank you," Audrey said, her chin dropping.

"Don't mention it." It was really the least I could do after warning everyone off from the assholes she worked for.

"Come with me," my mother said, taking Audrey by the elbow. "Let's put together a quick supper."

Audrey's eyes lit up. "I love your kitchen. Put me to work." She turned to me. "We still need to talk about apple prices."

It would be a quick chat, but I wasn't ready to burst her bubble. Not yet, anyway. I pointed at the dead pig. "This takes some time," I explained, which was a huge understatement. "Jude and I will do the submersion and the scraping. Then we'll take a quick break for dinner. We'll talk then."

"Can I watch you do the butchering part?" she asked.

"Um..." *But I was trying not to be an asshole.* "Yeah. After we handle the submersion and the skinning."

The words sounded gorier than I'd intended when they came out of my mouth, but she didn't flinch. "Okay. Cool," she said.

Every time I thought I had this girl figured out, she surprised me.

* * *

The day kept on delivering surprises. My newest employee proved to be an unflinching assistant in the outdoor abattoir, which I'd set up under an awning on the back of the cider house. For hours, Jude helped me scrape and skin the pig. When we finally stopped for dinner, I apologized to him. "I know you were supposed to finish working hours ago. Here you are on your second day, and I'm already taking advantage."

He shook his head. "What I need in my life right now is more work and less thinking. It's all good."

Even so, I walked him back to the farmhouse, where Mom and my sisters had saved us our meals. "What's for dinner?" I asked in the way of men everywhere.

"Chicken salad salad," Daphne said. "It was Audrey's idea. Chicken salad—on a salad. Because it's tastier that way. There are walnuts and dried cherries in it. And couscous."

"And because I really like saying 'chicken salad salad,'" Audrey admitted from her perch on a barstool.

"Sounds good," I said, trying not to stare at Audrey and the way her slim fingers held her iced tea glass.

After I gobbled down my dinner, she followed me back outside to where Zachariah had taken a shift with the butchery.

"The temperature is dropping," she said as we walked together through the grass.

"It's never too hot in the evenings here," I agreed. "Even if the day is a scorcher, it just cools right off at night." I loved Vermont. Maybe I hadn't planned on moving back here right after college. But I did love the place.

"Where did you go after graduation?" she asked, reading my mind. "You got drafted, right? The Packers, was it?"

"Good memory," I said, surprised that she even knew. "Late round, though. I made it onto the practice squad, and I was hoping to make the roster the following year."

"Didn't work out?" she asked.

"Well, *probably* wouldn't have. That's what I tell

myself, anyway. My dad had a heart attack and died that October."

"I'm sorry."

"Thank you. Anyway—I left the team and came home to run things here."

"Oh wow," she said softly. "Shame you had to give up football."

"No big," I lied. Making the call to stay in Vermont and run our family farm was the biggest decision I'd ever made. But nobody had expected my healthy forty-nine-year-old dad to die suddenly. I thought I had ten or fifteen years to decide whether I wanted to farm. Instead, I was farming full time by age twenty-four and feeding three siblings, my mom and my grandparents.

We approached the worktable where Zach had finished the prep work. "I gutted it," he said as we approached. "Then I removed the head. Thought you'd want to get right to the, uh, more ordinary cuts first."

Zach had zero experience with women, but he was obviously more of a gentleman than I'd ever be. We always dealt with the head first, but it was kind of gory. "Thank you, Chewie," I said. I guided Audrey over to the sink where we both scrubbed our hands. "So, we'll take the shoulder roasts first," I said when we were through, and Zach handed me the knife.

I risked a glance at Audrey, who was frowning down at about two hundred pounds of gutted, skinless pig butterflied out on our giant steel-topped table. Then she ducked her head and saw, unfortunately, Tauntaun's head sitting right there in a bucket, the eyes practically staring at us.

"Wait!" she cried, looking agitated.

Oh boy. "If you feel nauseated, you can step outside."

Audrey whirled on me. "Griff Shipley, don't you dare throw away that head without removing the cheek meat."

"Come again?"

"You heard me. No—I'll do it." She bent over and dragged the bucket out where it would be accessible. Then she held out her hand, asking for the knife.

Dumbfounded, I handed it to her. Bending over, she grabbed the pig's ear. Then she slipped the tip of the knife under the skin. "The cheek meat is the only part of the animal that is both lean and tender. It makes a great braise, with Szechuan spices. I guess in a pinch you could go Italian—tomatoes and wine. Some garlic. Fresh oregano..." She kept cutting, the big knife making a dainty circle around the pig's face.

Beside me, Zach nudged my elbow in disbelief. The look I gave him said, *I know, right?* Even the new guy hid a smirk behind his hand.

Audrey laid a piece of meat on the platter my mother had put out for this purpose. Then she flipped the head around and cut again on the other side. After she liberated that piece, she nudged the bucket back underneath the table and looked up at me. "Can I keep going? I've never butchered a shoulder roast before. And this part will be for blade steaks, and then there's the loin..."

Marry me, my brain offered up as I gawked at her bloodied hands and bright smile. Note to self—don't cross Audrey again, at least not if there's a well-sharpened chef's knife in the vicinity. "Sure, go ahead," I said eventually. "I'll wrap the cuts."

Audrey watched me walk around the table to our sealing gizmo, all primed with a roll of fresh plastic. Once again, her eyes lit up. "Ooh! A vacuum sealer. There's a fun toy. We might have to switch jobs later." This girl was full of surprises. Humming to herself, she plunged the knife into the pig and began to carve. "You want these cuts big, right? But this is my first time, and I'm not sure I can get this roast out in one chunk."

Hell, neither could I, and I'd done this a dozen times already. "Just do your best. This is for farm use. It's not a beauty contest."

Zach just stood there watching, amusement growing on his face. Eventually I shooed him away. "You go eat. We'll hold down the fort. In fact—you're off the clock. Send my mom or May out later to take some things to the freezer."

Zach gave us a cheery wave and a grin that was more knowing than I wished it was. Then he walked away.

Audrey made another cut like she was born to it. "Look at that! All one piece," she crowed. "Pass the trophy."

Damn. "Those fuckers at BPG have you in the wrong job."

She snorted. "Gosh, you think? Story of my life."

"Why, though?" I asked. "Shouldn't they just let you loose in a kitchen?"

Audrey looked up, her face sad. "If I had a penis and a French accent, I'd be *running* one of their kitchens. I can't even get a line job."

"Then why do you stay there?"

"Six more weeks," she said, frowning down at her work. "Then I get to pitch them a restaurant idea. If they like it enough, they'll back it. But I'm in competition with about twenty other people, some of whom have both the penis and the French accent. And I don't have my idea formulated. I'm not panicked yet, though."

That sounded like the very definition of a long shot. Tougher than making it onto an NFL roster, maybe. "What happens if you don't win the prize?"

She shook her head. "Then I'm an unemployed girl with a culinary degree. I can always get a kitchen job somewhere. I won't starve. But having my own restaurant won't happen. Or they might offer me a job *somewhere*. Hey..." She pointed at the meat. "This is gorgeous. You don't sell your pork, right?"

I shook my head. "Nope. This is just to feed the people who produce the apples. I could buy a lot of meat at a big-box store. That would be a fuck of a lot easier. But we can't stand the idea of feeding factory meat to the people who pick the organic apples and milk the healthy cows. It's just not the right thing to do."

"No cutting corners with Griff Shipley," she teased.

"Well, really," I said, my voice betraying irritation. "It wouldn't be ethical."

"Was it *ethical* to warn all the farmers in the county away from a potential sale?" she asked.

"Yeah." It came out a little too forcefully. "It was ethical if making a sale to you had no potential to increase business at a better margin. BPG is only shopping in Vermont because they already pissed off the Massachusetts farmers. I found a discussion of it on an ag forum after you drove away. They'll drop us like a dress on prom night if we dare to demand reasonable compensation."

Her shoulders slumped. "Great. They're going to send me to freaking Canada next week, I'll bet."

"Hey, Canada is only two hours away. I'd better make a few calls."

"Griff!" she said, raising the knife, pointing it at me. "That's not funny."

"Sorry." I really needed to stop teasing this girl. But something about her got under my skin in all the ways there were. "Um," I pointed at the low-cut top she was wearing, feeling like a creeper. "You got some blood on that shirt, I'm afraid. Afterward I'll show you how to get it out." Naturally, my brain served up a mental image of her removing that shirt.

She raised an eyebrow at me, as if reading my mind. "Thanks for the help," she said dryly. "But every girl becomes an expert in getting blood out of fabric right around her thirteenth birthday. Cold water and soap. It's not rocket science."

"Uh, right." I felt myself blushing. "Do you want me to take a turn?"

"Am I doing it wrong?"

"No."

"Then no. Here..." She flipped a blade steak onto the platter. "Wrap this up, Farmer Griff."

She eventually let me do some of the work. We switched jobs when dusk came, bringing pink light to the sky beyond our farmhouse. Jude and Zach were off the clock for the night. But Mom and May popped in from time to time to remove our handiwork to the freezers in the house, to turn on the lights and to bring me and Audrey each a glass of my cider.

"Ooh, score! I love this stuff," she said appreciatively, and I couldn't help but feel a burst of stupid pride.

It was pushing midnight when I finally suggested we stop. Reluctantly, she let me put the rest of the carcass in the cooler. "I butcher earlier in the season than most people. It's not because I want lean pork," I explained, hosing off the work surface. "It's because I need to have this finished well before I need the cool room for apples. It wouldn't be sanitary to store them together."

"Gotcha," she said, washing our cider glasses in the sink.

I didn't know where the evening had gone.

Butchering was usually a chore, but I had Audrey's feminine laugh—and sharp tongue—to keep me company.

The gory remnants I sealed in a big plastic bin. "This will get composted tomorrow," I explained. "But if I left it out, we'd attract coyotes. And raccoons. Hear that?" I paused, pointing toward the distant forest. The animals' throaty, snickering conversation could be heard in the trees.

"That's...a raccoon?"

"A bunch of 'em. They're active in the dark."

"And coyotes? Right on your property?" She peered into the dark, looking concerned, and I had to bite back a laugh. "They're after my chickens, and so are the raccoons. Or at least the chicken feed. They don't want you. You're too much trouble."

"That's what everybody says," she whispered, then smiled. It was supposed to be a joke, but I had the feeling it was only halfway funny to her.

"Come on," I said, beckoning toward the bunkhouse, into the night. "We're done now." I switched off the overhead lights, but it didn't quite plunge us into darkness, because the moon was nearly full, and it shone down through the clear skies, illuminating the stones of the bunkhouse.

"Zach said he got my bag out of the car," she told me as we began walking. "That was nice of him."

"Now you know who's the gentleman on the premises."

She gave me a quick poke in the side. "Not you."

"Damn right."

Audrey laughed. "Even though you're giving up your room to me tonight. Isn't that what a gentleman does?"

"Peer pressure," I explained.

"Ah, well. I'll take it."

A silence settled over us, and I became keenly aware of how near we were to each other in the dark. Audrey stuck so close beside me that her hand grazed mine. I could hear her breathing, and it filled my head with dirty ideas. I wanted to make her breathe even harder...

In a nearby tree, a barred owl hooted. It was the same *her-her-herr-herr* that I heard every night of my life. But Audrey went rigid.

A chuckle escaped before I could stop it. "She wants a nice juicy field mouse. Or maybe a chipmunk, if she's feeling ambitious." I reached around and put a comforting hand on her bare shoulder. That was a mistake. Because her silky skin under my hand shot a new bolt of awareness through my body.

Audrey lifted her hands and squinted at them in the dark. "I really need to clean up, or I'll leave your room looking like a crime scene."

"I know. Me too." I nudged her in the direction of the bunkhouse's far side. "That's what the outdoor shower is for. I'll show you."

My father had built the outdoor shower when I was about ten years old. It was a way of offering our temporary help a cleanup spot outside the house. But he'd done such a great job on it that I'd taken to using it myself whenever the weather was warm. As a kid I'd liked to bare my ass to the elements. Still did.

"There aren't any coyotes in there, right?" she asked as we approached the wooden stall.

"I'll chase 'em out just for you," I promised. "Here." Poking the door open, I checked the place out. The dry end had a spa bench and a place to hang clothing on hooks. There were a couple of fresh towels waiting there already, courtesy of my thoughtful mother. My father's hand-hewed ledge ran the length of the rectangular enclosure, and shampoos and soaps waited beside the shower itself. "Go ahead," I told Audrey. "I'll fend off the vicious predators while you rinse off the blood."

"Don't mock a girl who can trim a pork loin like a pro." She brushed past me into the stall and shut the door. I was taller than the wall, so we ended up staring into each other's eyes even as she lifted her top over her head and tossed it aside.

Arousal tightened my body everywhere. I knew I needed to look away. But her eyes held mine, like a taunt. She reached behind her body, her shoulders jumping as she unclasped a hidden bra.

Jesus Christ.

I finally turned away, my back to the wooden stall, my eyes on the stars above. Behind me I heard the gentle swish of feminine clothing, and just the sound made me hard. I took a deep, even breath and tried to think of other things. I picked out the stars for Ursa Major overhead.

The faucet squeaked once and water began to rain down behind me. "It only takes a few seconds to heat," I said. But my voice came out as a rasp. Because *I'd* taken only a few seconds to heat. And I didn't know if I wanted to cool down.

Desire made a man feel alive. There was no shame in it. Even if I knew it would have no outlet—I'd go to sleep horny and alone in one of the empty bunks tonight—it was a good thing. It was a fresh kind of energy, one I hadn't felt in way too long.

Back when Audrey and I had hooked up in college, I hadn't appreciated that yet. A crazy night was just something I thought I deserved after winning a game. A fraternity party. The keg in the corner and the red plastic cups. That was my life at the time. I'd been happy, but I didn't know how rare that kind of freedom was.

The night she'd turned up at my frat house after her breakup, I'd danced with Audrey and then taken her to bed without a second thought. We were both after the same thing that night—a little reckless joy. On the dance floor she'd wrapped her arms around my neck with a knowing smile, and I'd kissed her before the first song was even over.

It had been only an hour later when I had her naked on my bed, gripping the headboard while I...

"Mmm," she said from the shower, and my pulse kicked up a notch.

None of that, asshole, I reminded myself. The noise she'd made was only the sound of someone who'd stepped under a perfect spray of warm water after a long night of work.

For several minutes I counted stars and beats of my heart and any other damn thing that could be counted. Finally the water shut off, and I heard her rustling with the towel. It was so quiet that the sounds of water droplets escaping down the drain weren't enough to drown out my ragged breathing.

Swallowing hard, I gripped the fabric of my T-shirt and hauled it over my head. This was going to be the fastest shower in history. And cold, too. Then I'd deliver Audrey to the door of my room and pack off to a bunk bed.

But I didn't account for the look on her face when I turned around. The moonlight revealed droplets of water clinging to her cheekbones and eyes flashing with unexpected heat. Her gaze traced a line across my shoulders. Then it rose slowly to meet mine. Her lips parted slightly, then she blinked in surprise.

"Here," I rasped, my hand on top of the door. "Switch?"

She dropped her gaze and gave the door a tug.

Swinging it open partway, she slipped between the frame and my body, the knot of her towel scraping across my bare chest.

Then she stopped, her chin tilting upward. Her expression was a dare. And I always took a dare.

I dropped my head, finding her jaw with my lips. Then I traced a slow line up her cheek, breathing in the faint scent of my own soap along with the clean scent of mostly naked, willing girl. When I pushed my tongue into her ear, she let out a moan that probably startled the owls high up in the trees.

Chapter Eight

Audrey

The minute Griff Shipley had taken off his shirt, my body turned traitor. And by the time he put his mouth on me, whatever self-restraint I'd had flew away on the sweet Vermont breeze.

I tipped my chin to give him better access while he dropped a line of shameless kisses down my neck. When he nipped me at the juncture of my shoulder, my hands shot out unbidden, landing on his rippling chest. His body was hard and warm, and the feel of his full lips grazing my skin was making me crazy.

"Fuck," I gasped. And I meant it as an order, not an exclamation.

He took a step forward, and I took one back. Then we repeated that dance step twice more until my backside met the ledge running across the stone wall enclosed by the shower stall. "This what you want?" he rumbled into my ear. "You want my hands on you?"

His roughened thumbs stroked the skin of my breasts just above the towel, and I gasped his name like an overeager fool. Griff still thought of me as an airhead sorority girl. And I was about to prove him right.

Griff grabbed my chin and kissed me. It was no dainty peck, either. He gripped the back of my head and took me hungrily. I opened for him immediately, because there was no point in being coy when you've already invited the man to feast at the table of *you*. Pressing against his big, solid body, I pushed my tongue into his mouth.

We were doing this. I was about to do the nasty with Griff Shipley up against a stone wall his grandfather built a hundred years ago.

"You didn't answer me," he grunted, startling me. "What do you want, Audrey? You want my cock?" The second he said the word, my lady parts shimmied in response.

I didn't know if I could answer. It was one thing to have a ten-minute-stand against a wall. It was another to beg for it.

But then he eased back, waiting for my answer. And the loss of all that hungry attention? Not good. Not good at all.

"Just this once," I whispered.

He chuckled so low and deep that I felt the vibrations through his chest. Capturing my face in two hands, he lifted my chin, forcing me to look up at him. "Just this once, huh?"

The glint in his eye was ten percent mocking and ninety percent heat. That ten percent irritated me. Not enough to stop him, though. Let's not get crazy.

"Better make it memorable, then," I said with more bravado than I felt.

His grin was so arrogant I wanted to wipe it off his face. "Darlin', I'm gonna fuck you now, and you can tell me some time later if it was memorable."

At that I gave a whole body shiver. And it wasn't because Griff parted my towel with one thick thumb and cast it aside so that I felt the sweet nighttime air *everywhere*.

"Mmm," he said slowly, cupping one roughened palm under my breast. His appraising gaze was like a wall of heat, warming me on every inch of skin where it landed. "Just as good as I pictured while you were showering."

His shameless hand dipped low. He looked me straight in the eye as he dipped two thick fingers between my legs. And they slipped right where I wanted them, because I was already soaking wet and ready for him.

God, what a cheap date I was.

He threw his head back, making a low, guttural sound. "Unzip me," he ordered.

I couldn't obey right away, because his fingers continued to torture me. I let out a shudder first. Then my shaky hands fell to his belt. After a minute of fumbling he shoved my fingers away, yanking the belt free and unzipping himself in one go. With my prize in reach, I shoved down his jeans and boxers. I gasped as his ambitious erection sprang up to greet me. He was thick and beautiful and just what I wanted.

In fact...

Grasping his hips in both hands, I pushed him a step backward. Then I leaned over and took the fat crown into my mouth.

"Oh fuck," he panted. He grabbed a fistful of my hair. "Take more," he ordered. "Suck me."

The rasp of his voice pulsed through my body, filling me with desperation. And his musky, salty taste made my head spin. I was going to give him just what he wanted, because I wanted it, too.

But first he was going to have to learn some patience.

I eased back slowly, circling my tongue around his head as if I were taking a contemplative first taste of a new gelato flavor. Then I kissed his tip once. Twice.

His groan was low and agonized. "Audrey," he warned.

But I would not be rushed. I dragged my tongue down the underside of his shaft, which had him grumbling out a string of half-formed curses. His hips twitched with impatience, but he did not beg me aloud.

Stubborn, this man. And now my slow pace was just torturing the both of us.

Capitulating, I opened wide and swallowed him down the best I could. My lonely lifestyle hadn't provided any practice in a long time, but I gave a good, hard suck and was rewarded with a bellowed groan. I cupped his heavy balls in my hand and bobbed my head until he put a big paw under my chin and tugged me upright.

I leaned against the wall, beckoning to him, hoping to move things along. If I was going to have an ill-advised quickie with my former hookup, I wanted it to happen right away, before I came to my senses.

But I was unprepared for the intense look in his eyes when he backed me up to the wooden ledge on the stone wall. As if he could see all the way through me. The chatter of self-criticism running through my head silenced itself under the weight of his stare. He lifted a hand to my cheek and just held it there, as if to ground me. *Focus*, his serious eyes suggested. *Or you'll miss it.*

My heart gave a nervous little jump. I put my hands on his massive chest and closed my eyes. His heart beat out a steady rhythm under my hand, and I took a deep breath, readying myself for whatever came next.

The crinkle of a wrapper punctured the silence. I looked down to watch him roll on a condom he'd produced from his wallet. The sight of his hand wrapped around a thick erection made my mouth water.

He kicked off his jeans and shoes. "Come here, baby," he whispered, grasping my bare ass and lifting me a few inches until I was perched on the ledge attached to the wall. It wasn't very deep, so I had to rest my hands on his shoulders to keep from sliding off. Our heads lined up as we both looked down to watch as his cock pointed thick and strong right at its target. He eased my knees further apart, opening me up, and I could hear myself panting from anticipation. "Aw, yeah," he said, closing the distance.

I leaned forward, my arms draping around his neck as his fat cockhead stopped right at my entrance. He circled there for a moment, and I held my breath as he teased my clit. When he repeated this motion, I gasped out a command. "Do it already."

With an eager grunt he pushed all the way inside. I was suddenly full of Griff Shipley, and he was a lot to handle. My body gave a happy spasm around his thick length.

"Christ. You missed me that much, princess?"

I buried my face in his neck to try to get my bearings. If he looked at my face right now, he'd see how badly I needed this. And I didn't want to give him the satisfaction.

With a groan, Griff began to work his hips. His hands skimmed down my back and came to rest between the wall and my ass. I had a faint notion that he was trying to prevent my skin from scraping against the stone wall, but all my thoughts popped like fragile bubbles when he gave me a good, hard thrust.

I was being fucked by Griff Shipley under the Vermont stars. And it was overwhelming.

Kissing my way down his chin, his beard tickling my skin, I sucked on the cord of muscle between his neck and shoulder.

"*Fuck*, baby. Give me your mouth. I want it."

Ignoring the request, I nibbled on his skin. The massiveness of his body was such a turn-on. He was an unyielding wall of a man. I just wanted to stay right here—literally pressed between a rock and a hard place. Forever. I rolled my hips forward to meet him, and the extra contact made me see stars in front of my slammed-shut eyes.

"Ungh. So good," he muttered, slowing down to grind against me. A big paw of a hand scooped my chin off his shoulder and angled my mouth up to his. He slipped that hand behind my head and then forced his tongue into my mouth at the same time he thrust hard.

The double assault had me whimpering into his mouth. I capitulated completely, wrapping my legs around him. I stopped fighting the thought that this was a bad idea. For many lovely minutes, with Griff pounding into me, this was the *only* idea. Our kisses were bottomless. His, eager, rhythmic grunts echoed through my chest.

Someone was moaning, and I think it was me.

His desperate groan rumbled through my mouth and down into my soul. That's when every muscle in my body tightened around him. Griff slowed down then, as if trying to put off the inevitable. "Mmm," he groaned just before sucking on my tongue.

Then it was all over but the cryin'. With a gasp I let myself be carried away on the fleeting bliss of this man's handiwork. Pleasure erupted in my core, zinging everywhere at once. Griff gave an answering shout and went rigid, the muscles in his neck standing out like mountain ridges. He yanked my body close one more time. Our hearts pounded against each other.

For a few moments we just panted together, spent. I held his sweaty body tightly, certain in the knowledge that many acres of awkwardness would stretch between us now.

I heard the squeak of the faucet, and then warm water began to rain down on us. Griff disengaged our bodies, lowering me carefully to the wooden slatted floor. I grabbed my hair to keep it out of the spray, and, as he tucked me against the wall, we took a sixty-second shower. After wrapping a towel around me a moment later—a dry one—he picked up our shoes and clothes off the bench and steered me out into the night.

The stars were brilliant overhead. We were so far away from any cities that it was the best view of the night sky I'd ever had. "There's the milky way!" I whispered suddenly. I'd never seen it so clearly before— that hazy arc overhead the way it looked in textbooks.

Griff's eyebrows lifted in the dark. "Yep. It's there every night."

He thinks I'm an imbecile.

Putting a hand at my lower back, he guided me into the bunkhouse. Just inside, he pushed open a door on the right. My duffel bag had been set on the double bed. A bedside lamp made a pool of yellow light in the corner, illuminating an antique quilt on the wall and a deep cottage window showing a square of blackness.

"I'll show you the bathroom," he said quietly.

"Okay," I whispered, darting to the bag for my toothbrush and then following him into the room across the hall.

He left me alone to take care of business. When I came out again, we traded places wordlessly. Griff disappeared into the bathroom and shut the door.

That was it, then. But what do you say to the man who you just banged unexpectedly in his outdoor shower? *Thanks? Nice knowing you?* (Biblically. Again.) I tiptoed into his bedroom. It was awfully spare. The only sign of personality was a paperback thriller on the nightstand and a pair of reading glasses.

Aw. Somehow it softened Griff's image to know he wore glasses when he read in bed.

Leaving the door ajar—just in case he planned to visit—I lifted his quilt and slipped between the sheets. I was pretty sure that Griff's mom had snuck in here and put fresh sheets on the bed. But it still smelled piney and Griff-like. I rolled my face into his pillow and took a deep, surreptitious breath.

Hearing a noise in the hallway, I lifted my chin to listen. A moment later Griff appeared, still wearing his towel. With one quick yank he cast it aside. Then I watched in surprise as he lifted the quilt and nudged me. "Move over, baby."

I made room, and he stretched his wide frame across the bed. Then he reached over to my side of the bed, lifting me as if I weighed no more than one of his goose-down pillows. I landed halfway on his body, my head tucked onto his shoulder, my bare ass in one of his big hands.

Holy cannoli. I was *cuddling* the world's grumpiest farmer.

His body relaxed even further as he got comfortable. His thumb stroked my skin, leaving shivers in its wake. I risked a sweep of my hand across his ribs, and he twitched. "Sorry," I said immediately.

The low, unfamiliar rumble I heard next turned out to be a chuckle. "S'okay," he whispered. "Just ticklish."

That was charming and unexpected. So of course I had to do it again. I never did have any impulse control. My fingertips traced lightly down his chest until he twitched again and then grabbed my hand. "Enough of that, princess." He kissed my palm and then placed it firmly in the middle of his chest.

I stretched to kiss his cheek, my face skimming through the surprisingly soft beard on the way to finding his smooth skin. He made a soft grunt of surprise and then sighed. His arms tightened around me. The moment was unexpectedly tender. Nothing like the awkward dismount from a drunken college hookup.

He was so warm and solid beneath me. I could touch him all night long and never get bored. "Goodnight, Griff," I whispered into the dark.

"Goodnight, baby," he rasped. "Sleep now."

And I did.

Chapter Nine

Griffin

Dawn came before I was ready. It's always hard to get up at five-thirty. But that morning was especially brutal, seeing as I awoke with a naked angel draped over me and a rock-hard dick.

My body wanted more. So it was a blessing that Audrey stayed asleep as I eased out from underneath her. When I left the bed, she let out a sleepy sigh and curled her sweet body around my pillow. I stared down at her a moment longer, daring myself to recall last night's hijinks in the shower. Just...*damn*. She and I were a dangerous combination. We needed cautionary signs like the ones hanging in the tractor shed over the cans of diesel fuel. WARNING: COMBUSTIBLE.

The sound of the bunkhouse door closing behind Zach or Jude got me moving. I got dressed and spent thirty seconds in the bathroom, trying to make myself presentable. Then I hustled out across the meadow to the dairy barn where my two employees had begun the day's work without me.

"Morning," Zach said, handing Jude the shovel. "Shall I start the cow parade?"

"Sure. Send 'em in."

Zach turned around. "Okay...what the hell?" He pointed, aiming at my neck.

Fuck. I clapped my hand over my skin like the guilty man I was. Should have looked a little closer in the mirror this morning.

Jude bent over a pile of cow shit and began to shovel, but I could hear his snicker.

Zach frowned at me, looking confused. And then I saw the moment he understood what he was looking at, because a flush crept onto his cheekbones. He bit his lip and turned away, embarrassed.

Zach wasn't the kind of guy to judge me for hooking up with Audrey. But he was—at twenty-one—the oldest virgin I knew. Whenever sex came up in a movie or in conversation he always got a little red-faced. "Let the milkers in," I prompted.

"Sure," he said quickly, sprinting toward the door to admit the first two lucky heifers.

We began the milking in silence. Eventually Zachariah put some music on our beat-up old radio because he swore that the cows enjoyed classical guitar. I disinfected another Jersey's bags and then hooked 'er up to the milking machine. This was a job I could do on autopilot. Some mornings I did my best thinking during the milking.

Not today, though. My thoughts were not on the usual cider strategy or farm business. Instead, my mind kept wandering toward Audrey's soft skin and eager hands. And why was I calculating the distance to Boston? It was about one hundred fifty miles, give or take.

Right, I reminded myself. The two-and-a-half-hour drive was discouraging. My schedule didn't accommodate a girlfriend even if she was two-and-a-half *minutes* away. My life couldn't handle yet another person who would depend on me not to let her down.

There were plenty of those already.

But, hell, she was tempting. I'd be living off memories of last night for a good long time. I knew I'd lie in my bed and stroke myself thinking about the way she gripped me with her whole body and the sweet sounds she made when she came.

"Griffin? Y'okay, there?"

I looked up fast to see Jude standing over me. "What?" I'd missed what he'd said.

"I just wanted to know what you want me to do with these bales of hay I'm pulling off the back of the truck. You seem a little *tired*, though." He smirked at me. "I could ask you later."

Busted. I gave him a surly grunt and unhooked the cow from the milker. "Use the fork to fill the feed troughs in here. Careful not to hit any of the girls on the nose."

He gave me a smart-ass wink and turned away. I still didn't know what to make of this kid. He seemed like a good worker. And if I didn't know his history, I'd probably think he was a godsend.

As I considered him, one thing gnawed at me. A day ago I'd sat across the table from Jude telling myself that it would never be me who got hooked on anything. And here I was feeling a serious addictive pull toward a certain hot little chef with a strong will and a wicked tongue.

Yeah, no candidates for sainthood here. Except Zach, maybe.

The milking went fast with three people. Then it was time for breakfast. "You two head in," I told Jude and Zach. "I gotta grab something from my room."

"A little early in the season for turtlenecks, Han," Zach said, his ears turning pink.

"Shut it, Padawan," I grumbled, and Jude laughed.

Audrey was not in my room when I ducked in to grab a tattered button-down from my closet. The shirt covered most of the damage. Then I put on my game face and headed for the house, washing my hands while

I listened to the chatter in the kitchen.

"How do you *do* that?" May asked. "If I tried it, there'd be eggs all over the ceiling."

The husky laugh that followed made my blood run hot. *Christ.* Just the sound of her was like a drug. "The chef who taught us eggs was a real masochist. I don't know if he was ever in the military, but he was such a drill sergeant that I wanted to brain him with my frying pan. But it worked. He made me fold so many omelets that now they come out perfectly every time."

I realized I was just standing there, the hand towel in my fist, eavesdropping like a creeper. So I manned up and went into the kitchen. "Morning, ladies," I said, heading for the coffee pot.

"Yo," May returned. "We are having ham and cheddar omelets with garlic-scape sour cream and maple-glazed bacon."

"Damn." My stomach growled. "I'm free for that."

"I'll bet you are." My sister shoved an empty plate at me. "They're made to order, though. You're in line behind Dylan."

That left me leaning against the kitchen counter and trying not to ogle Audrey's ass in the little denim skirt she wore. Long, smooth legs stretched from beneath its hem, and it was a struggle not to think too hard about how they'd been wrapped around me while we...

Christ.

I was just a few feet away, and the urge to touch her was strong. I wanted to kiss the satiny skin just in front of her ear and run my hands down the silky ponytail she'd donned at some point between waking up in my bed and cooking in my kitchen.

Hands off, I reminded myself. After helping myself to Audrey like a buffet last night, the least I could do was avoid embarrassing her in front of my family.

Something about Audrey really turned my crank, though. It was there between us whether I liked it or not. Every hour she spent in Vermont served to remind me of exactly how hot for her I'd been in college, too. As I watched her flip a perfect yellow omelet onto Dylan's plate and then give him a big smile, I felt an unfamiliar yearning in my gut. There was no woman in my life, and I wasn't in the market for one. But someday I hoped to find someone. And maybe she'd glance at me over her shoulder the way that Audrey did now and then lick her perfect lips.

After my little brother walked away, she asked, "What'll it be, Farmer Griff?"

You. "Uh, I like everything."

She quirked one perfect eyebrow as if to say, *I noticed.*

"Um, ham and cheese," I said. "Please."

"Coming right up." She turned her back to me again. Apparently we were playing it this way—as if last night never happened. I watched as she tossed a handful of chopped onions into the pan, where they began to sizzle.

"I didn't say onions," I said without thinking. They weren't conducive to the goodbye kiss I'd need if I was going to let her get into that little rental car later and drive away.

"Too bad," she sang. "They're good for you." She added a handful of chopped green peppers, too.

That was fine, because I really did like everything. But her willful disregard for my order brought on a familiar prickle of energy. This girl pushed my buttons on purpose. *All* my buttons. "Why'd you ask me what I wanted, then?"

"Just to make you feel empowered," she said, cracking two eggs at a time over the side of the bowl. If I tried that, there'd be egg on the counter and my body and probably the floor. But her eggs plopped neatly into the bowl and she tossed the shells into the compost bucket in a perfect arc. Then she picked up a third egg.

"Two is fine," I said quickly.

She cracked it anyway. "You need to keep up your strength," she said in a low voice, and just the implication made blood rush to my groin. "It takes energy to call every farm within fifty miles and warn them away from me."

I groaned inwardly. "I sure am sorry about that." It had been a rash thing to do. Even if I believed that BPG Group was the Evil Empire, it hadn't been necessary to make her job more difficult.

She used a whisk to quickly scramble the eggs. Then she poured a dollop of cream into the bowl and stirred again. "As soon as I can get a tire, I'm out of your hair."

Hair made me think of wrapping my hand around hers.

Audrey poured the eggs over the sizzling vegetables. Then she picked up the pan and swirled the mixture in a perfect circle so that it resembled a photo shoot for a culinary magazine. She watched the pan on the fire for some hidden sign. (Or maybe she was simply avoiding my gaze.) But then, when I was about to ask a rude question just to get a rise out of her, she grasped the handle and flipped the yellow disk into the air, catching it again like a Jedi flipping his lightsaber.

"I still don't know how she does that!" my mother crowed, entering the room behind me. "Griff, it's a little hot for flannel, no?" She squeezed my elbow on her way to the coffee pot.

"It was, uh, cold in the barn this morning," I lied.

Only then did Audrey break character. She snuck a look at my neck and then looked sheepish.

Awesome. Women regret me even before breakfast.

Ham and cheese were layered down the center of the omelet, which she folded tidily. It was beautiful and suddenly I was starving. "Plate," she demanded. I held it out and she turned the omelet onto the porcelain surface with a practiced twist of her slender wrist. "Who's next?" she called.

I stood there with my plate in my hands, wondering what to do. Note to self—the next time you have a one-night stand, don't do it in the midst of your entire family. "You should eat breakfast, too," I said softly.

"Already done," she said without even a glance over her shoulder. "The bacon and the sour cream are on the dining table. Enjoy."

Oh, but I did.

But now I was dismissed. *Again.* Didn't it just figure.

Chapter Ten

Audrey

And the Academy Award goes to…Audrey Kidder, for her performance in The Morning After.

When Griff left the kitchen, I heaved a sigh of relief. If he'd been all touchy-feely this morning, his family would think I was a ho. And not the kind you use in a garden.

I was washing the omelet pan when May Shipley took it out of my hands and set it in the sink. "Sit," she said. "Have coffee. Stop working. Mom and I feel guilty enough already."

Reluctantly I followed her into the dining room and poured myself a little glass of juice. I took a chair beside May, and the men all stopped their conversation to tell me it was the best omelet they'd ever had.

"It's just eggs," I said. I'd never been able to take a compliment, probably because I never got very many. I grew up in a compliment-free environment. My mom wanted an achiever, which I failed to become. Seducing football players was my kind of fun, and I started young. She bought me sweater sets, and I bought black lingerie to wear under them. My teen years were a series of screaming matches over my hair, my makeup, the length of my skirts.

Good times.

From my pocket, my phone bleated. Loudly. "Sorry," I said quickly, pulling it out to silence it. I didn't recognize the number. Whoever it was, he could wait.

I drank my juice and listened to Griffin explain to Jude why he needed to see the newest *Star Wars* movie.

"The spoilers made it all the way into the prison," Jude argued. "I already know who dies at the end."

"Doesn't matter," Griff insisted. "See it to witness the franchise's return to greatness."

My phone chimed with a text, and then chimed again. "Sorry," I repeated. "It's not usually like this." I dug out my phone and read the text message. Then I read it again. "Whoa."

"Is everything okay?" Mrs. Shipley asked.

I looked up quickly. "Of course."

Her face relaxed, and then May spoke up to explain. "It's been a couple years now. But when my father died so suddenly, we all learned to be a little freaked out by unexpected phone calls.

Ouch. "I'm sorry. When my phone rings it's usually because I've done something wrong again."

Mrs. Shipley smiled at me. "That can't always be the case."

"Pretty often! But not today." I couldn't quite wrap my head around this sudden stroke of good fortune. "I've been recalled to Boston to work in one of BPG's most chic kitchens, starting tonight. It says to show up for kitchen prep at three-thirty. They'll probably put me on salads or something boring, but still. It's a cool opportunity. God, I hope the text was really meant for me."

May laughed. "Why wouldn't it be?"

"Eh. I'm not their favorite employee. And the chef in charge is a real macho asshole. They all are, but him especially. I wouldn't be invited into his kitchen unless there was a true crisis. He probably had a temper tantrum and fired his whole kitchen, or something." I'd bet money on it.

"Wow. What kind of food will you be cooking?"

"This place is all about modernist cuisine. Like a piece of tuna, frozen to negative a million and cut with a band saw into a precise cube, then seared with a polka-dot pattern and plated with a foam around it tasting of mango and pine nuts. It's really over the top. Not my favorite kind of cooking, but it will look great on my resume."

They all stared at me as if trying to figure out why anyone would want to cut tuna with a band saw. And, at that moment, I couldn't understand it myself.

"I hope you enjoy it, honey," Ruth Shipley said. She set down her coffee cup. "Now, we have to talk about last night."

Across the room, Griff choked on a bite of omelet while I simultaneously broke out in a sweat.

"Griffin, your brother told me the most outlandish thing before he went to bed. He said that you want to sell some cows."

It took me a moment, but after I replayed those words in my brain a few times, I was pretty sure "sell some cows" was not a sexual innuendo, and that Ruthie Shipley was not referring to me.

Griff relaxed, too. He took a sip of coffee before answering. "It's something we need to consider. We could reinvest the proceeds in the cider operation. There's a higher margin to be made in alcoholic beverages than in milk."

"But, *Griffin.*" Mrs. Shipley touched her throat in shock. "Your father worked his whole life to build up..." She swallowed hard. "I can't understand why you'd do that."

Griff set down his mug. "It was a great business for a while," he said carefully. "But the price of milk is down, and the rent's going up."

His mother's eyes widened. "But...Smitty won't turn us out. We could speak to him about the rent."

Slowly, Griff shook his big head. "The land is more valuable than it used to be. He's probably got offers to sell. Good ones. Our lease is up, Mom. If you were him, wouldn't you consider all your options?"

"I suppose." She stood quickly and carried her plate into the kitchen.

There was an awkward silence until May asked, "What if we sink money into the cidery and it fails?"

Griff tipped his head back and laughed at the ceiling. "That is the big question, isn't it? Can I at least finish my eggs before I settle our destiny?"

With a sigh, she gathered her dishes and followed her mother into the kitchen.

Meanwhile, I sat there feeling like an eavesdropper on this family drama. Although I wasn't the only one. Zach and Jude were studying their empty plates pretty carefully, too.

The silence was broken by the sound of tires on the gravel driveway outside. Zach got up and pushed the lace curtain aside. "Oh, it's Wilson. He's got the tire you need."

Griff's gaze lifted quickly to mine, as if he'd forgotten I was here. He looked a little sad for some weird reason.

I hopped out of my chair. "He delivered the tire?"

"He owes me a favor," Zach said.

"Let me find my checkbook."

Zach shook his head. "He's gonna bill the rental company."

"Oh. Thanks."

Just like that there was no more reason to stay at the Shipley farm.

Zach and his buddy from the tire place had the new tire on in less than ten minutes. Mrs. Shipley hugged me and thanked me for helping in the kitchen. Then she thanked me for helping with the butchering. "Is there anything you need for the drive back to Boston?" she asked.

"Just my bag. I'll pop into the bunkhouse and grab it," I said, doing my level best not to blush to a medium-rare shade of pink. The word "bunkhouse" was probably going to make me all hot and bothered for the rest of my life.

I nipped into Griff's room to remove my duffel from the bed that I'd made before breakfast. Even now I felt the urge to drop my face onto his pillow one more time and take a final breath of Griff.

Was that creepy?

Probably.

So I gathered up the tattered shreds of my dignity and got the hell out of there.

The car sat in the driveway, ready to go. Griff and his guys had moved on to a discussion about washing out a fermentation tank. When I approached, Zachariah and Jude each gave me a friendly wave and then drifted away, leaving only Griff and I beside the car. I tossed my bag into the trunk thinking, *now what?* Do we shake hands? Kiss? What is the post-hook-up-I'll-be-in-touch-about-the-cider protocol?

"So," I said, closing the trunk.

"So," he said, cocking his head to the side and smiling down at me.

That smile packed a punch, and it stole my focus. "It's been...interesting."

"Aw." He actually rolled his eyes. "Interesting? *That's* the review I get? I'm pretty sure the earth moved."

"Well..." My cheeks heated. "You're a farmer. It's your job to notice the earth. I know I burned off some crucial brain cells last night. I'll be lucky to find my way back to Boston."

His smile grew wider. "Come back if you get lost. You know where to find me."

I did know where to find him, and it was unexpected. For five years I'd forgotten about him, and all the things that went wrong for me at BU. But now I'd be thinking about Griff for quite some time. The man left an impression. Even now I felt the pull.

It was definitely time to hit the road.

"I'll, uh, make sure your ciders get into a sommelier's hands."

Griff's eyes crinkled at the edges. "Thank you."

"You never know," I said, opening the car door. "People all over Boston could be drinking it in the fall. At twenty-four bucks a bottle."

He snorted. "Hey. Not so fast." Before I had a chance to react, Griff had moved around the car door and into my personal space. Given our height difference, my eyes were at beard level. His full lips said, "I get a chance to say goodbye, right?"

I swallowed hard, because I *hate* goodbyes. If there was such a thing as goodbye-a-phobia, I definitely had a bad case. Griff's big body came closer, the warmth of it engulfing me. With two of his thick fingers, he tilted my chin up to meet his gaze.

"Hey," he whispered. "You okay?" His brown eyes searched my expression.

"Of course," I bit out.

Then his mouth was on mine, his lips full and warm. I wrapped my arms around him without waiting for an invitation. And he kissed me slowly and deeply, while I clung to him like a well-made mayonnaise on a spoon. His tongue made a hungry pass over mine, and I knew I'd be tasting him all the way home to Boston.

When he pulled back, I wasn't ready.

"That's just a little something to remember me by," he whispered.

As if I could forget. "Later," I said, trying to keep things light. And why did that seem so hard all of a sudden?

"Goodbye," he corrected, backing away.

Right.

I got into the car and started the engine while Griff watched, an unreadable expression on his face. He folded his brawny arms across his chest as I turned around.

He gave me a single wave, and then I headed the other way, down the drive and out of his life.

Part Two

August

Cooking is like love. It should be entered into with abandon or not at all. –Harriet van Horne

Chapter Eleven

One Month Later

Griffin

It was Saturday night, and we were all exhausted, as usual. Apple-picking season had begun for the earliest varieties. After we'd consumed about ten thousand calories each of Mom's cooking, my cousin and Zach and I drove over to The Mountain Goat for beers.

I'd avoided the Goat, as we called the place, since springtime. My ex-fuck-buddy managed the place, and she'd been unhappy when I broke things off with her.

It had only been a week ago that I'd ventured back into the bar. My cousin Kyle liked to go out, and since he was staying in the bunkhouse to help out with the harvest, I manned up and showed my face at the Goat. Zara ignored me, which I expected. She didn't poison my drinks, so I figured I was doing all right.

Tonight we'd met up with Kyle's younger brother Kieran, who was leaving soon for training with the Drug Enforcement Agency. I chose the back corner of a big, U-shaped booth that wasn't too cramped and gave my cousins a view of every woman who walked in the door.

"Zara just gave you a look," Kyle announced as soon as we sat down. "Like, a laser death-glare."

"Uh-huh," I said. "Be a good little farm boy and buy the first round?" I put a twenty on the table. Kyle was a cheapskate. He never shelled out for beer unless there were women present.

"I'll get us a pitcher," Zach said, hopping up, leaving my money on the table.

"Why can't you be more like him?" I asked Kyle. Of my two cousins, Kyle was the talker, while Kieran was quieter. Truthfully I was a lot closer to these two than my own little brother. Dylan was ten years younger than me, while my cousins were closer to my own age. I was twenty-seven, Kyle was twenty-five and Kieran twenty-three. We'd been picking apples together since we could walk and drinking at the Goat since we were legal.

"So why did you break it off with Zara, anyway?" Kyle asked, jutting his chin toward the bar. "I thought she was cool. And, I mean..." He gave her a long, appraising look. "You could do a lot worse in this town."

"It was never supposed to be serious," I said, drumming my fingers on the table top.

"But that's what she wanted?" Kyle asked.

"She didn't give me an ultimatum. We always said it was just sex. But I got sick of feeling guilty when I didn't ask her home for dinner or make more of an effort." Nothing against Zara—she was a great girl. But there were too many people counting on me already. It stressed me out too much to add another one.

Kyle gave me a skeptical look. "You stopped banging the hottest woman in the county because you felt guilty?"

It wasn't as simple as he made it sound. "She'd been dropping hints. Said she wanted to spend more time with me. I didn't want to string her along, is all. Didn't seem fair."

"If you say so," he said in a way that really meant *you're a big fucking idiot.*

Maybe I was, because the last month had been a grind and not the good kind.

And it would only get worse. Late summer and early fall were our busy season, when we all worked our asses off. My cousins had spent the day picking Zestars and Yellow Transparents. Zach and the twins took apples and cider to the Norwich farmers' market, and I'd spent the day with Jude cleaning the tanks and fixing up the cider house. Starting next weekend, the descending hordes would arrive, parking up our meadow, picking apples and buying cider. And somehow—while weaving between the selfie-taking weekenders—I'd have to press as many apples as I could during that busy time to make this year's vintage of Shipley Cider.

Zach returned to the table with a pitcher and four glasses. I poured him the first one, then handed beers across to my cousins. "Cheers," I said when my own was ready. "Here's to good weekend weather for the next two months."

Kyle grinned. "Here's to horny tourists showing up at the Goat during leaf season to fuck me."

I snorted. "They'd better have hotel rooms. Because the bunkhouse is off limits, and keep your tail out of my truck."

"Man, this is a tough crowd for a Friday night." He took a deep drink of his beer. "Guess I should have drunk to good weather, because I'm gonna need that, too. For fucking al fresco."

As usual, Zach blushed deeply at all the sex talk.

Another Friday night at the Goat, ladies and gentlemen.

While we'd been pouring our beer, a pair of perfectly shapely legs had passed through the edge of my sightline. My traitorous brain went immediately to Audrey Kidder, as it so often did these days. Every time I got in bed, I imagined her there beside me. Every time an unfamiliar car pulled up the drive, I watched to see who would get out. But it was never a hot blonde with an attitude. It was always a portly feed salesman or one of the twins' friends.

Meanwhile, family dinners were tense, because we spent a lot of time discussing the future of our dairy business. Smitty had sent over a new lease with a term of five years and a built-in rent increase for each successive year. We had sixty days to sign, which sounded like plenty until you factored in selling off a dairy herd.

Good times.

I took another gulp of my beer and wondered why I'd come out tonight. There was beer at home, and I seemed to have brought my troubles with me.

"Dibs," Kyle said suddenly. "I haven't seen her before. Wow."

I didn't swivel my head for a look. The poor girl—whoever she was—didn't need a whole table of dudes leering at her. Kyle was about to put on the full-court press, anyway.

But Zachariah began to chuckle. "You're not first in line there, Kyle."

"Why? I don't see a ring."

"She and Griffin..." He cleared his throat.

At that, I gave in and turned my head, and my daily fantasy snapped into place. "No way." Lo and behold, Audrey Kidder sat on a barstool talking to Zara. If Zach hadn't said anything, I'd probably have thought my eyes were deceiving me. I'd been spotting Audrey Kidder out of the corner of my eye at farmers' markets for weeks. But it was never actually her.

Until now.

"What?" Kyle yelped. "Bullshit. I'm gonna go buy her a drink." He pressed a hand down on the table and made to rise.

I reached across the table and clamped his hand down under mine. "No you're not."

"Really," Kyle drawled. "Look who's all territorial all of a sudden." He shook off my hand and leaned back in his seat. "Well. Go get 'er, then. This will be entertaining."

Great. The last thing I needed was an audience when I talked to Audrey. And what the hell was I even going to say to the girl? *Hey, since you left I've been playing our night together over and over in my mind obsessively. Have a beer with me and my nosy family?*

"Annnnd we've been spotted," Zach said cheerfully. He lifted a hand and gave Audrey a wave.

"Move," I nudged Zach. If she was back in Tuxbury, I was going to talk to her, audience or not.

Zach got out of the way, and when I stood up I saw Audrey whip back around toward Zara, who had leaned over the bar and, with narrowed eyes, whispered something to Audrey.

Fuck.

Chapter Twelve

Audrey

Of course I'd expected to see Griff Shipley again in Vermont. It's just that I thought it might take longer than an hour to run into him. I wasn't ready for that mountain of a man to turn up in the bar where I'd just ordered a chicken Caesar salad and a beer. I needed to get my bearings before I faced down all that hotness.

The bartender—Zara—was warning me away already. "Watch out for that crew. Bunch of assholes, except for the blond kid. He's a sweetie. The Shipley boys think they're God's gift, though. Griff's self-centered and Kyle's a manwhore. Nobody knows what Kieran thinks, because that man doesn't do a lot of talking."

When I'd stolen a look at their table, I'd been surprised to see two more Shipleys than I'd met before. There was a clear family resemblance, too. They were all big-shouldered, rugged men with strong jaws and thick hair. I wondered which one Zara had run afoul of.

The answer arrived at my shoulder about sixty seconds later.

"Evening, ladies." Griff's deep voice seemed to vibrate right through my chest. I wished it wouldn't. The next few weeks would be a lot easier if I was immune to Griffin Shipley.

"Evening," Zara muttered. "You need something?" Her dark eyes dared him to ask her for anything.

"Just need to say hello to Audrey," he said, dropping

a hand on my bare shoulder. My skin heated beneath his hand, and I fought off a giddy shiver. My libido was like a Golden Retriever puppy, ready to jump all over him and lick his face.

Down, girl.

Steeling myself against all that hotness, I looked up at him. "Evening, Grumpy Griff."

The corners of Zara's mouth turned up. But then her gaze traveled down to his hand, which was still on my shoulder. And the girl's dark eyes filled with something like a mixture of irritation and hurt. She turned away, heading down to the other end of the bar.

"Come sit with us," he said, his voice rumbling right through my core.

"I'm waiting for my meal," I piped up. "And something tells me the bartender doesn't like you. If I'm at your table, she might never feed me."

He chuckled, the sound low and rich. "Well, it's a risk."

"What did you ever do to her?" I asked, taking sides with a woman I'd known for about three minutes.

"Eh, it's what I didn't."

We stopped talking because Zara came toward me again, my salad bowl in her hand. She plunked it down in front of me, then Griff picked it right up. "Put this on our tab," he said, taking the roll of silverware out of her other hand.

"Yes, master," she sniped, giving him a salute before marching off.

"Whatever you did or didn't do, you might want to consider apologizing," I said as I rose from the stool, grabbing my beer.

"I'll take it under advisement." He carried my dinner over to a vintage wooden booth where three guys watched my approach with fascination.

"Hey there, Audrey," Zach said, jumping up. He held out a hand, offering me the inside seat.

I slid in, and Griff sat beside me, setting my salad down in front of me. Zach pulled up a chair to the end of the table.

"These chuckleheads are Kieran and Kyle, my cousins," Griff explained as I began to eat my salad. "Boys, say hi to our friend Audrey."

"Hi-to-our-friend-Audrey," they droned in tandem, then laughed and high-fived each other.

Griff shook his big head as if in pain, but I had a feeling that Kyle and Kieran were going to be fun. The night was looking up. And the salad I'd ordered really wasn't bad. If a restaurant had a decent Caesar salad, I knew it was worth going back again.

Of course, I'd probably come here every night like a loser if it meant sitting hip to hip to Griff Shipley. Pathetic much?

"So. How are things?" I asked, cutting my chicken with my fork. "Where's the new guy? I wondered if he'd work out okay." I shoved a bite into in my mouth, wishing I hadn't said it. I didn't mean to advertise the fact that I'd thought about the Shipley farm every day since I'd left it.

"Jude is doing great," Zach volunteered. "Mrs. Shipley's been feeding him up. Tonight May drove him to a Narcotics Anonymous meeting in Norwich."

"That was nice of her."

"It really is," Griff agreed.

"Let's see..." Zach put his chin in his hand. "The peaches are almost done, and the apples are just beginning..."

"You have peaches?" I squeaked. "Damn. The things I could make with tree-ripened peaches." I gave a shuddering sigh just thinking about it. Peach *cobbler*.

Ginger-peach muffins...

"Whoa," Kyle said with a grin. "You okay over there? They're just peaches. The wasps like those trees, too. Just yesterday I got stung on my bare..."

"Quiet, moron," Griff barked. He turned to me. "Did BPG send you back to Vermont?"

"They sure did. Their old approach wasn't working, so they upped their budget. I think the numbers are decent now. Guess I'll find out." I knew there'd be some new problem, though. There always was.

"How did you like that kitchen where you were temping?" Griff asked, his forehead furrowing into a thoughtful expression. "The high-tech place."

I was surprised he even remembered. "It was fascinating, and I learned a lot about cutting-edge foodie technology. But the kitchen was sort of...joyless. And the chef was a dick. They all are. He didn't bother learning my name for the first two weeks. The last two weeks he spent grabbing my ass and calling me 'Tawdry.' That was his funny little joke."

Griffin made the grouchiest face I have ever seen on him. And that's saying something. "This asshole is the *boss?*"

Kieran spoke up for the first time. "Can't you report him to HR?"

"I could," I said, picking through my salad. "But they don't care what he says as long as he's getting good reviews and selling out of forty-dollar truffle dishes in his dining room. Besides—this company is going to fund my dream, even if they don't know it yet. So I don't want to be the girl who's accusing them of a hostile work environment."

Nobody spoke for a moment, but Zach's face went all endearingly gloomy.

"That sucks, princess," Griff said eventually.

"Yeah," Kyle agreed. "This calls for more beer. I'll get it so Zara doesn't poison it."

Kieran chuckled. "It's like clockwork—there's a woman present, so Kyle finds his wallet."

They all chatted about the bar and about picking the rest of the peaches while I finished my salad.

"How long are you in town?" Griff asked when I pushed my plate away.

Kyle waggled his eyebrows at Griff, who silenced him with a Griff Glare.

"At least a couple of weeks. I'll have to drive around a lot to find all the produce they're looking for." There wouldn't be anyone from BPG around to monitor my daily activities. That meant lots of time to explore and eat local peaches. I could even try cooking them in the crappy little kitchenette at the motor lodge where I was staying. I was looking forward to a little unstructured time away from the stressful kitchen where I'd worked so hard for the last month. The bottom of the foodie totem pole was a lonely place.

"The cranberries won't be ripe for a while," Zach was saying to Kieran. "You're heading out of town at the wrong time."

"Wait, you have cranberries, too?" I asked. "I thought you needed a bog for that."

Griff shook his head. "Big commercial growers flood the field to make the harvest easier. But the plant itself grows anywhere you put it."

"In November, Mrs. Shipley makes her famous apple and cranberry pie with a crumb topping," Zach said, leaning back in his chair and closing his eyes. "It's my favorite time of year."

"Truth," Kyle said, sitting down again with the pitcher. "That pie gives me a foodgasm. It's pretty much the reason I work the orchard in the first place."

"Naw," Griff scoffed. "It's because of my winning personality." He pushed my beer glass toward his cousin for a refill.

At the same moment, Griff's free hand landed on my bare knee, spanning so much width that his fingertips grazed the sensitive skin on my inner thigh.

I gave a whole-body shiver.

"You okay?" Kyle asked again.

"Fine," I said quickly, taking another gulp of beer. But those naughty fingertips stroked slowly across my skin, firing up every nerve ending in my body. My brain began to short circuit, sending sparks flying willy-nilly in every direction.

If he kept that up I was going to do something very, very stupid. So I did what was necessary. Slipping my hand under the table, I pushed his hand off of my knee. "You are not a nice man," I said under my breath.

"Not true," he returned quietly. And as his hand retreated back to its own territory, it took mine with it. Griff's big fingers closed gently around my own, and for reasons that were a mystery to me, I let them.

Griff flattened my hand onto his leg, my palm spread out on his muscular thigh, my fingertips grazing his bare quad where his shorts ended. The hair on his leg felt surprisingly soft under my fingers, and I fought off another shiver as a fresh memory from our recent night together slammed through me. *My back against the wall, his legs flexing repeatedly as we...*

Gah. I didn't know how a girl was supposed to stop thinking about a thing like that.

"Who's doing the Norwich fair tomorrow?" somebody asked. "I went last week."

"I'll take it," Griff said as his fingers slid down the back of my hand. "Jude will come with me."

"Bring us back some donuts," Kyle requested.

They kept talking, but all my focus was on my hand and the way Griff was stroking it with just the lightest touches. Then he lifted my hand into his and massaged my palm with his roughened thumb, teasing me with a slow caress that had me thinking about other places he might be touching...

I wanted to lie back and close my eyes. I wanted to throw myself at him again.

But I wasn't going to do it.

I wasn't.

Really.

His tricky fingers curved around my wrist, making me feel deceptively fragile compared to his great bulk. Who knew that the wrist was an erogenous zone? I'd begun to prickle with awareness everywhere. And he was only *holding my hand.*

"Sleepy?" Kyle asked me as my eyes went to half-mast from pleasure.

"Mmm?" I shook myself. "It was a long drive up here after a long day at work."

The conversation went on, but I was fixated on Griff's touch. Those naughty fingers brushed my leg again, but only the outside. Maybe I really *was* "Tawdry" because I regretted shoving him away from me. Unbidden, my leg drifted ever so slightly closer to him beneath the table. Griff chuckled quietly, then skimmed his palm over my bare knee again.

I stopped breathing.

Those thick fingers spread, caressing the tender skin of my inner thigh. Then his hand slipped upward, under my skirt. "You know where I found some vole damage?" he asked, though I could barely focus on the words. "By the Greening trees, the ones beside the Pippins..." He drew a little map with his finger on the table, and the other three men focused their attention on whatever he was telling them. Meanwhile, a single finger passed lightly up my thigh, between my legs, over the cotton of my panties.

I bit down on my lip to keep from whimpering. In my life I'd done some irresponsible things. Tonight I felt myself on the verge of one more.

"You okay, Audrey?" Zach asked me, cocking his head to the side like a puppy. "You're kinda flushed."

"Uh," I said, trying not to pant. "I think I need some air."

Griff's hand retreated instantly. Then he slid out of the booth. "I'll come outside with you."

"There's something I needed to ask you, anyway." And there really was. If I could just stop lusting after him for ten seconds, I'd planned to ask for his help.

He took my hand and led me outside. The summery air smelled so sweet I wanted to drink it in. But the only thing I'd be drinking in was Griff. He pushed me up against the wooden clapboards and kissed me.

Apparently Griff and I didn't do slow and subtle. Our tongues tangled about two seconds into that kiss. He tasted like a potent elixir of heat and man and beer. And I wanted every drop I could get. His big hands landed at my waist, where they nearly encircled me. I wanted to stay there, pinned by Griff Shipley, forever.

I'd always been a practical girl.

Not.

When we came up for air we were both panting. I tipped my head back against the wall and looked up at the brilliant display of stars. "Is this what we do?" I asked with a wheeze. "We attack each other at every outdoor opportunity?"

"Apparently," he mumbled, bending down to suck on my neck. My girl parts shimmied, hoping he'd never stop, unless it was to use that incredible mouth elsewhere. "Is that what you wanted to ask me?"

"What?" I gasped, pressing my legs together against the ache. "No. I..."

He lifted his head and waited.

God. My breasts were heavy and my lips were swollen. "Just know that I enjoy revenge."

"Yeah?" His big, sinful mouth curved into a smile. "I'll remember that. Now what did you want to ask me?"

"Uh. It was a favor. Wanted to ask for..." His thumb caressed my cheekbone, and it was hard to stay focused. "...help."

He made a low sound in his throat. "What kind of *help?*" His hips pushed against me, and I felt the most glorious erection pin me to the wall. While he waited for my answer, he ran his fingers through my messy hair.

"Um..." I took a deep breath, calling on the last few brain cells I still had left. "I wondered if you'd introduce me to some farmers. You told 'em all not to talk to me. But now my prices are so much better."

His eyes fell shut, and he sighed. Then he backed off a few crucial inches, taking his hands off my body and standing at least a foot away.

I braced myself for his rejection.

"Yeah," he said, opening his eyes. He studied me, his expression thoughtful. "I could do that. Sure thing."

"Really?" I squeaked, putting both hands on his broad chest.

"Really," he repeated. "You can come to the Norwich farmers' market with me tomorrow morning. It's the biggest market in the area. Lots of farmers in one place."

"Great," I breathed, looking up into his rugged face. *Kiss me again,* I inwardly begged.

Instead, he gently removed my hands from his chest.

"W...why'd you do that?"

He sighed. "You asked me for help with business. I'm not gonna be like that asshole chef who's grabbing your ass when you're just trying to get a job done."

"But...but..." I stammered. All the nerves in my body (particularly the ones below my waist) screamed, *Noooooooooo!*

"Besides," he said, reaching for my hand. "I drove my guys here tonight..." He kissed my palm, and the soft brush of his beard taunted me. I wanted to feel it everywhere. He must have seen it in my eyes. Because he placed my hand at his neck, then dipped his head to kiss my jaw again. His voice dropped low and smoky. "The things I want to do to you would take all night, anyway. If we ever get a chance, I want you all spread out underneath me."

Unggh. The idea had me absolutely throbbing. *Tawdry Audrey at your service.*

"But not tonight," he whispered. "Not in a parking lot, princess."

I said nothing at all for fear that I'd start begging. So instead I just stared up at him like a puppy hoping for one more treat. He leaned in and gave me a single, soft kiss. When he pulled back, I wanted to reach for him, but I made myself stand still.

The back door banged open and Zara lurched into view with a plastic bin in two hands. She stopped short when she saw us, her eyes tracing the narrow distance between me and Griff. Jerking her gaze away, she took two steps forward and slammed the bin to the ground, the recyclables rattling around with a deafening crash. Then she stormed inside and slammed the door.

"Is that your girlfriend?" I asked. *Please say no.*

"No, baby." He sighed. "It never got that far."

Oh. But it was obvious they'd had something. Of course they had. Zara was beautiful. Griff Shipley probably had every woman for a hundred miles pining for him.

Don't fall for him, I ordered myself. *Don't you dare.*

"Where are you staying?" Griff asked. "Not like there are a lot of options. It's either The Three Bears Motor Lodge or a hotel in Montpelier."

"The, uh, motor lodge," I confessed. Until that moment I hadn't realized that I'd chosen the option closer to the Shipley Farm. *Thanks, subconscious.*

He chuckled. "Is your room okay? I always wonder how Mrs. Beasley keeps that place up. She's about ninety."

"She looks it."

"I'll bet. She doesn't retire, though, because then there wouldn't be any visitors to spy on anymore."

"Oh."

A silence fell over us. Griff just stood there in the moonlight, looking down at me, as if I were a puzzle he was trying to solve.

The main door opened this time, and Griff stepped back just as his cousins came out. Kyle looked from Griff to me and back again. "Everything okay?"

"Just fine," I said quickly.

Kyle nodded at his cousin. "Thought you'd want to get back."

"Yeah," he said, lifting a hand to the back of his neck. "Dawn comes soon enough. Where is your car, princess?"

God, I hated that nickname. "It's right there."

"You need directions or..."

I shook my head. "It's two miles down the road, Griff. Even a fuck-up like me can find it."

Kyle laughed, but Griffin looked like he'd tasted something sour. "I'll pick you up at seven-thirty," he said.

"In the *morning?*" I squeaked.

His bearded face broke into a smile—and the man's smile was *potent.* "Be ready, princess. It's a long day selling apples." He turned away and headed toward his truck. All four guys got in.

I headed for my rental car, because what else was I going to do with the last bit of a Friday night in Tuxbury, Vermont?

I noticed that Griff waited until I'd left the parking lot and turned in the proper direction before he drove away into the night.

He really did think I was supremely incompetent. Just like everyone else did.

Chapter Thirteen

Griffin

It was nearly impossible to work a fourteen-hour day on the farm and then lay awake half the night. But somehow I managed it.

As a quarter moon rose and set outside my window, I lay there staring at the ceiling, listening to a nearby barred owl hoot, while my problems chased each other around in my head.

I was a selfish man at heart. We all are, I suppose. But saving our farm required a level of selflessness that was difficult to maintain. I'd told myself that I could do it—I could give up football and run this place the way it had always been run. I could employ my father's brand of Yankee ingenuity to forge on, selling milk and apples to bring in cash for things like clothes and cars and tuition. And doctor's visits for gramps and Dylan's contact lenses.

Every day I got up before dawn and worked like a cart horse without complaint.

But somewhere along the way I'd begun to dream, and dreaming was dangerous. In my mind's eye I'd built a modern brewery in the cider house. And I'd ripped out some of our least interesting apple trees to re-graft them with cider varietals. In my dreams I spent my days blending fascinating, complicated ciders and shipping them to eager buyers.

At some point I'd begun to draft a short but crucial list of things that I just plain *wanted*. But wanting wasn't allowed. Not for me. Not right now, anyway. My family was already freaking out over my plan to sell off part of our herd and reinvest in the brewery. It could work, though. We could prosper.

Or it could fail and I'd let everyone down.

The worst-case scenario was that we'd have to sell the farm. And go...where, exactly? If the farm failed, I'd have to get a job that paid well. I had a college degree in chemistry, so I was theoretically employable, but in a city, where I never wanted to live. At best I could live in a goddamn suburb surrounded by neighbors who poisoned their lawns every other week to keep the weeds away.

Fuck. I'd be that asshole who lectured the neighbors about the evils of commercial herbicides, and told their kids to stay off my organic lawn. I'd keep my blinds shut so I wouldn't see how close together the houses were. Meanwhile, our hilltop farm would be sold to some asshole who'd tear down the farmhouse to build a six-bedroom manse with a four stall garage.

Yep, the million-dollar views were great here. It was just too damn bad we didn't have the million dollars.

Tonight I'd added yet another item to the list of things I wanted. And this one was as dangerous to my sanity as any other dream. Saying goodnight to Audrey had caused me physical pain—even harder to explain than my yearning to make a go of the cider business.

Around and around we go. My thoughts were like a never-ending merry-go-round.

I rolled onto my stomach and stuffed my face into the pillow. There was no reason why that girl should make me so crazy. I barely even knew her. That's what I was going to keep telling myself, anyway. It was just lust, right?

Right.

I didn't have time for a girlfriend, especially one who lived in Boston and didn't like me all that much.

I'd help her meet some farmers, and hopefully she'd get what she needed and go back to Beantown. As long as she and I were in the same area code, I wasn't going to be able to finish a thought, unless that thought involved her naked body.

Jesus. My cock thickened against the mattress just from the memory of the way she'd looked over her shoulder at me from the barstool. There'd been a challenge in her eye. *Don't tangle with me*, it said. *I may be cute, but I am fierce.*

I just wanted to fuck all that sass right out of her. I wanted to shut her up with my mouth and my hands until she came apart on my cock.

Instead, tomorrow we would sell a thousand dollars' worth of apples and cider and introduce her to a bunch of farming nerds. What a party.

I locked my arms together under the pillow and forbade myself to think about her anymore until morning.

* * *

Thank god for coffee.

Six hours later I drove up to the motor lodge in my pickup, the back loaded with fruit and cider. The place where Audrey was staying was trapped in the 1950s. It wasn't one big motel but rather a bunch of tiny one-room cabins. The sign out front boasted Color TV, and someone had added at the bottom: 3 Bars of Cell Phone Service. But it was cheerful enough. Mrs. Beasley kept each cabin's window box stuffed full of petunias, though we all knew the flowers were just an excuse to peer into her guests' windows as she watered them.

There was no sign of Audrey yet. Jude and I sat in silence for a moment, scanning the blue doors, waiting for one to open. And then the one on the far right popped open and Audrey came out in another one of her tiny denim skirts that killed me, her long legs gleaming in the morning sunlight as she hurried toward the truck. She tossed her hair out of the way, exposing smooth, bare shoulders.

It was gonna be a long day. No doubt about it.

Jude opened his door and jumped out. Then he climbed into the back seat. For a convicted felon, Jude had surprisingly good manners.

Audrey heaved herself up and onto the truck's seat and slammed the door.

"Morning," I said, reversing out of my parking spot. "Sleep well?" *I didn't.*

"God, it's early!" She grabbed my coffee thermos out of the cupholder and took a sip.

"Help yourself," I grumbled. "Not like Jude and I need that. We've been up for two-and-a-half hours milking cows and loading the truck. But no big." The loss of a night's sleep obviously made me even crustier than usual.

"Oh, Grouchy Griff." Audrey took another sip of my coffee. "I brought you some lemon scones that I baked myself this morning. They are fabulous. It's a fair trade, I swear."

"Baked? Where?" I demanded. Nobody baked at Mrs. Beasley's motor lodge.

"There's a toaster oven in my room."

There was chuckling from the back seat. "So you just...whipped up some scones on the TV?"

"Yep." She leaned over and dug something out of her

shoulder bag. "Here, Jude. Taste the greatness."

She handed something over the seat. A moment later Jude began moaning.

"Everything okay back there?" I grumbled.

"Oh, *hell* that's good. Can I eat Griff's?"

"Nope!" she sang. "A girl needs some leverage sometimes. Coffee?" She passed my thermos back to him, too.

When it came back in my direction, I grabbed the thermos and set it down. As if I needed any more of it. I was jumpy already. Audrey smelled like fruity shampoo and lemon scones. That, and her teasing smile made me hungry for about a hundred different things, only a few of which were food.

I pointed the truck south toward Norwich. As the crow flies, it wasn't very far. But the drive took most of an hour because the roads in Vermont didn't often go where you needed 'em to.

"Shame about all this traffic," Audrey said, stretching her golden legs out in front of her.

"Yeah," I said automatically.

She burst out laughing. "What are you thinking about? Because you didn't even hear what I said, did you?"

"I could hazard a guess," Jude muttered behind me.

"Just hungry," I grumbled, giving Jude a glare in the rear-view.

All the teasing fell out of her voice, which became soft. "Would you like a scone, Grouchy Griff?"

"Yes please, princess."

She placed one in my palm, and I took a bite. Sweet, crumbly, lemony goodness broke across my tongue.

It wasn't easy to hold back my moan, but I managed. Just barely.

* * *

We pulled up to the usual mayhem—men and women hauling bushel baskets and coolers off truck beds while their children ran around like little maniacs.

The weather was nice today, which meant we'd see the maximum number of customers. The Norwich market was the regional mother ship. It was the only market where the booths stayed put all week long and where musicians entertained the crowd. It was something of a spectacle.

Jude and I carried the goods from the truck to the stall. Setting up was easy enough except for the extra complication of swatting away Audrey's help every time she tried to lift an apple crate.

"Jesus, Griff!" she argued when I snatched another crate out of her hands. "It's not that heavy."

The truth was that I couldn't stand the sight of a pretty girl doing work that was really mine. But the perky princess wouldn't want to hear that. "You're not covered by my workers' comp," I said by way of explanation. "Your job is to stand there and look pretty."

She rolled her eyes, then pouted for a moment, perking up again when she spotted the baker's goods on the neighboring table. "Ooh, *donuts.* Hey—how come you guys don't make cider donuts for the tourists at your farm? There's nothing like a hot cider donut with cinnamon sugar."

"No time," I said, setting our scale on the table and balancing it. It was nine o'clock—opening hour. A child ran down the aisles clanging the bell, and the buyers pounced. The early customers were always families with young children and retirees. As the morning wore on, we'd see fewer locals and more tourists.

During August, this market was the very picture of

abundance. Farm-fresh eggs, loaves of country-style bread and fresh-picked everything. Abraham's—my neighbors'—stall was catty-corner to mine. The Apostate Farm sign hung over a table loaded down with organic vegetables in every color. Red and golden beets. Orange and purple carrots. Yellow crook-neck squash and blindingly beautiful tomatoes that had survived last month's blight scare.

I weighed the first bag of apples of the day at one minute after nine. "That'll be six dollars," I pronounced, rounding down. We always rounded down to the nearest fifty cents, because it made the transactions faster and it signaled good will. Of course, we carried higher prices per pound here in Norwich than anywhere else. But that was our little secret.

The buying was brisk. "Eight dollars," I said to the next person. "Six-fifty," for the next. And then, "Two bottles of cider, twenty four dollars, please." The action continued for a while and when there was finally a little break, I handed Jude the money belt. "Can you hold down the fort for a few? I want to introduce Audrey to some farmers."

"Sure."

As it turned out, Audrey didn't need a lot of help. After I'd introduced her to the decision-makers at the three biggest organic farms, she got right in there. "Oh! These are glorious!" she said of a picturesque display of winter squashes. "Omigod, is this an ambercup?" She hugged an orange squash like a long-lost child. "I never see these in Boston! They have the best flavor and texture. It's so moist and buttery."

I stood there like a dolt, watching her wrap the old farmer around her finger. She whipped out a wallet and bought a squash. Then she fawned over some heirloom tomatoes before finally getting around to mentioning her produce-hungry employer.

It took me a few minutes to realize that I wasn't needed anymore. I went back to my own stand, where Jude handed over the money belt without a word and began restocking the tables with apples from our truck and lining up the cider bottles with the labels facing the same direction.

Jude had been with us a month now, and the kid always caught on quickly. Last week I'd watched him handling a fast bunch of transactions without relying on the calculator to check his math. Yet right after he'd arrived, Jude had let slip that he got Cs and Ds in high school.

He was a puzzle I was still trying to figure out.

The morning slipped into afternoon as I sold an ocean of apples and cider. I kept my prices higher at this market than at some others, because Norwich had plenty of cash, and the attitude that went along with it. "When will the Crispins be ready? I want *pie*," an old woman complained. "These won't do."

"We don't get Crispins 'til October," I said gently. *Nature doesn't care about your pie.* "The Zestars will bake up for you just fine, though."

She sniffed unhappily and then bought ten pounds of Zestars. People are weird.

Audrey eventually staggered toward my booth, weighed down under bags of vegetables, with a squash under one arm and a perfect tub of late raspberries balanced on one palm.

I ducked out of the stall to grab some of her booty before it all went crashing down and managed not to get yelled at for helping.

"Thank you," she breathed.

"Why'd you buy all this stuff?" I asked. "Don't tell me you're making squash in the toaster oven at Mrs.

Beasley's."

Audrey shook her head. "Nope. That's a gift for your mom. Here, have a six-dollar raspberry." She popped one in her mouth.

I found a place for all her things in an empty apple crate. "Why'd you go shopping? I thought your asshole employers were supposed to foot the bill."

"Credibility," she said, crossing those silky arms. "Buying some things makes me sound serious."

"You already sound serious," I heard myself say. *Seriously delicious.* But really—her enthusiasm for ingredients was obvious. Who wouldn't want to sell produce to a girl who practically orgasmed over the balance of sugars and acids in a purple heirloom tomato?

"Hope so." She sighed. "But it might not even matter. It's pretty late in the season. Lots of these farmers' produce is promised to restaurants who offered fair rates right off the bat."

"Crap. I was worried about that for you."

She nudged me with her elbow. "Careful, Griff, you almost sound helpful right now."

Damn it, I did.

"Can I play store? Maybe Jude needs a break?"

"Sure. Bet he'd love a break."

Audrey took over the apple selling while I stacked some fruit and listened to her charm the pants off my customers. "These have such lovely perfume," she said of my Zestars. "I'd sauté them and serve them with a pork roast."

Great. Now I was starving.

"Um, Griff?" I heard her ask a few minutes later. "Do you take these?"

Audrey held up a paper Market Money voucher—the ones I'd designed for our customers who were cashing in food stamps. I'd forgotten to tell her about those. Meanwhile, the woman standing in front of her jiggled a toddler on her hip and wore an embarrassed frown on her face.

"Of course," I said quickly, darting over to help. "Are these yours?" I asked, checking the scale.

"Yeah," the customer murmured.

The apples on the scale didn't quite weigh out to the five bucks on the voucher. "You've got more coming. Hang on." One more apple would have done it, but I grabbed four and bagged them all up together. "Here you go. See you next week. We'll have even more variety as the season goes on."

"Thank you," she said quietly, taking the bag.

"That was nice of you," Audrey said when the woman had disappeared into the crowd.

"Clean food isn't just for rich people."

Audrey shook her head. "I promise not to tell any of your old football friends that you're a softie. Your secret is safe with me."

"You have a customer," was my only response.

An hour and a half later we were back on the road. The fair was over, and I'd sold nearly every apple I'd brought and fifty bottles of cider. Before we got back in the truck I bartered a bottle with Fran of Fran's Flatbreads in exchange for three of his generous slices with chicken, olives and feta.

So my belly was full but I was feeling undercaffeinated after my long, sleepless night. "Tell me about your family," I said to Audrey, hoping she'd keep me awake. "You met mine already."

"That won't take long," she said. "I don't have a father."

"Everyone has a father," I argued. "Basic science,

princess."

"I passed seventh-grade biology, Griff. But when my mother decided she wanted a child, she picked the fanciest fertility specialist in Boston and chose a vial of Harvard sperm to be my father."

"Ah. Okay."

"See, my mother hates men. *Hates.* So getting married was out of the question."

"She's...an angry lesbian?" I guessed. Jude snorted in the back seat.

"No, that would be more interesting. She's just *angry.* She wants to singlehandedly bust the glass ceiling for every woman in America. She runs a big venture capital firm. She's on the board of directors at a dozen different companies. As far as I can tell, she wants women everywhere to become money-hungry assholes, just like men."

"Sounds like a fun person," Jude said.

"She's a peach," Audrey said. "The second time I failed out of college, she cut me off. She sold my car and cut up my credit cards. She told me to figure it out for myself."

"Ouch," I said. "I'm sorry."

"Nah." Audrey grinned at me. "Best thing that ever happened to me. Mom didn't realize that you can't hound your kid after you cut her off. She thought I'd stick around for daily lectures and doses of humiliation. But I moved out. It was rough at first—working shitty kitchen jobs and couch surfing for three weeks until I started getting paychecks. For the first time in my life, there was nobody telling me I was a worthless piece of junk."

Fuuuuck. That had to be an exaggeration. "She said that to her own child?"

"Oh sure." Audrey waved one pretty hand in the air.

"Mom just assumed I'd get straight A's like she did. But that just wasn't in the cards. She even called up the sperm bank when I was in high school to ask if they'd discovered any issues with that donor. I think she wanted to sue them. Fun times."

I found myself white-knuckling the steering wheel and had to force my hands to relax. "Jesus. Sorry, babe."

"It's *okay*," she insisted. "Know what's funny? She thinks that I went to culinary school just to spite her."

"Why?"

"Because women have been cooking for millennia, right? And she views herself as a crusader for equality in the boardroom. She thinks it's embarrassing that I want to be a chef and assumes I chose cooking just to make her look stupid. It's the only thing I ever excelled at, though. Somewhere out there is a sperm donor who's really savvy in the kitchen."

I drove the next few miles in silence, wondering what it would be like to have your only parent reject you. My family and I had some difficult decisions to make about our farm's future. But my parents had always told us that we could do whatever made us happy. Whether we chose farming or something completely different, it was always up to us.

Meanwhile, Audrey spun around on the passenger's seat to talk to Jude. She slung an elbow over the back of the seat, and now I had an oblique view of her tight, sexy ass. Hell. It was a long enough drive already.

"So what did you cook in the prison kitchen?" she asked our favorite felon.

"Lots of ground beef, because it's cheap."

"That makes sense."

"Right. But you should have seen this meat. Swear to God—the cartons were stamped: *Grade D But Fit for Human Consumption*."

"Omigod!" Audrey shrieked. "It's the 'but' that really gives you pause, right?"

Her butt sure made me want to pause.

Their conversation went on in the direction of the myriad things a guy could make with ground beef for prisoners. They were discussing the difference between a goulash and a stew when I felt a small hand slide onto my belly. The heat from her palm warmed my Shipley Farms T-shirt.

It was nice, but inconvenient. It gave my body some big ideas.

"I think a goulash can have a tomato base, or not," Audrey mused to Jude. Then she slid her hand an inch lower, her fingertips reaching the hem of my shorts. As she continued her conversation with the man in the back seat, those fingers popped the button on my shorts.

Oh. Hell.

I let out a long, slow breath and stared carefully ahead at the road. But that hand skimmed under my T-shirt, across my belly. Then it plunged down between my shorts and underwear, landing on my cock, which twitched to life inside my boxers. She cupped me, her thumb slowly stroking me, coaxing me harder.

Remembering to breathe, I inhaled carefully. Yeah, she'd *said* she'd get even with me. And here I'd thought it was nothing but an idle threat.

Gritting my teeth, I tried to conjure up last night's Red Sox score. But my dick was now hard as the bat they'd used to win the game. So I catalogued my mental to-do list. That sucker was long enough to deflate any boner. Or so I thought. When that failed, I tried reciting the periodic table. *Hydrogen. Helium. Lithiummmmmmm.* Her hand tortured me through the fabric of my underwear. I was so hard I'd begun to ache.

My first chance at relief came when I exited the

highway and stopped at a light. I thought she'd turn around and leave me alone. But as I shifted into first, Audrey took the opportunity to suddenly slip her hand inside my fly and stroke me with a firm grip.

"Arghff," I said.

"You okay?" she chirped. "That was an odd noise."

I grabbed her hand and yanked it out of my pants. "Just fine," I said, turning onto the two-lane road toward home.

Audrey went back to her conversation with Jude. They were talking about side dishes now. Probably. My brain felt muzzy and thick. I was hard and leaking for her and desperate to see the finish of what she'd started.

Not in the truck, though.

Goddamn stubborn girl. Nothing like a taste of my own medicine to make me grumpy.

We were three miles from home when her hand returned, stroking me slowly over my shorts. I bit down on my lip to keep from groaning. Then I knocked Audrey's hand away a second time and sped the rest of the way home, tortured by her proximity and the husky sound of her laugh whenever Jude said anything funny.

God, I wanted her so badly. And she knew it, the little vixen.

When we pulled up the drive I was ornerier than I'd been in a long time. And hard as one of the fence posts I'd be setting into the ground this afternoon.

That's when I realized that I'd forgotten to drop Audrey back at the motor lodge. "Sorry. You don't have your car. Zach can run you home," I said as I killed the engine.

"No problem!" she said cheerfully. "I need to give all this produce to your mother, anyway." She reached down onto the floor of the truck where we'd stashed the vegetable crate.

I was trying to subtly tuck away my aching dick and zip my shorts, when she scooped up the fucking winter squash and set it at my knee. "Be a dear and carry this into the house, will you? I know you hate it when I carry things." She gave me a cheeky grin I would have liked to wipe off her face with my tongue.

Then I carried that fucking squash in front of my crotch all the way indoors.

I almost had myself under control by the time Zach announced that he was ready to drive Audrey home. She gave me a polite thank you for the market introductions and a cheery, knowing smile. Then Zach took her home.

As I was stacking all the empty apple crates outside the cider house, a dusty blue Jeep drove up. A man my late father's age climbed out and approached me. "Griffin Shipley? I'm Amos Appleby."

Ah. He was another of my mother's church friends. "Hi, Amos," I said, offering my hand. "What brings you up our hill today?"

"Cows," he said, shaking my hand. "I heard you're thinking of selling off your herd."

"Well..." I said slowly, wondering where he'd heard. I'd mentioned it to only a few farmers. "Yeah, that's under consideration. You interested?"

"Sure thing," he said with a grin. "When would you want this to happen?"

"Uh," I said as my mother approached.

"Amos! This is a pleasant surprise."

"I came to talk about cows," he said. "But if you had a piece of that apple pie you bring to the church supper sometimes..." He chuckled.

But my mother's face had fallen. "Griff wants to sell, but it isn't decided," she said quickly.

"I see." The man's smile slid off. "Sorry to trouble

you."

"Why don't you leave me your number?" I whipped out my phone.

Amos glanced between me and my mother. "Ah, okay. You folks think it over, though." He gave me his digits and he was on his way.

My mother and I stood there in the driveway. "I don't want to sell," she said softly. "But it's not me who milks them every day."

"Mom, I'm not doing it because I want to sleep in, okay? The milking parlor across the road is antiquated. New gear costs more than twenty grand. And the rent is going up. This isn't just a wild hair I'm having."

"Could we get a few more years out of our milking rig?"

"We already did. And the price of milk is going down. The price of good cider is higher. I'm just trying to be smart."

Mom sighed. "Okay. I trust you, Griffin. If you say we should invest in cider instead of milk, I'll stop worrying about it."

Aw, hell. "I don't have a crystal ball. But our business is going to change whether we want it to or not. We're getting pinched on our operation across the street. I'm just trying to make the best of it."

She squeezed my elbow. "It's just scary to try a new business."

"Don't I know it." My biggest fear was talking my family into this change and then bombing somehow. Although I really didn't think that would happen. "You know—you talk as though the dairy was the only thing Dad left behind. He taught me to make cider. I watched him blend ciders every year of my life."

Her face gentled. "He said it was a lost art."

"Not lost on me."

"Come on," she said, tugging me toward the house. "If we're going to do this, someone has to tell Dylan."

"Christ. We'll arm wrestle. Loser breaks the news."

"August Griffin Shipley! That's not fair."

Laughing, I followed her inside.

Chapter Fourteen

Audrey

I spent the next two days following up with the farmers Griffin had introduced me to in Norwich. The prices I'd been given were acceptable on about half the vegetables on my list. So that was something. But quantity was definitely a problem. I could have made an order for three times the amount they offered me.

"If you'd spoken up in April, this would be easier," they told me.

They were right, of course.

And because I was shopping in August, the job would take more than a few days. I'd have to cobble together more produce from more farmers to complete BPG's shopping list. Whatever I couldn't find, BPG would have to buy from wholesalers. They'd lose out on local mystique and bragging rights, but the world wouldn't end.

My job might, though.

Bumping around the country roads of eastern Vermont in my rental car had a few perks. When I discovered that quite a few farmstands sold local cheeses, I bought a box of crackers and a pocketknife at a general store in Norwich called Dan & Whit's. The sign in their window read, *If We Don't Have It, You Don't Need It.*

I snacked on good cheese, crackers and the plums that had just come into season. Even if the work wasn't going so well, the food was amazing.

I sent vague little updates to my boss at BPG, just so he wouldn't forget I existed. "I found a new farm for organic herbs!" I said in one email. I never gave him any numbers. I didn't want Bill Burton to know I was struggling. Disappointing him seemed like a good thing to put off.

He wasn't the only one I would disappoint this week. An email popped up from my mother, and I did not delete it as I usually did. In the first place, the subject line read URGENT. And secondly, I needed to know if she was meddling in my job at BPG. Did she even know I worked there? Had Burton told her?

Audrey—

You are expected to submit your résumé to Mr. Roger Smith of CarterCorp next week, or by August tenth at the very latest. At my urging, he is holding an interview slot for you. The job is: Nutritional Director for CarterCorp's Executive Dining. You would work regular nine to five hours while reviewing and revising the company's in-house corporate cafeteria menu offerings. The pay is exceptional for your line of work, with full insurance and benefits.

Don't keep Mr. Smith waiting. This is an amazing opportunity for you. And by holding this slot, Smith is doing me a great favor.

—K.K.

P.S. Should you need any assistance with your résumé, send it to my assistant and she will take a red pen to it.

I read the message three more times, each time growing a little surlier.

It probably *was* a great job—the sort of position that would help any new chef pay off her credit cards and start her career. And nine-to-five hours were as rare as wild truffles in the foodie world.

But I would not be applying. I didn't want any job that was handed to me as a favor to my mother. It was bad enough that her long, ambitious shadow had kept me from losing my job at BPG. This would be a thousand times worse. CarterCorp was one of my mother's most active investments. I didn't want her pity job, and I really didn't want her to think that I was only surviving my twenties because she'd rescued me again. Whatever they would pay me at CarterCorp, it wouldn't be worth it.

That said, I was purposely avoiding any glimpse of my bank balance, and avoiding emails from my pothead roommate asking when he'd get his money back for the weed I'd accidentally stolen from him.

Things were not going well. But I'd rather take a crappy short-order cook's job than get another handout from my mother.

I deleted the message and went back to sorting through my list of farmers.

There was one farm in particular that I avoided for several days to give my hormones a break. But that didn't mean I hadn't thought about Griff. As I explored Vermont's gravel roads, it was hard to think of anyone else.

And why was that?

He and I had chemistry and a thin past. Twice now our intense attraction had gotten the better of us. Each time, though, there were extenuating circumstances. Back in college, he'd been my rebound guy. When the cheating scumbag known as Bryce had broken my heart, I'd felt it deeply. When I'd called him out for hooking up behind my back, he'd said some hurtful things. He'd called me a "stupid little rich bitch" and "uptight," too.

I was not uptight! An uptight girl would not have given Bryce a blowjob while he Skyped with his parents.

Demanding that my boyfriend be loyal did *not* make me uptight, damn it.

When I'd shown up at a party at his frat, I'd hoped Bryce would see me. I'd wanted him to watch me pick up someone else and go home with him.

As it happened, Bryce didn't show that night. But I forgot to care. Griffin had been there, his eyes on me from the moment I walked in. He'd made me feel beautiful at a moment when I'd been feeling like a cast-off. My night with him had been so hot that I'd gone back for seconds a week later.

But then doubt had set in, especially when I'd told my mother that Bryce and I were through. "You can't trust a man, Audrey," she'd said for the hundredth time. "They want sex, and they want freedom. That's how they're wired."

My mother wasn't a warm person, and she wasn't a nice person. She was sharp as a chef's knife right off the whetstone, though. And I'd believed her warning about men.

When Griff had invited me to dinner after our second tryst, I'd hesitated. He'd been a senior and a football star. He'd pegged me as an easy lay. Which I obviously was.

Trusting another man not to use me wasn't something I was ready to do. I never called him back or saw him again—until last month.

On Tuesday I drove back to the Shipley farm. My brief hiatus from seeing him didn't stop my tongue from hanging out as I parked in front of the cider house. Griff and his boys were all out there *shirtless* stacking crates of apples. It was apples, bulging biceps and rippling pecs as far as the eye could see. Zach was the only one who dove for a shirt when I got out of the car. Jude— who was heavily tattooed—ignored me. Kyle actually flexed, then gave me a wink. Showoff.

And I don't even know what Griff did, because I was trying so hard not to stare at his eight-pack and the happy trial running down toward his...

Crap. I was a terrible businesswoman. Mentally undressing your vendor was definitely a no-no.

"Afternoon," Griff rumbled. "How's business?"

"Not bad. I bought a lot of fennel today."

"That's *fenn*tastic," he quipped, wiping sweat off his forehead.

"Omigod. You did have your sense of humor surgically removed, didn't you? Did it leave a scar?"

Kyle snorted. "Are we done here?" he asked Griff. "It's almost lunchtime."

My eyes tracked toward the farmhouse. I was always looking for an excuse to visit the Shipley kitchen.

Griff looked at his watch. "In half an hour. Can you kids paint the sticky traps in the Cortland rows?"

"Yes, O great one," Kyle said.

Griff led me into the cider house. "What's shakin?" he asked, walking over to one of his tanks. He put a hand on its shiny metal side.

"I need to talk about cider. How much, and how many bottles."

He put his ear against the tank. "Hear that?"

Alone with a half-naked Griff, I put my ear against the tank to humor him. At first I didn't hear a thing. But then there was a gurgle. And another one. It was as if I'd pressed my ear against the belly of a great beast who was digesting his dinner. "What is that?"

"The sound of yeast converting sugar into alcohol. The sound of fermentation."

"The sound of money falling into your pocket."

He cocked a great, bushy eyebrow. "Is it? I gotta tell you—I'm really on the fence about doing business with

BPG. I don't trust them. And I never do business with people I don't trust."

Sigh. "You're very principled, Griff. Ask anyone. But if BPG pays you a reasonable price, why wouldn't you sell? It could be really good for your business."

He stroked his beard. "What are they offering?"

"Six bucks a bottle. But I don't know if that's reasonable. I need to hear it from you."

Griff faced me. "For how much?"

Crap. I should have known that, right? "They didn't say."

He was quiet for a moment. "Listen, seven bucks is a comfortable price for me. But I could get down to six if I absolutely had to. The size is a little tricky. I can only give you a thousand out of last year's vintage. That's not much. But my new stuff will start shipping in…" He looked up at the ceiling beams. "December. You could have everything that's ready before New Years. I'd have to put in two more tanks, but if I did, I could produce up to six thousand bottles for you. That's two hundred fifty cases."

"Do you want to, though?" Putting in extra tanks sounded like a big deal.

"I absolutely do." He stared me down with those serious eyes, the ones that always took my breath away. "An order from BPG could get me halfway to where I need to go. Is this really gonna happen?"

It was. But I didn't want to tell him until I had my boss's word. "Let me go call them." I turned and trotted for the door.

"Wait!" he called. "Aren't you staying for lunch?"

The offer surprised me so much that I turned to check his face to see if he was serious. And it was hard to say, because his expression was as cautious as ever. I took one more hit off the yummy sight of him—one big hand on his cider tank, his T-shirt edible chest on display—and then I gave him a quick excuse and got the heck out of there.

* * *

Back in my motel room, before I picked up the phone to negotiate with my overlords, I asked myself a question. WWMBMD? What Would My Bitchy Mom Do?

She and I never got along, but the woman knew how to drive a hard bargain. You couldn't live in her house for twenty years and not learn a thing or two.

"*Seven* dollars a bottle," I told Burton Jr. over the phone. "You tasted it last month. Your sommeliers are going to love this bottle. You can mark it up to twenty-four bucks because there's a lot of story here. The same Vermont family has been making this cider in small batches for four generations." I was pretty sure that was true. "You should see this hilltop orchard. Twenty-thousand apple trees, and not just the usual picks. It's all heirloom fruit, and they have such pretty wooden fermentation barrels..."

"Hmm."

"You'll make a good mark-up, and it's still cheaper for the customer than a bottle of wine. Everybody wins."

"Well..."

I held my breath in the silence. This was my third call to BPG. I'd been working on the guy all afternoon. *Come on, Burton.*

"Will he make us a special label with our name on it?"

I closed my eyes and tried to guess what Griff would say about that. He wouldn't mind, right? "I think so. But you have to give him final approval, so everyone is happy with the branding."

"Right," he said noncommittally. "Well, if you can get him down to six-seventy-five, I'll take the six-thousand units."

Somehow I kept my tone neutral. "I'm pretty sure I can do that," I said slowly. "I'll call you a little later to confirm."

"Let me know," he said and hung up.

The second the line went dead, I squealed. Then I grabbed my purse and ran outside, leaving my crappy little cabin behind. Fifty yards away the lace curtains moved inside the owner's little house. Griff wasn't kidding. The old lady kept tabs on everything that moved.

I drove two miles to The Mountain Goat and took a seat at the bar.

"Hey lady," Zara said. "How's tricks?"

"Bring me the finest Greek salad in all the land!" I cried. "It's been a good day."

She smiled, and the diamond stud in her nose twitched. "You want chicken on that?"

"Yep. I'm living it up. Another day of not getting fired is a good day. I'd love a beer, too. A..." I looked at the taps. "A Switchback. When in Vermont..."

"Coming up."

I made myself drink half the beer before calling my boss. "Hey," I said. "I got him down to six-seventy-five."

"Good work, Audrey! I'll make a note of it."

"He'd, uh, like to get something in writing," I added. These things were above my pay grade but I was pretty sure that promising someone forty-thousand dollars worth of cider was a little different than shaking hands over a few pallets of cabbages.

"Okay. I'll send a note down to contracts."

"Great. Gotta go! Thanks." I got off the phone as Zara plunked a salad down in front of me. But before I dug in, I made one more call.

"Hello?" The voice that answered the phone at Shipley Farm sounded too perky to be Griff's.

"Hi, this is Audrey Kidder calling. Is Griffin available?"

"Sure! Hey Griff—it's *Audrey*."

I heard a snicker before the phone abruptly changed hands. "Princess?" Griffin barked. "What's up?"

"Six-seventy-five for six-thousand bottles," I said.

"Come again?" he said slowly.

I spoke more directly into the phone, though it wasn't really loud in here. "Six dollars and seventy-five cents, six thousand times. That's forty grand, big guy. I'm not *that* bad at math, no matter what Mommy says."

"That's what I thought you said. *Shit*. Okay."

Hmm. His reaction wasn't exactly how I'd imagined it. His indifference was confusing to me. So I decided to bail out of the phone call and cut my losses. "I'd better go. They just handed over my Greek salad."

"At the Goat?"

"Where else?"

He chuckled. "Good point. Okay. Eat up. You'll need the energy."

The phone went dead before I could ask why.

Whatever.

I ate my salad and nursed my beer. When there was only a half inch left, I considered ordering a second one. But a girl had to celebrate modestly if she was ever going to have her own apartment.

The last drops of ale had just been consumed when I felt a big body looming over me. I looked up to meet Griff's laser stare. "Hi," I squeaked.

He said nothing, only took a twenty out of his wallet and threw it down on the bar. Then he took my hand and tugged me off the barstool.

"Where are we going?"

"To celebrate," he said, guiding me past the rest of the evening crowd.

"Celebrate?" I echoed as we reached the cooler air outside.

"Fuck yeah." He pushed me up against the clapboards and cupped the back of my head. "You feel like celebrating?"

All my girly parts spasmed. But I tried to play it cool anyway. "How do you want to celebrate?" The question came out husky and desperate. My whole life I'd never been any good at playing it cool.

He grinned suddenly. "Got two choices. We could drive to the Whippi Dip for some soft serve. What's your favorite flavor? I'll bet you're not a plain vanilla girl." His roughened thumb skimmed my cheekbone.

"Um…" What was the question?

A smile teased his full lips. "Now, if you don't feel like soft serve, Plan B is driving you back to the motor lodge, where I fuck you 'til you scream my name. Your pick."

There's no way I managed to hide the whole-body shiver that ran through me. "Is, uh, the soft serve organic and blessed by virgins under a full moon?"

"Doubt it." His eyes crinkled at the corners as he smiled down at me.

"Then I suppose I'd better go with choice number two."

He kissed me so fast I didn't even see it coming. But suddenly my hands were pinned to the wall on either side of me, and Griff's mouth pressed hungrily down onto mine. Throwing all appearances to the wind, I opened for him immediately. He thrust his tongue over mine and groaned.

All of me shimmied.

Chapter Fifteen

Griffin

The taste of Audrey Kidder always made me lose my mind. Plundering her mouth right there outside The Mountain Goat, I gave up trying to fight it.

I didn't know why this feisty little woman had such a debilitating effect on me. Maybe I'd never figure it out. All I knew was that she stirred me up in a way that no one else did. I wanted her in every way a man could want her. I wanted her in my bed, underneath me. I wanted her up against this wall.

I even wanted her to sit beside me on the way to the market, giving me lip for everything I said. And I wanted her hanging out in the kitchen putting cherries in the barbecue sauce and chatting up my sisters.

Fuck, I had it bad.

My hands were full of her sweet curves, and I was already drunk on the taste of her and as hard as the logs in my woodpile. Only the sweep of headlights as a car turned into the parking lot brought me halfway back into consciousness. With a Herculean effort, I broke our kiss and took a half-step backward.

Audrey blinked up at me, looking as dazed as I felt.

"Keys, princess," I ordered.

"What?"

"Your keys." I held out my hand. "To your rental car."

She fumbled into her purse and handed them to me. Aiming at the parking lot, I pressed the button. A late-model Rav4 blinked to life. At least they'd given her four-wheel drive this time. It might keep her out of ditches. Grabbing her hand, I walked her over to the passenger's door, which I opened for her. Then I climbed into the driver's seat and slid the seat back by about ten inches.

We were halfway through the four-minute drive to the motor lodge before she said, "You're driving my car."

"Yep. Otherwise Mrs. Beasley will tell the whole world I spent the night in your room." The place came into view, and I steered her vehicle toward the parking spot with the worst view into the main house. Then I popped Audrey's seatbelt because she was still in a daze.

When I opened her car door, though, she looked up at me with need in her eyes. She jumped out, grabbed the keys out of my hand and used one to open the door to her tiny cabin.

I began undressing her the second the door clicked shut. I stripped her out of her top and threw it on the dresser. She reached for my fly and unzipped me. Then we were kissing again and stripping and kicking clothes away and stumbling over to her bed. I grabbed the quilt and yanked it down. The last thing I did before lying down was to grab the strip of condoms out of the pocket where I'd stashed them on my way over to fetch her from the Goat.

Tearing one off, I handed it to her. Then I pulled her naked body onto my thighs until she was straddling me. Lifting both arms, I skimmed her soft curves until she purred. She was silky under my work-beaten hands. If I didn't know better, I'd think she was too pristine to want my rough hands on her body. But I already knew with Audrey that what you see was not always what you got. Beneath her girl-next-door facade beat the heart of a perfect sinner.

If there was a more attractive package on the planet, I'd never met her.

She had the packet half open when my hands cupped her breasts, my thumbs gently scraping her nipples. Her head dropped back on a gasp, and she shuddered with desire as I stroked her tits.

"Do your job, baby," I prodded. "You can't have my dick until you do."

Audrey clenched her body against my thighs and sighed. Then she sheathed me with shaking hands.

"That's it," I coached her. "Now I've got to make sure you're ready for me." I skimmed a hand down her belly until my thumb dipped between her legs. We both hissed as I met slickness and heat. "Aw, yeah," I panted. With her and me, everything always happened in a mad rush. For once I thought I might slow it down a notch. "Come here, princess." I lifted her by the hips and pulled her up onto my chest. "Come closer. Farmers like to get dirty."

Her pink mouth fell open and she whimpered.

"That's right. Come here. All the way." I tugged her perfect ass closer. The musky scent of her desire hit me like a rush. So I coaxed her up my body until I could reach what I wanted with my tongue. "Mmm," I groaned as I licked up the center of her for the first time.

"Oh, Griff," she moaned above me. "Oh God." Her hips moved in little jerks as I began to explore her with my tongue. Her thighs were tense on either side of my body as she strained to hold herself aloft.

I tickled her thighs with my beard and chuckled. "Here, baby," I said, lifting her hands off the headboard and placing them onto her breasts. "Work these for me."

Her eyes widened, but she did as I said, cupping her breasts and tweaking her nipples. Fuck, it was the hottest view I'd ever had in my life. I grabbed her ass and pulled her over my mouth again. We *both* moaned, and then I was practically drowning in willing, horny girl. *That's it*, I inwardly coached her, because speech was impossible. *Ride my tongue.*

"Ah. Ah. Ahh," she bit out as she moved. The sounds she made were almost too much. My poor, ignored cock ached for want of attention. "Oh," she moaned. "Grifff..." She ground down on my mouth. Hottest thing ever.

She was close, but I wasn't ready to let her go there yet. I grabbed her by the hips and shifted her down my body again. "Up, princess."

Audrey rose up on her knees on command. I positioned myself beneath her and then grabbed her hips, impaling her on my cock. She gave a yell of shock and pleasure, then tried to ride me. But I held her fast to my hips with a firm grip.

"Please," she begged.

Christ. She was so hot and tight that I needed a minute to calm down. She struggled against my grip but I would not relent. "Who's the best fuck you've ever had?" I growled.

She dropped her chin, her silky hair hanging down, covering those perfect tits. "Y-you are," she gasped out. "It's not even a c-contest."

"Aw." I squeezed her hips. "Good answer, baby. I feel like giving you a reward." I let up on her hips. "Go on. Take what you need."

With a grateful moan, she began to ride me with short, purposeful thrusts. Her cheeks were pink, her eyes heavy with desire. And here I'd thought the best views in Vermont were of the foothills. This was the sexiest thing I'd ever seen—her breasts bouncing in time to the excited sounds she made. But something was missing. I tugged her shoulders down until she was spread out on my body, and I took her mouth in a greedy kiss.

Her fingers threaded into my hair, and she moaned into my mouth.

Heaven.

Stressful week be damned—I had everything a man could ever ask for at that moment. I knew Audrey wasn't mine. She lived hours away, and she'd be gone before the month was out. For this brief moment, though, everything was right with the world.

I wrapped my arms around her body and rolled us over. She landed on the pillow, hair spread everywhere like an angel's, wide-eyed and looking up at me like I hung the moon. Her sweet expression was what did me in. Desire snaked down my spine, frying all my control. I thrust my hips forward as she arched up for a kiss. The tension was too much. "Come, princess," I begged, grabbing her thigh in one hand and yanking it up onto my body. The next thrust had me seeing stars. "Oh fuck," I moaned. I dipped into her mouth, swallowing her answering moan, and felt her tighten everywhere around me.

Just like that, I was done like dinner.

Grunting like a beast, I poured myself into her, just like I'd wanted to do every damn minute since her last trip to Vermont.

Beneath me, Audrey clenched and shuddered. I thrust once more, slowly, just for her. And her moan was like liquid pouring through my soul, seeping into all the empty places I didn't even know I had.

My body finally went slack. I rolled to the side, pulling her with me. With a satisfied sigh she pushed her face into my neck, and we both worked at catching our breath.

"That was..." she whispered. "We... Urrmh."

My thoughts exactly.

Then she pulled herself together and finished a sentence. "This beats the snot out of soft-serve ice cream."

My laughter was so sudden it startled me. I had to hold her tightly to my chest so that I didn't bounce her clear off of me. "Don't know what it is about you, princess," I admitted when I finally stopped laughing. "You make me crazy."

"I like you crazy," she whispered.

"Mmm." Sifting my fingers through her soft hair, I had the loopy, impractical idea that we might just belong together for keeps. Audrey was a hoot. She made me forget all the stressful parts of my life.

"Sure like the way you celebrate," she purred as her smooth fingers trailed through my beard.

I turned my head and trapped her fingers between my lips, giving them a nibble before letting them go.

"Hoped you'd be happy about the price I got for you," she whispered.

Right. The cider. Funny—but the celebration was at least as exciting as the news we were supposedly celebrating.

Probably more so.

"It's a fair price, baby." I gave her a quick kiss. "And the big order means I can invest in some sizeable tanks. My family won't be quite so freaked out about the changes I'm making around here with an order for forty grand in cider."

"Mm-hmm." Audrey trailed her lips across my collarbone and then down my chest, where she began dusting me with kisses.

"Got to order those tanks tomorrow so I can fill 'em

up next month." I could just picture them, standing in my cider house, bubbling away. Fermenting the progress on which dreams were made.

Audrey made a soft sound of agreement. But then she kissed her way up my neck, and I forgot about cider tanks for the second time tonight.

Chapter Sixteen

Audrey

Griffin was so quiet that I thought he'd fallen asleep. As men do.

After a few minutes, though, he heaved a sigh and went into the little bathroom. I heard the sound of the shower running. When he emerged a few minutes later, I expected him to pull on his shorts and go. But that's not what happened.

He lay down on the bed again and pulled the covers up over both of us. "This place is kind of a dump," he said, chuckling. "Looks like Mrs. Beasley renovated in the seventies."

"Eh, it's rustic," I said. "The room I rent in Boston is less cheery than this." I thought of my pot-smoking pastry-chef roommate and all the dirty dishes he'd probably piled in the sink in my absence. If I weren't around to give him a glare, he'd live like a pig.

Griff made a noise of disapproval. Then he pulled me onto his big body. "Doesn't seem right that your mother won't help you land on your feet."

I looked down at him. "I'm *on* my feet. My life isn't stylish, but I pay for it myself." And, damn. That came out a little too forcefully. But I was touchy about this. Nobody could say that I wasn't pulling my own weight.

He smiled up at me. Then he ran his thumb down my nose so tenderly that it left me blinking with surprise. "Maybe I worded that badly. But the whole reason I want money is so that I can give it to my family. That's why I work so hard."

Dropping my head onto his giant shoulder, I thought

that over. "It's not the only reason," I argued. "You like what you do. Otherwise you wouldn't give speeches to anyone who will listen about cider apples and consolidated pest management."

"*Integrated* pest management."

I pinched his ass.

He pinched my boob.

"Ow!"

"You started it," he teased, his fingers caressing the skin he'd tweaked only a second earlier.

Griff Shipley was surprisingly cuddly after sex. I wracked my brain to try to remember what had happened five years ago in Boston after we'd done the deed. I supposed we'd slept together then, too. But at the time I'd probably assumed it was because he didn't want to get up to walk me home...

"You're right," he said.

"What?" My mind had wandered.

"I do like what I do. It's just that I'm not sure I ever had a choice."

"Oh." He'd told me that first day—when my car had been in his ditch—that his father had died. "Didn't you intend to run the farm?"

He was quiet a moment. "I hadn't decided. Football was still important to me. Still thought I could make it onto a roster."

"You could have," I said a little too quickly. I loved football, and I went to every home game at BU. Every time Griff Shipley had taken the field in his tight pants, my eyes had been glued to his very fine ass. Not that I was about to admit that I paid way too much attention to him well before we ever hooked up.

In fact, I'd done something quite obnoxious. When he'd introduced himself to me at the frat party, I'd made him repeat his name.

"Something funny?" he asked as I smiled into his shoulder.

"Not a thing." I cleared my throat. "Maybe you won't farm forever. You're young. Some day you'll have choices."

"I'm here at least until Daphne and Dylan get sorted out. And most days I'm happy," he said quietly. "I like the work. What I don't like is the pressure. We're always one bad crop away from bankruptcy, you know?"

"Football players are always one bad game away from a debilitating injury," I pointed out.

"True."

His fingers stroked my hair, and I began to drift on the sweetness of it all. My thoughts became misty as his hands wandered across my neck and down my back. He cupped my backside, pulling me tightly against his body. I woke up fully when I realized there was a very hard dick poking me in the belly. "Again?" I mumbled.

"You should be so lucky," he murmured.

"Poor thing, you've got no self esteem."

He laughed and moved his hands onto my breasts. His smiling mouth moved to cover mine, and then we were kissing again, his beard chafing my face.

I loved it.

After a while he slipped me onto the sheet, face down. I heard the crackle of a condom wrapper. Then big hands spread my legs and reached between them.

I pushed my face into the pillow to muffle my gasp. There was something dirty and wonderful about the way he handled me. Every touch was a *command*, as if I'd been placed on this earth to pleasure him. Judging from the way my body responded to his touch, perhaps I had.

Maybe I should just get it over with and change my legal name to Tawdry. I'd need a new set of business cards, though...

"Oh-fuck-gaaaahhhh," I moaned as he pushed inside.

He chuckled into my ear at close range. "That's my girl. She wants my cock however I give it to her."

Guilty. I slammed my eyes shut and tried to memorize the way this felt. His burly body surrounded me. Thick arms boxed me in. Muscled legs held mine tightly together. I'd been immobilized in the most perfect way. And now he was dropping wet, open-mouthed kisses onto my neck, gently sucking on my skin.

I let out another moan and tried to buck my hips. But I could barely move his great bulk.

"Going somewhere?" he whispered.

"Get on with it."

He chuckled. Then he gave his hips the slowest pump in the history of sex.

I growled into the pillow.

"Okay, baby," he whispered, kissing my neck. "All right." He picked up the pace, and I nearly wept with gratitude.

As Griff whispered sweet, dirty things into my ear, I let go. My thoughts melted like a stick of fine butter. I stopped thinking so hard and let him carry me away again.

* * *

Several hours later, I opened my eyes to a sunny morning.

I knew right away that Griff was gone. It was too cool in the bed, for starters. That man's body was like a furnace. And it was too quiet. Disappointment sliced through me, even if I knew he and I didn't have a snuggling-and-out-to-breakfast relationship.

We didn't have a relationship at all.

That's when loneliness set in. Hard.

This always happened to me, too. It was why I didn't have many one-night stands. It wasn't that sex embarrassed me. I wasn't ashamed. It's just that if something was good, I wanted more of it. Like a good brown butter sauce or salted caramels.

It was probably a good thing that Griff had bailed already this morning. I'd have probably freaked him out by suggesting we get together again tonight. And I wasn't in Vermont for Griffin Shipley. I was here for *me*.

In the little bathroom, the shower squeaked to life. When I stepped under the spray, the water was warm and steady. So at least I had that going for me. Today I needed to find someone to sell me both fingerling potatoes and honey. (But not together, because ew.) My job could be worse. I could be digging ditches. I could be the dishwasher at a diner.

Though if I effed up one more job for BPG, that dishwashing gig was a possibility.

But first, coffee.

Once showered and tidy, I gathered my farming notes and phone. Keys in hand, I opened the door to my little one-room cabin, almost stepping on a note that had been left just inside my door.

Princess—wish we could have breakfast, but I'm off to milk 50 cows. You called the house phone last night, which means I don't have your number. Here's mine. 802.228.4331. —A.G.S.

Aw.

Okay, Audrey, I coached myself. *You are not going to get all giddy about this note. Nope. Bad idea.*

Leaving a girl a note after two rounds of toe-curling sex was not all that romantic. It meant nothing. It meant that Griff Shipley wanted to keep things cheerful with his new fuck buddy. He'd probably left Zara fifty notes when they'd been together, right?

Right.

And what difference did it make, anyway? Griff was tied to his farm and his cows. I was going to build a foodie empire in Boston any minute now. It was a relationship with no future. Correction—it was a...*sex fest* with no future.

Damn shame, though.

I got in my rental car and drove two miles to The Mountain Goat. If I were a smarter girl, I would have already figured out if was open for breakfast.

There was one car in the parking lot, which told me nothing. So I pulled in.

Now that I thought about it, hadn't Griff left his truck here last night? He'd said it was intentional, so Mrs. Beasley wouldn't gossip.

Ouch. He didn't want all his neighbors to know about our boinkfest. Which was probably because he didn't want his *family* to know.

While I might be deep in lust with Griff, I'd already fallen head over heels for his family. Given the chance, I'd move right into his kitchen. I wanted to be one of the lucky Shipleys who called Ruth "Mom" and set that big oak table for twelve every night. I would play Frisbee with Dylan and braid Daphne's hair.

This was the secret fantasy that every only child had occasionally. Over the years I'd appropriated dozens of my friends' families, mentally inserting myself into their happy mayhem.

Then again, if I were a Shipley, that would make Griff my brother. *Ew.* Bad plan.

A tapping on my car window pulled me out of my reverie. I turned quickly to see Zara's questioning look.

Whoops.

I opened the car door and stepped out. "Hi. Sorry. I was just wondering if you were open in the mornings for, you know, coffee."

Zara slowly shook her head. "I've thought about it. We have to take deliveries in the morning, so there's usually someone here. But, no. Never figured that into the business plan."

My gaze traveled to the wooden building. "You own this place?"

"Nope. I manage it." Her mouth turned hard. "But a woman can run a bar, you know. You don't need a penis for everything."

"Sorry," I said quickly. "I'm, um, familiar with the problem."

She raised her pierced eyebrow. "The problem of penises?"

"Yes. *No.*" *Hell.* Which penis were we talking about here? Heat crawled up my neck. "I know, um, a bar can be run with a vagina. Well, not *with* the vagina but..." I coughed.

Zara startled me by laughing. "You really do need coffee, don't you?"

"Yup."

She jerked her chin toward the shuttered restaurant. "Come on. I just made a pot to help me wait for the bread delivery."

I galloped after her like a happy pony. Free coffee? That would get me out of my lonely funk.

Zara stopped at the side of the building to tug two bins full of beer bottles out into the open. It must be recycling day. Then she kicked open the door and headed through the dining room to a coffee pot behind the bar. She poured two mugs and grabbed a quart of milk out of the reach-in below the bar. "Here," she said. "Have a seat."

I hoisted myself onto the same bar stool I'd sat on last night and poured a dollop of milk into my mug. Then I took a deep gulp of it. "Ahh," I sighed. "Thank you."

She eyed me over the rim of her cup. "Speaking of penises."

Uh-oh.

"Griff's truck spent the night in the parking lot here."

I should have known that an interrogation would come with the coffee. It was probably worth it, though. I decided to play dumb. "Did it?"

She rolled her eyes. "Just don't fall for him, okay?"

I'm sure I failed to hide my wince. "We, uh, used to hook up in college. Nothing serious."

"Oh," she said slowly. "So you know how it is."

"Yeah." I really did. He was like any bad habit—tasty and hard to resist.

"He loves his apple trees and his family. And that's a lot of trees and a giant family. So it's almost as if they use up all his emotional availability. Half the county has it bad for Griff Shipley."

"I'll bet."

Zara cupped her coffee mug in her hands and sighed. "There aren't many single men around here, either. All the good ones move away, where there are better jobs."

"But not you?"

She shook her head. "I like it here. But it's lonely."

"You can be lonely anywhere," I told her. "Trust me." That was probably too much truth-telling, but hey—I hadn't had a full cup of coffee yet.

Zara measured me with her eyes. "You're a fancy chef of some kind, right?"

I snorted. "Only in my own mind. But someday it will be true." I said this often, but I also believed it.

Because good guys ultimately won out, and karma was real.

"What brings you to Vermont?"

Zara was interrogating me now, but I didn't mind, because the coffee was dark and aromatic. "Business. I work for a big restaurant group that needs to up their farm-to-table game. It's my job to fill up their shopping cart with produce."

"Huh. My uncles have an orchard and the pears look really good this year."

"Pears?" I perked up. "That's not on my list, but I'll bet my overlords would want some."

Zara smiled. "Let me write down the address, and I'll call them and tell them to talk to you."

"Yay!" I drained my coffee. "This is great. Thank you."

"Don't mention it," she said with a frown. Zara seemed uncomfortable with affection. Or enthusiasm. I hadn't quite figured her out yet. She jotted something on a cocktail napkin and then handed it to me.

I tucked the address into my purse. "If you're here in the mornings, you should *sell* coffee."

"I've thought about it." She glanced around the room, as if picturing the place full of caffeine hounds. "But that would require adding on some even earlier hours. You can't just walk in and start selling coffee, right? I'd need pastries, too..."

"Good point." And now I was craving pastries, damn it. I put my mug on the counter. "I'd better go. Thanks for all your help."

She gave me a wave and plucked my mug off the bar. "Later."

I went outside and got in the rental car. It was time to scope out some pears and find something for breakfast.

Chapter Seventeen

Griffin

The morning I woke up beside Audrey was a good one. Even though I had to jog two miles to my truck at dawn and then put up with all the smirks in the cow barn, I was a happy man.

And it wasn't just the sex. Everything seemed to be going right for a change. When I told her about the big order from BPG, my mother's mind was put at ease. Nobody panicked when I bought a set of three fermentation tanks that were larger than anything we already had. I got 'em used, too, from a guy in Massachusetts who was sizing up after just two years.

That's how things would go for me, too, right?

The next few days had me feeling so optimistic that my helpers began to tease me. "Can you, like, snarl at us? Just once? It's weird seeing you smile all the time," Kyle complained.

"Creeps us out," Jude added.

They needn't have worried. My mood took a hit when a late afternoon windstorm did some damage to the apple trees at the front of the property. I probably lost twenty bushels of fruit when the storm knocked branches off several of my trees.

"What do you want to do with these, boss?" Zachariah asked, showing me the immature fruit he'd begun to fetch off the ground. "Odds are they won't ripen up even if we try sweating 'em."

"Never tell me the odds!" I quipped, earning a grin

from Zach. I took the apple out of his hand and took a bite. It was hard, of course. But worse—the starches hadn't converted to sugars yet. *Hell.* They'd make terrible cider. "Compost."

"Sure thing," he said, helpful as ever.

My mood continued to sink as the week ground onward. This was the most stressful part of the year—when I had a great crop hanging on my trees, but it couldn't be harvested yet. All that potential was vulnerable to Mother Nature's whims.

But the buzz kill was that Audrey hadn't called. I don't know what I was expecting, really. All I knew is that I wanted to see her again. And if she only had a few days to be in Vermont, why the hell wouldn't she want to spend 'em with me?

Eventually I did what I should have done already. I got in my truck and I drove by the motor lodge. But Audrey's rental car wasn't out front, and her cabin was dark.

Maybe she'd gone back to Boston already without bothering to tell me. I spent the night alone re-reading a couple chapters of *The Lord of The Rings*, because Zach had just finished reading it for the very first time, and I'd been chatting about it with him. It was hard to feel lonely while touring Middle-Earth.

I went to sleep at nine. If I couldn't have Audrey, at least I could have eight hours of sleep before my five o'clock wakeup. The next day I spent hours reading and rereading our latest round of organic certification paperwork. I hated the parts of my job that had to be done at a desk. What good was it being a farmer if you were trapped indoors?

When I finally went outdoors to check on the day's work, Zach nudged me. A Rav4 was coming up the drive.

"Ooh, it's Griff's girrrrrlfriend," Kyle sang.

"What are we, twelve?" I growled to hide my excitement.

After parking the car, she unfolded her long legs from the driver's side and shut the door. I watched hungrily. Audrey was unnecessarily beautiful. She was like the butterflies I saw every day hovering over the meadow—they were more stunning than all the other pollinators. It didn't really seem fair to the bees who did the same work.

"Hello," I said walking toward her car.

She turned her chin up to look at me, an appraising look on her face. "Hi there."

"Thought I might hear from you before now," I said slowly.

Audrey squinted at me. "The contracts department hasn't given me any paperwork for you yet."

I stared her down. "Ah, well. Guess there's no reason you'd stop by, then. What was I thinking?"

She blinked first, dropping her chin and turning to wave at Zach who was trotting toward the dairy barn in search of my little brother. Then she looked back up at me and frowned. "What's the matter? What'd I do?"

"Nothing," I said quickly. What did I expect, anyway? "What can I help you with?"

Her expression turned sheepish. "I've come to beg you to sell me some apples."

There were other things I wished she'd beg me for, but apparently that topic was off limits. "Let me guess. The price isn't great."

"Well, it's double what they offered before. Two bucks a pound. But they want something interesting. Some kind of heirloom variety that the pastry chefs can make a fuss over."

"In other words, they want the best thing I've got for

a cheap price."

"Yeah." She sighed. "But maybe you could just sell me a small amount? I've been having to piece things together all over the place. So a few bushels would really help me out."

"Of course I can." And I couldn't resist reaching out to push an errant piece of hair out of her face.

Her eyes lit up. "Really? And you have something good and weird to sell me?"

"Yeah." I thought about it for a second. "I have a few Blue Pearmain trees."

"Are they *blue*?" Audrey looked positively giddy.

"They're blue*ish*. Blue for an apple. Henry David Thoreau wrote about 'em. They were his favorite variety. That ought to give your snobby pastry guy a big boner."

"Totally!" She put both hands on my chest. "This is awesome! Thank you so much!"

Swear to god, nobody ever looked so cute and sexy talking about apples before. "You're welcome." I grabbed her hands. "Now come with me for a few minutes. I want your help with something.

"Really?"

With her hand in mine, I walked toward the cider house, and she galloped along beside me. "This is the fun part of my job."

"Your job has fun parts?" She said in a bubbly voice. "I thought it was all tireless labor. Uphill to the orchard both ways..."

"Someone cracks herself up." I squeezed her hand. "The fun part is tasting and blending."

"That *does* sound like fun. Show me."

Oh the things I'd like to show you. "Come on in," I said, pushing open the cider house door and flipping on some lights. "Have a seat. I need to grab a few things."

Chapter Eighteen

Audrey

I perched on a stool while Griffin puttered around, setting things on the tasting bar. He put out a half-dozen wine glasses, several beakers, metal measuring tools and a notebook with the month and year scribbled onto the cover. Then he fetched five growlers—gallon-sized glass jugs—and lined them up on the table.

Watching his muscles flex as he worked was my new favorite activity. All week I'd felt a tingle in my girly parts whenever I remembered our recent night together. Being alone with him now was the best kind of torture.

But Griff was all business. "Welcome to my laboratory," he said, flipping open the notebook and then swapping two of the growlers' places in line.

"This is very fancy," I remarked. "I'd have paid better attention in science class if there were tastings involved."

His big brown eyes lifted to mine, and they were amused. "I have a degree in organic chemistry because I knew it could come to this."

"Wow." Organic chemistry? For some reason I'd thought he was a communications major like the rest of the jocks I knew. But my crush was smart—too smart to get involved with me.

He tapped the top of a growler with his pencil. "So here's the goal. I have to choose two blends to enter in a competition. Each entry costs three hundred bucks, so it has to be good."

"Ouch."

"I know, right? But it's the American Tasting Society. They're fancy."

"That's intimidating."

"A little. Winning would be a really big deal. Good for business."

"I'll bet. I've never won a prize."

He looked up from the jugs he was arranging on the table. "Culinary prizes are hard, right? It's a snobby world."

"That's not what I meant. I mean, I've never won a prize *in my life*. Did you have field day in elementary school? Wait—you probably won everything. It was probably your favorite day of the year. But I never once won a ribbon."

He gave me a curious smile—the kind you give crazy people. "Field day was good to me. But it was a tiny school, and I was big for my age."

"Ah. Well. My luck continued into high school. Awards Day at the end of the year was my nemesis. The worst was junior year. My mother took an afternoon off work, which was a Very Big Deal. And we were supposed to go out for sushi to celebrate the beginning of the end of high school. But here's what happened—literally everyone in my private school class got an award except for me. Best in English, Best at Latin, etc. There were dozens of prizes. I hoped Mom wouldn't notice, but when it was all over the principal asked everyone who'd won an award to come up on stage for a photograph. And I was the only one in my class who was still sitting in the junior's row. My mom was so embarrassed. We didn't even go out for sushi. She said she'd lost her appetite."

Griff was studying me now, his jaw tight. *Ugh.* I didn't know why the man always caused me to babble on like an idiot. "Anyway. Let's taste some cider."

"Um..." He looked down at the jugs under his hands as if he'd never seen them before. "Right. Okay. So these five ciders are arranged in order of complexity." He touched the first one on my left. "From simple and bright—" He pointed at the last one. "—to downright funky."

"You've put them in funk order," I suggested.

"Yeah. I need to find two winners. And I'm hoping to submit two that taste quite different from one another."

"Because you don't know what the judges will be in the mood for," I guessed.

"Exactly. So let's taste." He lifted the second jug in line and unwrapped a piece of rubber tape from around the cap. Then he opened it and poured an inch into each of two glasses. "This is a fairly simple creature. Smell."

He handed me the glass, and I put my nose inside its bowl and inhaled. I was met with a delicious, fruity, tart scent. "Mmm. It's grassy. Not as fruity as I would have thought." I hesitated before taking a drink. "Do you taste and spit?" That was how this sort of thing was done by winemakers—so they didn't spend all their days drunk. I didn't want to look like a lush in front of Griff.

"You can spit if you want," he said. "But we're not going to taste too many things. So I'm just gonna swallow."

Okay, then. I took a taste of the cider in my glass, making the delicate slurp that's taught in a wine-tasting class to maximize both aroma and the contact with my tongue. And *wow*, it was good. "It's lovely. I get a nice burst of both tart and sweet."

Across the table from me, Griff was giving the cider his own taste. He tipped that big burly head backward and swallowed, his Adam's apple working. He was at least as tasty as the cider. I fought the urge to circle the table and taste the cider a second time right off his tongue.

Watching a hot guy drink good liquor was hot

enough. But a hot guy who could *make* good liquor? Was there anyone sexier in the world? No there was not.

Griff lined up two more glasses and opened the growler on the far left. "Compare it to this one."

"Happy to help out!" I lifted my glass dutifully and sniffed. "Smells fruity." I tasted. Then I tasted again.

"What do you think?"

I set down the glass. "I could drink this all day, but it doesn't shout 'blue ribbon.' It's a little citrusy, and doesn't know as many secrets."

Griff tipped his head to the side and gave me a sexy smile. "Good girl. That's exactly what I think of it, too. You know what? You're pretty good at this."

I felt my cheeks grow hot as the unexpected compliment washed over me. Wasn't that ridiculous? It's not like he'd praised my ability to perform neurosurgery or disarm Iran. "Well," I said, hoping to hide how ridiculously happy it made me to hear that I'd done something right. "That brings the number of things I'm good at to *two*." I swirled the golden liquid around in my glass. "Cooking and drinking."

When he spoke again, his voice was like gravel. "I can think of a couple of other things off the top of my head."

"Griff!" I warned. "We're working here." But at least I wasn't the only one still thinking about the other night. Even if Griff only saw me as his sex toy. I pushed my second glass into line with the first one. "Keep it coming. Let's taste the funkier stuff."

He opened the third jug and poured. "Have at it."

This one had a different nose altogether. I inhaled twice to try to define its scent. "Spicy. Cardamom? And honey." I took a careful taste. "Interesting! I'm still getting honey. Or...guava, maybe. And there's a muskiness that the other two don't have. I think this one is a contender."

Once again I watched while he let the cider roll around on his tongue. Was there tasting-room porn out there on the internet somewhere? If not, there should be. His dark eyes fell closed as he swallowed.

Wowzers.

"Hmm." He studied his glass as if he might see visions appear in the liquid. "Let's try something." He poured the remaining cider into a measuring cup and then back into his glass. Then he took the second jug and poured some measure of it, dumping that into the glass, too. Then he scratched a little note onto his pad. "You first."

He passed me the new blend, and I sipped it. "Hey!" I sipped again. "That's great. It's softer than the third one all by itself." I handed the glass over and he tasted it.

"I like it. Okay, that goes in the 'maybe' column, too." He uncorked the fourth one and poured me a shot.

It had a real whiff of...age to it. Like old books in a liquid form. I tasted, and it was nothing like any cider I'd ever had. "Wow. It has quite the bitter finish, but I really don't mind."

He tasted, too, while I tried not to ogle him. "Yeah. To me this is *cider*. This is the real deal. But I could still blend it back a couple of clicks. Now let's taste one to put hair on your chest." He opened the final jug and poured. "This one will have you singing 'Funky Town.'"

"Whew," I said after a sniff. It was potent. But there was something awfully alluring about that rich, musky odor. It was... I sniffed again. So much like...

"What do you think?" he demanded after a sip. "Too much? It's musky. Heady. It has a good mouth feel but it's kind of unpredictable."

I closed my eyes and tasted. On the tongue, it was a

much more typical cider. But the nose was thrillingly deviant. It suggested *danger*. I inhaled deeply in my glass and then laughed.

"Now it's funny?"

I shook my head. "You won't like my tasting notes. You're going to say I'm crazy."

"You hate this one?"

"Not at all," I said quickly. "But the scent, it's like..." I laughed again.

"Tell me. I can take it."

"*Sex*," I blurted out. "It smells of sex."

Griff choked on the sip he was taking. "What the hell?" Closing his eyes, he sniffed his glass again. His eyes popped open. "Fuck."

"Exactly."

"I've bottled..."

"Fucking."

Griff shook his head. "Well, that's a first. Can't say it's got any commercial appeal, but..."

"Of *course* it does! Who wouldn't appreciate sex in a liquid form? *Jesus*. And here I thought you were a businessman. You *have* to enter this one."

"Why? Because it amuses you?"

"No! Because the judges will be drawn to it, even if they don't know why. This thing isn't judged by robots, right? Everybody likes sex, and nobody gets enough of it."

"Don't they?" His big eyebrows lifted. "I could help you with that problem."

"Focus, Griff. We have a contest to win, here. We're going all psych-ninja on them with the sex blend. It's stealthy."

He frowned. "The one thing this cider is *not* is subtle. Let's blend it down a little and see what happens."

Figures. I always came on too strong, too. "Fine." I picked up the second jug in the line and poured a dollop into the sex brew. Then I tasted it again. "Nope."

"Too acidic, I bet?" Griff asked.

"Yeah." I set down the glass. "I know what it needs but I don't know how to get there."

He measured out a small pour of the sex cider and swirled it around in his glass. Then he added half as much of the acidic cider, and another portion of the second jug. "Two parts E to one part A and B," he muttered, making a scrawled note in his book. "Here. You first."

I put my nose in the glass and inhaled. "Mmm. Smells like a summertime nooner."

Griffin threw back his big head and laughed. "Interesting observation. Since it's summertime and..." He checked his watch. "Coming up on noon."

Thanks, subconscious. I tasted it. The new version tasted more like apples. "It's fruitier now, which is nice."

Griff nodded thoughtfully. "That blend should soften it."

"Totally." I took another sip. "We've eased it back from a hardcore-bang cider to a romantic tryst. And the balance of sweet and sour works. How'd you get that right on the first try?"

"Practice, baby." He raised a hand to stroke his beard, and now I was staring at his full lips.

Damn. Why did this man have to be so freaking attractive?

I shook off the distraction and handed him the glass. "Taste it already. It's awesome."

Once more I got to watch Griffin Shipley in the throes of cider-tasting passion. The deep inhale at the mouth of the glass, the closed-eyed sip complete with pornographic mouth action. He tasted it three times, and then he set the glass down and made another scribbled note.

"Well?" I demanded. "You're totally entering this one, right?"

"I'll consider it," he said, writing.

"What? That's *it*? We identified the next blue-ribbon-category killer and you'll *take it under advisement?*"

Dark eyes lifted to mine. "Simmer down, princess. Everything gets tasted a second time before I decide. The nose is easily overwhelmed. Tomorrow I'll pour samples of the three contending blends and taste them again."

"I knew that," I said, hopping off the stool. "But I want my picture with the trophy after you win. There is a trophy, right?"

"Probably." He grinned. "I have to clean up a few things here. Then do you want to go skinny-dipping?"

"What?" The change in topic caught me off guard.

"It's kind of hot today, and there's still half an hour before lunch. We could cool off at the swimming hole down the hill. There's never anyone there, so clothes are optional. You probably don't have a bathing suit..."

I pictured Griffin removing all his clothes and wading into the water in front of me...

My girl parts quivered. "That's a tempting offer," I said quickly. "But I think I need to keep my clothes on when you're nearby."

"Where's the fun in that?" He gathered up a half-dozen glasses using the thick fingers of only one hand.

All business, I gathered the ones he couldn't get on the first pass. "Listen, I know you like me better when I talk less and strip more."

"That is not *even* true." The words were so vehement they startled me. "I don't like your employer, princess. Never said I didn't like you."

I thought that over as Griffin set the glasses down in a giant metal sink and turned on the water. If he didn't dislike me, why did he look so irritable whenever I showed up? And there was something else. "Look, I get it. We've had some fun together. Our, uh, favorite hobby is pretty irresistible. But I have a job to do. And you don't want people knowing about us. So maybe that means we shouldn't indulge."

He slapped the faucet handle down, cutting off the water abruptly. "I don't want people *what?*" He turned toward me wearing a typical, piercing Griff frown. It was so potent it should probably be its own word. *Griffrown.*

I couldn't take the heat. I looked down at my hands, still holding glasses. "You left your truck at the Goat." Hell, I was already calling the place by its local nickname. It was a sign that I'd become too attached. "So nobody would know you're slumming it with your college hookup. I'm not even offended. But maybe that means we should find a new hobby. Like paddle boarding. Or hiking. I hear the hiking is good around here."

"*Hiking.*" He said the word the way other people say "root canal."

I set the glasses down next to the other ones. "It's just an example."

He put his wet hands on my bare shoulders. Then he walked me backwards three paces until my back was up against a giant metal cider tank. When I looked up, I found his expression as hot as a blowtorch. "Princess, we're going to get a few things straight."

"We are?" *Good response, Tawdry. Searing.*

"One, I left my truck at the Goat to protect *your* reputation, not mine. Not everybody likes me around here."

"Like who? I thought you were related to everyone who mattered."

He gave a little snort. "Not quite. You bought some pears from Zara's uncles, right?"

"You heard about that?"

The big beard grinned. "Small town. Zara's family doesn't like me too much. I don't think they would have been so helpful to you if there was gossip."

I mulled that over. "So you left your truck right where Zara would see it? I'm sure she didn't appreciate it."

He winced. "That was unavoidable. She knows she and I are done, though. And Zara won't talk. She's good people."

"But not good enough for you." That just slipped out.

His eyes blazed. "It's not like that. Zara and I weren't a great blend. We were a simple and drinkable brew with no tannins. No complexity. No prize-winning juju."

I was pretty sure Zara disagreed, which was probably why the next thing I said came out sounding snippy. "I see. I guess a cider maker has to do his share of taste-and-spit on his way to greatness."

A nanosecond later, Griff's mouth was on mine, the kiss firm and demanding more.

I leaned back against the tank, hoping to stay aloof, if only on principal.

His full lips softened, brushing over mine. Then he dipped his head and stroked my neck with his bearded chin, the soft hairs teasing my sensitive skin. When he dropped an open-mouthed kiss under my ear, I held my breath. And when he slowly kissed his way along my jaw, I felt myself begin to capitulate.

His demanding mouth landed on mine for a second time, and I folded like a first-timer's souffle, molding my chest to his, parting my lips to be tasted.

As our tongues touched, he moaned long and low. Then he caught one side of my face in his big mitt of a hand and kissed me deeply. He tasted of cider and male hunger, and I felt that kiss everywhere.

After showing me exactly how pliable I really was, he drew back, breathing hard, eyes wild. "I like you plenty," he said.

"Okay?" Were we having a conversation? I couldn't remember.

"And I'm not afraid to say so."

"Um..." I took a deep breath to try to take in some brain-clearing oxygen.

"Come on." He took my hand and tugged me away from the cider tank. Then he led me across the room and blinking into the sunny day.

Just outside we ran into Jude and Kyle, both shirtless. The two of them were hosing down giant wooden barrels.

"Good work guys," Griff said. "And I need to mention how much I like Audrey."

Kyle shot us a quizzical look, but Jude just pressed his thumb over the mouth of the hose and turned the full force of the water on the next barrel. "Good to know."

"Very funny," I mumbled as he led me toward the edge of the orchards.

"Baby, I don't joke. No sense of humor, right? You said so yourself."

Fuck me, I had. "Where are we going?" I asked to change the subject. Row upon row of apple trees greeted us in long, orderly lines.

"Hiking," he said. "Your idea."

"But... Really?" Me and my big mouth.

He laughed. "I just want to show you the Blue

Pearmain trees. Come on. Down here."

We turned, passing dozens of apple trees, their branches full of greenish fruit with just a hint of ripening blush. "Wow, Griff. Good harvest."

"Bite your tongue," he said. "It's not a harvest until it's in the bank."

"Sorry. But there are a lot of apples on these trees. What are those?" I pointed.

"Honeycrisp. We put 'em here because that's what the people who come to pick want first. They're trendy for a reason. Great texture and flavor. They ripen slowly, though."

"Is it a drag having people crawling all over your property every weekend?"

He shrugged. "That's how it's been since I can remember. And they bring their checkbooks. We sell a lot of fruit that way, and it picks itself. If we didn't have the U-pick operation, we'd need to hire more day laborers. Speaking of which..." As we crossed a break in the trees, a group of men and women came into view. They were all wearing a kind of nylon bag on the fronts of their bodies, picking apples off the trees and placing them into the bags. There was a big wooden crate in the middle of the row, half full of apples.

"Afternoon!" Griff waved to them and got a few waves back.

"Hey." Zachariah came jogging into view. "You need something?"

"Nope," Griff said. "Just taking Audrey for a hike before lunch. Because I like her a lot. Even when she's talking."

Zach's eyebrows shot upward. "Um, okay? Is that all?"

"Lunch in a half hour," Griff said. "Audrey will be there, because..."

"Griff!" I smacked his elbow.

"What? I'm just telling it how it is."

"No. Now you're teasing me."

He shook his head. "Tough crowd here today, Chewie. See you at lunch."

"Sure, Han."

We walked on in silence, passing rows of apple trees. From the house and the cluster of farm buildings, it was hard to see how big the property was. But after walking past apple trees for a good ten minutes, the true scope of Shipley Farms became apparent. "You weren't kidding about the hike," I said, panting. It didn't help that we'd been walking uphill the whole way.

"I don't kid."

"Right."

"We're almost there, city girl. At least you're wearin' real shoes today. New kicks?"

Busted. "I bought them at Farm-Way." Tired of trudging around farms in my sandals, I'd wandered into a sprawling store in the little town of Bradford. That's where I'd found a pair of pink hiking shoes and some footie socks.

"What did you think of that place? We go there all the time."

"I thought it was hysterical." They sold shoes and clothes. And horse tack, chicken feed and wood fencing. "Where else can you buy a riding crop *and* local maple syrup? The place is like a Vermont BDSM supply shop."

Griff laughed and took my hand again. "Except the riding crops they sell are actually used on horses."

"That's just wrong." I sniffed. "Those horses need a safe word." Griff laughed again.

Onward we climbed. Just when I was about to start whining, Griff pointed at a group of trees. "Those are the ones. All the oddball trees are up here. My grandpa was the one who started putting in heirloom trees, and my dad added more. These are the Blue Permains. Those four." He pointed at some rather large trees. They had numbered tags hanging from them. All the trees did.

"How many varieties do you have, anyway?"

"Fifty-three."

"You have them all memorized?"

"Pretty much. There are a few lady apples—those are the little ones—I don't know which one is which unless I look 'em up. But those all go into the cider press so I don't really need to know."

I was out of breath when Griff finally stopped walking. I took a close look at the apples on the tree. Indeed, their skins had a cool, dusky hue. "When do they ripen?"

"October. Your overlords will have to wait a bit. How are they going to get all this produce, anyway? A few bushels of fruit from twenty different farms sounds like a pain in the ass."

"I don't know," I said, fingering one of the apples. "With help from their minions, I suppose? These are so pretty." They were still hard as rocks and mostly green. But there were dozens. Hundreds, maybe. The tree was just bursting with potential. If it wouldn't have made me look like a fool, I'd have taken a selfie with it, captioned: *close, but not quite.* The title would refer to me as well as the tree.

"Turn around. You haven't even seen the view."

When I looked back the way we'd come, I nearly gasped at the vista laid out before me. In the distance the Green Mountain range stretched across my view, their peaks looking slate-green and purple against the sky. But Griff's farm was the real stunner. The rows of fruit trees seemed to go on forever, orderly lines of fluffy green trees with thick grass between them.

"Wow," I said stupidly. "You must have spent your entire teenage years mowing."

"That is true. We let the grass stay pretty long, though. It cushions the apples when they fall. The best cider is made from ripe apples that have just fallen or are about to fall."

"It's so *big*," I said, trying to see the whole farm at once and failing.

"That's what all the girls say."

I punched him in the arm. "I'm serious. How do you keep all this up?"

"By never sleeping. Although I do have help."

Still. Griff wasn't even thirty. Until I'd stood here, I don't think I realized what a big job he had. "I'll bet you miss your dad," I blurted out.

"Every day." His voice became gruff. "I used to stand up here with him while he talked and talked about apples. He'd point at the rows and tell me all his plans, and I thought he'd be around a really long time to finish all of 'em." He lapsed into silence for a moment. "Now every day there's some small problem that makes me want to ask his opinion. Or I'll find some interesting thing out in the orchard and just want to show it to him, because I know he'd like to see."

Oh, man. My throat got tight. Here was Griff, a giant. A tough guy who worked all day for his family's dream. And he just wanted a chat with his dad. "He'd be so proud of you," I whispered.

Griff was silent, and the two of us looked at the vista for a moment. Then he took my hand in his and gave it a squeeze.

I squeezed back.

"Time for lunch," he said, his voice rough.

I followed him down the hill in the sunshine.

Chapter Nineteen

Griffin

When we got back to the house, lunch was set up underneath the canopy in the backyard. During picking season, we didn't fit around the table anymore.

Mom didn't call us out for being a few minutes late, because these outdoor lunches were a little more casual. Also, Gramps pulled up on his golf cart at the same time we arrived, and Mom never chided Gramps. He got a free pass.

"How are you, August?" my grandfather asked, clapping me on the back. He always called me by my true first name.

"Good, Gramps. And do you remember Audrey? I like her a lot."

"You like her *bra?* You say stuff like that and you'll get slapped."

Audrey snorted beside me.

"I said... Never mind. Let's have a hamburger."

The three of us queued up at the grill, where Dylan was flipping burgers. "Who wants cheese?" he called cheerfully.

"I do!" Audrey volunteered. "I like everything."

"I'll have cheese," I agreed. "Which I like, but not as much as I like Audrey."

"You're laying it on pretty thick," she muttered, laying out three paper plates and putting a bun on each of them.

"This one is for Audrey," Dylan said, shifting a

burger from his spatula to a burger bun. "It looks like the best one. You can't serve a chef just any old burger."

"You are adorable," she said, ruffling his hair. Dylan would probably slap anyone else who did that. But he was eating it up. "This all looks wonderful."

"Your family must feel a lot of pressure at the holidays," my mother said, standing by with a bowl full of potato salad. "Who wants to cook for a trained chef?"

Audrey snorted. "My mother has never made me a meal in her life. She thinks cooking is for losers. When I was nine, all I wanted for Christmas was an Easy-Bake Oven. I knew she'd never let me use the real one."

"Did she get you one?" I asked.

"No—she bought me a business suit and a scientific calculator. I wasn't even a little surprised. But I'd also told my grandmother what I wanted, and she got it for me!" Audrey grinned. "And she gave me a big supply of the tiny cake mixes you use in the little pan. It was heaven for about six months. But that summer my mother sent me away to math camp for three weeks. And when I got home it was gone. She threw everything away. All I had left was the weird little measuring spoon that came with it. I keep it in my jewelry box."

Audrey delivered this story while spooning condiments onto her burger. So she didn't see the shock on my mother's face. I saw Mom open her mouth and then close it again, at a loss for what to say about Audrey's so-called mom.

"Who wants ketchup?" Audrey said, holding up the dish.

"I do," I said quickly. "Have a seat, princess. I'll bring you a drink."

"Thank you, Griffin." She gave me a quick smile and walked away.

"I really like that girl," my mother said.

"That's my line."

Mom gave me a curious look, but then one of our day workers asked her for a Band-Aid for a scratch on his ankle. So she went to fuss over that instead of over me.

Fair enough.

I got two glasses of iced tea and joined Audrey at a picnic table. "Want to go to a movie later?" I asked.

Her burger paused on the way to her perfect mouth. "A movie? Where?"

"There's an old drive-in theater in Fairlee. I could see what's playing."

"Sure, Griff. That sounds like fun." Her gaze had snagged on something over by the grill. "Griff, is your mother limping?"

"What?" I looked at Mom. She was indeed favoring her right leg. I took a bite of my lunch and watched her try to serve potato salad while balancing with her hip against the serving table. *Hell.* That did not look right.

I waited until the throng died down to ask her about it. When my plate was empty, I took it up to the bin where dishes were to be stacked for washing. "What happened, Mom? Something's bothering your foot?"

She made a face. "It will be fine. I ran into the house for a Band-Aid. I shouldn't have been dashing around like a chicken, I guess. Tripped on the boot brush and twisted it a little. I'll ice it after lunch."

When the meal was over, I stuck around to help carry things into the house, and Audrey pitched in, too.

"Omigod—Griffin cleared a dish!" my sister Daphne crowed. "Alert the media!"

I gave Daphne a swat, and my mother frowned at me. "You can go out with the day workers, Griff. I'm okay."

She wasn't, though. I helped her to the den and then went to find an ice pack. When I came back and rolled up the linen pants she wore, I found her ankle had swelled to the size of a cantaloupe. "Mom, this looks bad. What if you broke something?"

"I didn't break anything," she insisted. "Just twisted it."

"Someone should look at it," I insisted. When I probed her ankle, she winced.

"But what if it's nothing? Why ruin an afternoon for nothing. Besides, I have two pork shoulders to braise."

"May can do it," I argued.

"Your sister went to Boston to visit Lark before classes begin again," my mother reminded me.

"I'll do it," Audrey said from the doorway.

"Honey, you don't have to…"

"I *want* to," Audrey insisted. "Let me help. Whether you have your ankle x-rayed or not, you should put your feet up."

My mother looked as if she wanted to argue. Mom was Ms. Capable, and I knew that sitting around while someone else cooked dinner would practically kill her. But Audrey wasn't wrong, and Mom knew it. "Thank you, honey," she said with a sigh. "I can still shell peas, as long as I'm sitting down."

"Of course you can," I said quickly. "And tomorrow, if that swelling isn't down…"

"I'll have it looked at," my mother promised.

"How do you like your pork shoulder?" Audrey asked. "Spice rub? Teriyaki flavor? Chipotle lime? Let's see if I've bookmarked any recipes…" She whipped her phone out of her back pocket.

There was nothing more I could do to help Mom, and I had to get back outside and take care of some business. "I'll, uh, see you later?"

Mom, Audrey and Daphne looked up from Audrey's phone. "Bye," Audrey said with a shy little smile that went straight to my dick.

Hell, I had it bad.

* * *

Hours later I sat down in a dining room that smelled like a four-star restaurant. I think I heard every stomach rumble in turn as Zach, Jude, my cousins and my brother took their seats.

"Wow," Dylan said, eying a platter the size of a small canoe. There was a mountain of pork so tender it was falling apart. And a heap of vegetables that smelled far more exotic than the fare that usually graced our table.

"Does everyone have a beverage?" Audrey called from the kitchen. I saw her dart past in an apron, her hair up in a knot on top of her head, tendrils framing her face. She must have felt eyes on her, because she looked up quickly and caught me staring.

Busted.

I got up again and went into the kitchen. This meal deserved a bottle of wine, so I grabbed two bottles out of a high cabinet and tucked them under my arm. The world's prettiest girl came zipping over to where I stood. "Take this," she commanded, thrusting a big bowl of rice into my free hand.

"This smells like..." I inhaled. "Coconut?"

"We're doing a little Thai thing tonight," she said, giving me a nudge on the bottom. "Put that on the table."

She followed me into the dining room, where my mother was just limping toward a chair to seat herself. I hated the sight of her discomfort.

"Hi Mom," I said, setting the rice down on the table. "I like Audrey. A lot."

"This again?" Audrey mumbled, darting back into the kitchen.

"We all do, dear. Though your sentiments would be more convincing when you're not drooling into her cooking, though. That's just a tip for you."

My grandfather walked in just in time for dinner, as always. He claimed a seat as my mother asked the inevitable. "How about tomorrow for moving into the farmhouse?"

"No thanks," he said, shaking out his napkin.

I went over to the cabinet where we kept the stemware. "Who needs a wine glass? Gramps? Mom?" I handed them out, putting glasses down for Audrey and all the guys except for Jude. When he'd first come to stay with us I'd offered him a beer and he'd told me that alcohol violated the terms of his parole. He'd said, "And even if it didn't, a drug is a drug. Alcohol was never my drug of choice, but I'm staying away from it."

Since then I'd always felt a little guilty about drinking in front of him. So we didn't do that very often.

Audrey came back with yet another giant platter of food, this one for the other end of the table.

"You're sitting here," I said to Audrey, patting the chair next to me. She raised an eyebrow, but then accepted the seat I pulled out for her.

Daphne bustled in with a giant bowl of salad. "That's the last of it!" she called. "Someone say grace because I'm starving."

"Why don't you do it, dear?"

Daphne bowed her head and said a nice, quick little prayer. And then we fell like wolves onto Audrey's cooking.

After the whole cherries-in-barbecue-sauce revelation, I knew to pile the food on my plate like a champ. The pork was delicious and flavored entirely differently than Mom's. It tasted of lime and basil and cilantro. The coconut rice was spicy and wonderful. But the vegetables amazed me more than anything. There was wilted spinach with a whiff of soy and ginger. And thinly sliced carrots that had been cooked quickly and then tossed in some sort of zesty sauce. I actually got hungrier with each bite I took.

Last time our family table was blessed with a sample of Audrey's genius, everyone moaned and carried on with loud praise. But this time everyone absorbed the bliss in relative silence. There were a few quiet words of thanks to Audrey, but nobody wanted to gush over food that poor Mom had wanted to cook for us in a more ordinary way.

As I glanced around the table, I saw Zach and Jude and Dylan shoveling it in almost guiltily.

That's when Mom threw down her napkin. "I would injure myself more often if it meant I could eat this. Well done, honey. Boys—it's okay. Be honest."

There was an immediate chorus of moaning and several offers of marriage. I think one of them came from me.

"God gave me another day on earth just so I could eat this," my grandfather crowed. "No offense to Ruthie."

"None taken," my mother said quickly.

Beside me Audrey gave a shy smile and blushed as the praise piled even higher. "You guys are fun to cook for. So I'll invite you all to my restaurant opening. Make sure to sit near the critics and enunciate clearly."

"Seriously," Daphne said, scraping up the last of her rice. "You should have your own restaurant. What kind will it be?"

Audrey fingered her fork. "I keep changing my mind. And the pitch session is just five weeks away. I need to choose an idea and stick to it. This week I'm vacillating between Mexican—because Boston is short on good Mexican food—and tapas. It can't be pub food and it can't be French, because BPG has plenty of that already."

"Whatever it is, I'm eating there," Kyle said, reaching for the serving spoon.

I snuck a hand under the table and gave Audrey's knee a squeeze. Just one, though. If this girl needed me to be patient with her, I would be.

* * *

Two hours later we were in my truck, heading for Fairlee on the back roads.

"What was the movie again?" she asked, rolling down her window to sniff the breeze.

It was work keeping my eyes on the road. I kept wanting to admire her. "*Independence Day*. The first one."

"Oh."

I sneaked a look at her. "You like aliens and Will Smith?"

"Sure. Well, I like Will Smith. Aliens I can take or leave."

The truck rolled to a halt at a four-way stop sign. "We don't have to go, you know. We can get ice cream instead."

She laughed. "You could eat right now?"

"No." Good point. There had been an amazing gingered apple crisp for dessert. We'd all rolled away from the table with full stomachs.

I drove on until we reached Lake Morey. The public boat launch parking lot was empty, so I pulled in and killed the engine. "If you don't want to watch aliens destroy the earth, we can just talk. Or go home and watch something else. I picked the drive-in because I wanted to spend some time with you." Crickets chirped outside our open windows. I watched Audrey, but she kept her face turned away from me. "Is something wrong?" I asked quietly. "Should I take you home?"

Her beautiful eyes darted toward me and then away again. "Nothing's wrong, Griff. Not with *you.*"

"With who, then?" I picked up her smooth hand from the truck's bench seat and kissed it. "Tell me how to make you happy, and I'll do it."

She made a small, frustrated sound. "I'm fine. But I don't do my best thinking when you're around."

"Why not?" I flipped her hand over and traced her palm with my lips. When I heard her breath hitch, I was pretty sure what was bothering her.

Audrey pulled her hand away and set it in her lap. "I'm kind of a wreck," she whispered.

"Not true," I said immediately. "You know I want you. Either you want it, too, or you don't. No reason to get all anxious about it." Stretching out my hand to find hers, I ran a single finger up her wrist and then her forearm.

She shivered, and I chuckled.

Chapter Twenty

Audrey

Here we go again. I was as good at resisting Griff Shipley as Homer Simpson was at resisting a donut. The way he made me feel only by touching my hand was probably illegal in several states. I sat there a moment longer, watching a little lake ripple in the first beams of moonlight. As if I were undecided. But what would happen next was as certain as the moonrise itself.

"It doesn't have to mean anything," I whispered, turning to face him.

"Uh-huh. Keep telling yourself that." He chuckled. "You forget I have a *degree* in chemistry." He dropped my hand, which was a disappointment. But then he slid closer to me on the bench seat. His hands scooped me into the air and deposited me into his lap.

I lay back against his great, firm bulk and sighed. "What am I going to do with you, Griff?"

His breath was warm at my ear. "I have a few ideas."

So did I.

His hands ran slowly up my ribcage. "I really like you, Audrey."

"You mentioned that earlier."

When he chuckled, I bounced a little from the motion. "But you think it's just for sex."

"Isn't it?" I breathed, already losing focus. "It's not like I'm going to stick around."

"That's not my fault, though," he pointed out. "And when you accused me of caring only about sex, you were right—"

"I was? Dude. That's no way to have your way with a girl."

"Turn around."

Not sure it was a great idea, I slid off his lap. Then I turned gingerly around until Griff pulled me onto his body. I was straddling him now, and blinking into his big brown eyes at close range. "What?" I asked, and it came out sounding snappish.

"You were right *originally*. You turn me on like nobody ever has." Griff punctuated this statement with one soft kiss. Then he pulled back, running one hand down my sternum, between my breasts and onto my tummy.

I quivered. Everywhere.

"Wanting you makes it hard to ignore that I've been lonely. That maybe I need more than fourteen hours a day of hard labor and a bed in the bunkhouse. I need *you* in my bed. In my kitchen..."

I snorted. My mother would stage a feminist intervention if she could hear that.

Griff shook his head. "That came out wrong. But every time I see you in my kitchen you look happy as a clam. You smile, and you get this look on your face like you're in the zone. It's nice. Makes me want to throw you over my shoulder and haul you away with me."

It wasn't easy to play hard to get while straddling Griff Shipley on the seat of his truck. I found that my fingers had wandered into his beard. I stroked his beard and asked, "Where else do you need me?"

Mom would burst a vessel if she heard that, too.

"Everywhere," he growled. "Want you in the cider house, tasting the blends with me. Want you sitting beside me in church, when I take Mom on Sundays. But after that I'll need you in the shower. Up against the wall..."

I kissed him then, pressing my lips against his, practically banging down the door to be let inside. Griff opened on a groan, his tongue welcoming mine. As usual, there was no time for small talk. We went from talking to making out like porn stars. One of his hands squeezed my ass while the other slipped a few inches beneath the waistband of my skirt. His fingertips hovered there, stroking the skin beneath my bellybutton, threatening to touch the good stuff, but never actually doing it.

Torture. I whimpered into his mouth and hoped that he'd hear me. And just for good measure, I unfastened the button on his jeans.

"I could drive you home," he panted between kisses.

That sounded like it would take too long. So I lowered his zipper.

He answered with a rumble and a voice like gravel. "We're going to fuck in the truck?"

It sounded like a dirty rhyming couplet. I plunged my hand down his abs to find his very hard dick peeking out of the top of his underwear. When I took him in hand, he moaned.

"One problem, princess," he ground out. "No condom."

I could have wept. "So what? I'm clean, and I'm good to go." Releasing him, I took a deep breath and looked him straight in the eye. "I know I'm flaky about some things. But not about birth control."

His gaze was heavy lidded. "I trust you, princess. Swear to God, I've never done it bare."

"Never?"

He shook his head.

"We don't have to." *Though I'll probably cry from disappointment.*

He lifted a hand to gather my hair and push it off

my shoulder. "Sweetheart, get on my dick. Do it now."

Quickly, I hiked up my skirt. Griff reached down and put a finger under the elastic of my panties. "Wait!" I yelped before he could snap them off of me. "I need these. I'm traveling."

"Fine." He pushed me up a bit so we could both tug down pieces of our respective clothing. "But don't ever tell me I don't have any manners."

"Ha," I scoffed. "You're a grouch. But a hot one."

"At least you could fuck me while you tell me all my flaws." He wrapped one big hand around his thick length and beckoned me closer.

As if I needed encouragement. I lined myself up over him and sank down, filling myself with him. God, this man. I let out a groan so loud that Griff's cows probably looked up from their hay. All the bluster left me. There was only this exquisite moment.

And I wasn't the only one who'd been rendered speechless. Griff threw his head back and gasped when I seated myself on him. "Jesus...fuck!" It was almost a shout. His chest heaved in and out against me, and he gripped my hips, holding me down. "Don't move...for a second." His eyes were slammed shut and his breathing was rapid. "Never guessed how good you'd feel with nothing between us. Like heaven."

Wow. I'd never seen anything so beautiful as Griffin Shipley nearly undone by lust. Leaning forward, I took his face in my hands, the soft fur of his beard ticking my palms. Then—unable to resist—I slowly clenched all the muscles in my core.

His eyes flew open again. "Fuck, princess." He released my hips and pulled me in until we were forehead to forehead, staring at each other. "You kill me. Every damn time. Just you."

My heart gave a little spasm even if I knew it was

just the horniness talking. So I figured I could shut him up if I kissed him. I slid my hands back into his hair and took his mouth. Hard.

But it backfired, because Griff Shipley knew how to kiss. He palmed my jaw and pulled me in, taking over the kiss, stroking my tongue, melting me like sugar into caramel. As our kisses grew ever deeper, I couldn't hold still anymore. I rocked against Griff's unyielding body, slowly at first and then faster.

Meanwhile, Griff made the most delicious noises. He dove so deeply into my mouth that I lost track of where I ended and he began. His palms wandered down to my bare ass, where they gave me the dirtiest squeeze. Then he used the leverage to work my body more roughly against his own.

The result stole all my executive function. There was only heat and bliss and the eager man beneath me. He gave a loud growl as we both lunged together for the finish line. I got there first as pulses of pleasure rippled first through my core and then everywhere at once. My toes curled so hard that both sandals ejected, forgotten, onto the floor of his truck.

His answering moan was like an aftershock, vibrating through my chest. Huge arms locked around me and together we shook with his release.

When it ended, I went limp against him. Our kisses slowed to a soft, mindless exchange of tongue and breath. Then I dropped my head with a sigh onto his great shoulder. How lucky that his body had so many fabulous places to hide my face. I never could look Griffin in the eye after our naked deeds. Being with him always left me feeling raw and vulnerable. I needed a few minutes to paste on my mask of indifference.

Anyone would.

He stroked my hair while I listened to his breathing

slow. Eventually he started to chuckle.

"What?"

"Sound carries across a lake," he said into my ear. "I hope we inspired a few people."

"Mmh." I couldn't be bothered to worry about who might have heard us. I was too busy worrying about how foolish I'd been to get naked with Griffin again. Not *even* naked. Tawdry Audrey had outdone herself again. And for what? I was slowly ruining myself for other men. Someday I might actually meet some available, decent guy who was interested in dating me. And God help him if he and I didn't have the chemistry I had with Griffin Shipley.

"Your bed or mine?" Griff asked.

That woke me up. I lifted my head off his shoulder and tried to fill my lungs with oxygen. He wanted to spend the night? "Um, mine?" If we drove up to his farm and walked past his family on the way to Griff's room, I might die of embarrassment.

"We left your car at the farm," he said. "We can stop there and get it on the way to the motor lodge."

Hell. "Your family is going to notice." *And think I'm a ho.*

He gave me a squeeze. "My family loves you."

But you don't, my brain offered up. And where did that come from, anyway? "It helps that I cook," I mumbled.

"Princess." He caught my chin in his hand. "You don't have any need to be embarrassed. It's nobody's business but ours."

It was nice that Griff thought so. But women had been judged since the dawn of time for who they slept with and how often. Speaking of which…I lifted my body off of Griff's, separating the two of us.

Caught off guard, he let out one more groan. "Jesus,

I'm addicted. Whose bed, princess? Cause I'm gonna need to do that again in about a half an hour."

"Mine," I said immediately. I'd never been known for my willpower. Besides, I could get up at dawn when Griff went home and escape with my car before his mom or younger siblings were awake to notice.

We tucked ourselves into our clothes and drove back to Tuxbury. Griff rolled down the windows and whistled along with the radio. Halfway there he reached for my hand and held it the rest of the way home.

I sniffed the crisp, Vermont summer air and let the wind tickle my face. Even in the midst of a bad decision, I could still live in the moment. And the moment was fine.

* * *

Twelve hours later I awoke to a knock on my cabin door.

I sat up fast, heart pounding. The room was bright with morning sunlight. And I was alone in the bed.

"Hello?" I called out. The clock said eight.

"Rise and shine, princess. Time for breakfast." He banged on the door again. "I've milked fifty cows already. Wake up!"

Stumbling on sleepy feet, I lurched over to the door and opened it, still trying to get my bearings. "I didn't hear you leave," I said.

Griff pushed into the room, laughing. "I noticed that. You were sacked out pretty hard." He backed me up to the bed, pushed me onto it and landed on top of me. "Guess I wore you out." He kissed my neck.

That woke me up. His big, hard body pressed mine into the bed. I clasped my hands around his head, loving the feel of his thick hair sifting through my fingers. This man was addictive.

He dropped a dozen fabulous kisses across the sensitive skin underneath my ear. But then he got back to his feet. "Up, baby. I have to take you back to your car before I spend the day pressing the first cider."

That sounded like fun to watch. I grabbed the hand he offered me and was hauled to my feet. "Can I take a one-minute shower?"

"I don't know, can you?"

"Griff!" I stomped toward the bathroom.

"I meant that literally," he said, sitting on the edge of the bed. "I thought women had a ten-minute minimum."

"Not this one." I closed the bathroom door behind me so I wouldn't be tempted to invite him in. Then I took a much-needed shower. Five minutes later I was dressed and slipping into shoes while I brushed my still-wet hair. "How's your mom? Did the swelling go down?"

He shook his head. "Negative. Daphne is going to drive her to the hospital in Montpelier for an x-ray. Mom insists she couldn't have broken it just by tripping. But I know she won't stay off that foot unless a doctor orders her to."

I grabbed my bag and phone. "If I helped with breakfast, would she sit down?"

"Maybe." He grinned. "Either way, I want to watch you flip eggs in the air while you boss me around. Come on, princess." He opened the door. "Make me an omelet I didn't order."

Something like warmth filled my chest. And then it was immediately chased by anxiety. Griffin needed a warning sign, like the kind they put over the pizza oven at the culinary school. *Danger, hot!* I had to be careful or I'd start picturing myself as a permanent part of his life. It was all too easy to imagine myself in that kitchen every day, teasing his little brother, helping out his mom.

Not only did I have the hots for Griff, I had a crush on his family, too.

Sitting in the passenger seat of Griff's truck on the ten-minute drive, I planned my restaurant pitch for BPG and tried not to stare at my favorite farmer behind the wheel.

By the time I ducked into Griff's bacon-scented kitchen, it was already a whirlwind of activity. And thank God. I was sure the family had spotted my car outside.

"Audrey!" Daphne called. "Can you do your super-fast chopping thing on these onions?"

"Sure." I stepped up to the counter. "What are we making?"

"Frittatas, I guess. I wanted to do quiche but I defrosted the wrong dough." She pointed at three risen balls of dough on the butcher's block. "That's for bread."

"Ah." My chef's brain spun like a roulette wheel and landed on an idea. "Should we just make little free-form pies anyway? If they're small, the crust won't need to be pre-baked. It's a shame to waste that dough."

"I guess? Show me."

"Divide those into six pieces," I said, pointing at the balls of dough. "Roll 'em out to a rough circle."

I attacked the onions while she worked. Ruth wandered into the kitchen a few minutes later. She moved so slowly that it pained me to watch. "Audrey! Thank you for stepping in. We're in a bit of a bind."

"It's no problem." I grabbed one of Daphne's little rounds of dough and began folding the edges up to try to shape it into a decent receptacle for eggs.

"We have little tart pans," Ruth volunteered. "Hold on." She limped toward a cupboard on the wall. Daphne darted over to help and came back with a dozen five- or six-inch metal pans.

"Perfect! These remind me of my Easy-Bake Oven." *Reunited at last.* I draped the dough over one of them and knew it would work. "Okay—break two or three eggs into here, then add the bacon. In a four-hundred-degree oven they'll cook up fast.

"They're so cute! Should we add some cheese?" Daphne grabbed the tin and got to work.

"Always a good idea," I agreed. "Some spinach would be nice, too?"

Our assembly line was in full swing when Ruth happened to ask, "How was the movie?"

"Great," I lied, and then was immediately sorry. "Uh, is there some parsley we can put on here?"

The pies took about twenty minutes to bake. Breakfast hit the table a little late, but early reviews were encouraging. "Looks like something in a magazine," Jude said when I handed over his plate.

"Smells like heaven," Zach agreed.

"I want the biggest one," Kyle said. "You're going to give it to Zach, aren't you? All the girls like Zachariah best. Isn't that right?"

"Ask Daphne." Dylan smirked. "She knows the answer."

His sister's face reddened and she turned quickly away.

Then Griff walked in. I didn't see him so much as I felt his eyes on me. A sizzle of heat climbed up my spine, and the air around me seemed to carry an electrical charge that wasn't there a moment before.

"That sure looks *good*," he said slowly. And I wasn't sure he meant the food.

My cheeks heated. "Let me fix you a plate." I grabbed the golden, doughy edges of a tart and tugged it quickly out of the pan, dropping it onto a plate.

"How do you not scorch yourself?" Daphne asked.

"I have asbestos fingers. Now take one of these for yourself." I flicked another one onto a plate.

While the pies had been baking, we'd let Ruth make the coffee. Then we made her sit down in the dining room.

"You're the official greeter," Daphne told her.

"The greeter?" her mother muttered. "Might as well just take me out back and shoot me." But she perked up a little when Grandpa Shipley shuffled in. "You're late! Ten minutes."

"I was gettin' the paper," he said.

"You'd be on time if you moved into the farmhouse."

He threw the paper on the table. "I'm not moving, because you'll watch everything I do. Hell, Ruthie. If I wanted someone to nag me, I'd get remarried."

She rolled her eyes. "I don't nag. I suggest."

"I *suggest* you leave me be," Grandpa said. He sat down in a chair and pulled the newspaper closer.

"Let me get your plate," I said.

"You should eat, too, princess." Griffin eyed me over the rim of his coffee cup.

God, was it just me? Or did everything he say sound dirty? "I will."

I hustled back into the kitchen and used the now-empty tins to set the last six pies to bake. Then I took one of the finished ones for myself and came back to the dining room just in time to hear Grandpa read a couple of lines from the front page of the local paper.

"The movie showing was interrupted again by the arrival of police cruisers and two ambulances." He looked up. "Exciting night at the drive-in last night."

Ruth cut into her tart. "Griff, you didn't mention any of this! Did the accident make a big mess?"

My gaze flew to Griff's. His expression flashed with a quick display of both panic and humor. "Well...I didn't really see it up close. Lot of people crowded around, you know? Didn't seem like a good idea to get in the way."

"You don't see a hay truck tip over every day," Grandpa said, slurping his coffee.

"You're right," Griff agreed. "Can I see that paper?" His grandfather passed it over. Griff scanned the article, nodding solemnly. "Yeah. Terrible mess. Took us forever to get out of there after the movie." He looked up and winked.

A tipped-over hay truck wasn't even half as messy as my feelings for Griff Shipley.

After breakfast I helped Daphne prep for lunch. She and her mom would probably be waiting around for an x-ray, so we made up big platters of lunchmeats and covered them with plastic wrap. "Aren't you going to stay?" she asked, giving me a pleading look that made me feel guilty.

"Nope. There are things I need to get done today." And it was just as well. I'd spent too much time already en famille with the Shipleys. They made me feel useful in a way that was rare for me. But hanging around in their kitchen wouldn't get me where I needed to go. "Do you mind if I take one of these last pies? There's someone I want to give it to."

Daphne just shrugged. "Take whatever you want! And come back to make them again tomorrow."

"We'll see. Good luck at the hospital."

She made a face. "Fun times in radiology! I'd better bring a book. Bye, Audrey!"

I got in the car and, after making a short drive,

carried a bag containing the bacon, egg and cheese pie to the kitchen door of The Mountain Goat and knocked loudly. Even so, I couldn't be heard over a radio which was blasting out some Guns N' Roses. So I opened the door and let myself in.

When I found her, Zara was scanning the contents of a walk-in refrigerator and singing along with Axl Rose.

"Hey," I said, tapping her hand gently.

"FUCK!" she shrieked, jumping away from me, slamming the door to the refrigerator, her eyes wild. "YOU STARTLED ME!" she shouted over the music.

I turned it down. "I noticed that. Sorry."

She clutched at her chest. "Jesus Christ. I think that took a year off my life."

"Bummer. But I brought you breakfast, so we're even."

Zara raised one inky eyebrow. It stood out like a slash mark against her pale skin. "You brought me...breakfast? Why?"

That's the moment I knew Zara and I had something in common. The look of mistrust on her face seemed awfully familiar. "Because I had an idea for you. About the coffee service you were considering. You said pastries would get you in here too early to make morning hours sensible. But you could do pies. They could be prepped by your chef the night before—the whole thing. They'd be waiting in the cooler on trays, and you'd just put them in the oven. You could charge four or five bucks, and it's mostly dough and a couple of eggs. The bacon would up the cost, but it's tasty..." I pulled my creation out of the bag.

"Wow." Zara grabbed a plate off the tall stack beside the salad station and slid it under the pie. "That's kind of a great idea. But why were you thinking about my problem?"

I shrugged. "It's what I do. I like solving kitchen problems. They're a lot easier than regular problems."

"True." Zara broke off a piece of crust and shoved it in her mouth. "Okay, I need a fork and knife. Coffee?"

"Of course."

We sat down at the bar and chatted while Zara ate. I was procrastinating. There was plenty of work to be done today, including a call I needed to make to my boss. But Zara was full of neighborhood gossip, which I could almost write off as gathering business intelligence.

"If you're dealing with the Honeyweights, ask Mr. Honeyweight for a price. His wife is a cheapskate."

"Good to know," I said, trying to remember if I'd agreed on a deal with that farm yet. My phone rang. I peered at the screen. "Sorry, one second. It's my corporate overlords. Hello?"

"Audrey," one of the Burtons barked. "There's a problem with transporting the perishables you're buying."

It took a second for that to sink in. "What do you mean?" I did a mental count of which farm goods were perishable. It was damn near everything.

"Last year when we were buying our farm-to-table products in Massachusetts, we asked our regular produce distributor to truck in our farm purchases. But we switched distributors a few months ago, and the new one can't accommodate our purchases in Vermont."

I turned that over in my mind for a moment, looking for a solution. "So how are all these vegetables getting to Boston?" If he said *they aren't*, I would throw the phone across the room.

"We're going to have to find another solution."

"By *we* you mean *me*, don't you?" I asked point blank.

He had the balls to chuckle. "That's right."

"Mr. Burton," I sputtered. "I spent the last week looking two-dozen farmers in the eye and promising that you were a good business partner."

"Don't panic, Audrey. It's not *that* much food. Nobody dies if we don't buy this stuff. The local produce is expensive, and if I can't get it to Boston on the cheap, BPG's shareholders won't be happy."

"What can I do to solve this?" My voice was shaking.

"I guess you need to find an inexpensive rental truck and drive it down yourself."

"Every Friday?"

He thought that over. "Yeah. You can drive up from Boston and bring the weekly shipment back. Either that or find a farmer with a truck and pay him a little something for his time."

Shit. I couldn't even imagine driving a loaded vegetable truck through Boston's North End.

God, the things I did for these jerks. But what was my alternative? "I'll find a truck," I said.

"Do that. But make sure there's enough on the back of it to make this worth our while. Gotta jump. Bye."

Click.

I put my head down on Zara's bar. It was either that or fly into a rage. Burton sat in his cushy Boston office, lecturing me about shareholder value. Meanwhile, *he'd* been the one to screw up his farm-to-table initiative from minute one. Every night I spent in the cheap motel was costing him. And all because he'd already burned through the goodwill of every organic farmer in Massachusetts.

What an idiot. And what an asshole.

"Bad day at the office?" Zara asked.

"You could say that. I need a truck and someone who's not afraid to drive it into Boston. Every week. For almost no pay."

"Sounds like a party." She mopped the bar, a thoughtful look on her face. "As much as I hate saying this, Griffin Shipley could probably help you. Not that he's all that generous with his time. But he's pretty invested in the whole farm-to-table thing. He has trucks. And his sister May drives to Boston a lot to visit her best friend."

I picked my head up off the bar and thought that over. "True..." But Griff hated BPG. On the other hand, his ciders had to get to Boston somehow. The produce deliveries were meant to start up in a week. But a month after that, he'd need to get his product into the city, so he could collect his big fat check. "I'll call him. He's gonna yell."

"Could happen," Zara agreed.

I dialed the Shipley household, hoping that someone other than Griff would answer. No luck.

"PRINCESS!" he boomed. "Got another flat tire?"

I adjusted the volume on my phone to avoid going deaf. "Not exactly," I hedged, resenting the implication that I was always bumping into shit and asking him to bail me out. If only it weren't true. "I've hit, uh, a snag, and I was wondering if you had any ideas for me."

"Hit me."

"Okay. Try not to say *I told you so*..." Then I explained the problem.

"Holy shit," he said when I was through. "I told you so."

"*Griff!*"

His laugh boomed into my ear. "Just a joke, princess. Don't rent a U-Haul. Get those assholes to pay a few cents a mile for one of my trucks and get them to pay one of my employees minimum wage for five hours each Friday. Oh—and make sure they're only expecting one drop-off location. I can't have my guys driving around Boston all day. Once the goods get into the city, it's their problem."

"That sounds entirely fair," I said, feeling the first hint of relief. "I hope they go for it."

"It's minimum wage. How much better could they do than that?"

"They pay me less than minimum wage."

There was a silence on the line. "Do you want to hear what I think of that?"

"Nope."

He sighed. "Didn't think so. Take care, princess. Thanks for all your help this morning."

"No problem. If your mom has to stay off her feet, I can help again tonight. Or tomorrow." Shit. There I went again, inviting myself into their lives. "Only if you need it," I hedged.

"Sounds good to me. I was thinking about ordering pizza. But that only works once or twice in a row. And we have to drive twenty minutes each way to pick it up."

"That's a pain. I'll call you later."

"I'll count on it. Bye, princess!" He hung up.

That had gone better than I expected. I was puzzling over the easy result when I saw Zara's face. "What's the matter?"

"Griffin Shipley calls you *princess?*"

"Uh, yeah. Isn't it awful?" My whole life people had assumed I was a pampered brat. I always had the newest clothes and went to a fancy school. And as payment, my mother told me every day what a great disappointment I was.

Good times.

I shoved my phone in my purse and zipped it closed.

"It's not awful." Zara's face had a dreamy look on it. "It's...wow."

"Why? I don't get it."

She sighed. "He thinks of himself as Han Solo, you know? He has a crusader complex a mile wide."

I snorted. "Yeah. So?"

"What did Han call Leia? *Princess*. I watched that fucking movie a dozen times to try to figure that man out. Never did crack the code. Looks like you did, though." She put her chin in a hand. "Seriously. I never saw Griff put any effort in with a girl before. Well done, sister."

"Um..." My head was practically exploding by now. I didn't think it was possible that Griff's nickname was anything more than a dig. But it was something to think about later. "Thanks for coffee. I have to run."

"Feel free to come back anytime you've brought me breakfast." She gave me a smile and a wave and I was out of there.

Chapter Twenty-One

September

Griffin

In spite of Mom's injury, the next couple of weeks were some of the best ones I'd had in a long time. The harvest looked good, and the weather cooperated. My guys picked apples like crazy. My new cider tanks arrived on the back of a flatbed truck. I scrubbed them out, grinning like a fool. This is what the big time looked like—three cylindrical steel columns in the corner of the cider house. When nobody was looking, I ran my hand over them, admiring the racking-off spouts at the bottom and the high-tech pressure gages at the top.

As August progressed, I cranked up the cider press every afternoon and juiced as many bushels as I could before dinner. Much of this juice went into one of my new tanks, while some of it was frozen for blending with later-season juice.

Mom's injury was healing slowly. When she'd first returned from the doctor's visit, I'd gotten all excited when she'd opened with, "It's not broken." But even as she'd said it, she'd winced on her way into the farmhouse.

"Not broken," I'd repeated. "That's great, right?"

Daphne had shaken her head. "It's a high-ankle sprain. Those take even longer to heal then a break."

"We'll see," my mother had said, holding her head up high.

It was just like Mom to assume that she could *will*

her ankle to heal. And hell, if anyone could, it was her. Mom was tough. But I made it my job to be sure she followed the doctor's orders to put no weight on it at all. They'd sent her home with a hundred-dollar pair of crutches and an irritated look in her eye.

At first, the pain and humiliation of being hurt made her irritable. There were moments when I considered handing over the trophy for Orneriest Shipley to my mother. I didn't know how to help.

But other people did. Jude surprised me by volunteering to help out with lunch prep. I'd forgotten that he'd said he worked in the prison kitchen. But Mom said yes, and he left the orchard at noon every day to pitch in. The first time I went into lunch and found him wearing her frilly apron I almost bust a gut laughing, and I think that was the point. It was hard for Mom to be snappish and depressed with Jude there to play the part of kitchen slave.

And then there was Audrey. She seemed to turn up every afternoon around the time that Mom usually started the kitchen prep. And Mom accepted her help in the kitchen more easily than anyone else's, even Jude's. Maybe because Audrey was a chef, or maybe because she was just so fucking adorable. My mother welcomed her assistance, and Audrey was kind enough to give it.

You have to make hay when the sun shines, as they say. So I did what I could to keep Audrey around when the workday was done. We actually made it to the movies for real. We even watched the film, while I drowned my lust-filled thoughts with popcorn and soda. And we went to the Goat now and then, where I was surprised at Zara's warmer greeting.

At some point I realized the greeting was for Audrey. Which just figured. She could win over anyone, and usually did. Some nights Audrey and I played euchre with Dylan and Daphne. We tried to let the twins be a team, but when things went badly they fought too much. So after that we played girls vs. guys.

The women clobbered Dylan and me. It's just the way of the world.

After most of these fun evenings, I followed Audrey home to the motor lodge and stayed the night in her bed. I'm pretty sure that undersized cabin of hers was nearly rocked from its foundation once or twice by our enthusiastic sex. We christened every surface of that shabby little room together. It was so, so good.

The Friday night after Mom's injury, Audrey and I lay in her bed, naked. "Can I ask you for a favor?"

"Another one so soon?" Her fingers walked down the centerline of my chest toward my groin.

I chuckled. "Not a sexual favor." I was already too satisfied to move. "I wondered if you'd pour cider for the tourists tomorrow. I'm trying to keep Mom off her feet."

She lifted her head from my shoulder. "Sure! I'll be giving out tastings?"

"Exactly. It's not brain work, but it's not digging ditches, either."

"Can I taste, too?"

"Of course." There was nothing I wouldn't have given her at that moment. Skin to skin with her was the only place I ever wanted to be. "One thing, though? Don't tell them any of the cider tastes like a blowjob."

She giggled into my neck. "*Fine*. I'll be very proper and boring. All your ciders taste like apricots or morning dew."

I rolled sideways and kissed her. And maybe it was the power of suggestion, but she tasted like apricots and happy girl.

* * *

Saturday dawned sunny, promising great weather and a whole lot of tourists.

I left Audrey snoozing in bed after setting her phone alarm for eight o'clock. Then I went home to prepare for the onslaught.

First up—loading the truck for the Norwich market. When that was done, May—returned from her trip to Boston—and Zach drove off together. I was sticking close today to keep an eye on Mom, who was quite put out by her injury.

She'd insisted on scrambling a big batch of eggs for breakfast, which she did with a crutch in one hand and a spatula in the other. After we ate, I set up a table outside the cider house and put the cash register there. Usually we put it on the tasting counter, but I knew she wouldn't stay seated if I left it there.

By a quarter to nine everything was ready. There were pumpkins piled high—those were grown by the Abrahams down the road at Apostate Farm. It wasn't just apples and cider that brought tourists to the orchard on a late August Saturday. They came for an experience, and we did our best to provide one.

Mom was in her seat, counting out change as the first cars pulled up, families sliding out of minivans, ready to pick Paula Reds and Ginger Golds. I became distracted by a pair of shapely legs unfolding from a rental car. When Audrey showed her face, she was smiling as brightly as the late summer sun. Damn, my farm looked better with her on it.

"Morning!" she called, swinging her purse.

I met her in the driveway and stole a kiss. She tasted like toothpaste and happiness. "Mmm," I said, wishing there were time for more of those. "Did you sleep well this morning after I left?"

She blinked up at me as we drifted toward the cider

house. "Sure. But what's the fun in that?"

No kidding.

"Oh, horses!"

Indeed, Dylan and Daphne were arguing feverishly in the driver's seat of Abraham's horse cart. They couldn't decide who would take the first shift driving lazy people the quarter mile through the orchard to the Ginger Gold.

"No," Daphne said, "we have to switch every hour."

"That's ridiculous," my brother argued. "Stop being such a little bitch about it."

Meanwhile, the two Percheron horses looked bored. One of them stretched his great neck down to sniff the hem of Audrey's skirt. She leapt out of the way. "Jeez. You're a little fresh, aren't you?"

I shoved the horse's nose out of the way, but I couldn't say I blamed him. "Kids, you're switching drivers every ninety minutes. Dylan goes first, and he's done at ten-thirty. End of discussion."

"What?" Daphne argued. "Ninety minutes is forever when you're driving this thing."

"Don't run over any customers," I added, turning my back to her. "Come on, Audrey."

She skipped along beside me. Cutest thing ever. "How much should I charge for a bottle of cider?"

"You don't have to take the money, Mom is doing that. But it's fourteen bucks if anyone asks."

"A bargain at any price!" she crowed. "This is going to be fun. I hope some people come inside to taste."

"Oh they will. You'll be slammed."

She gave me a shove. "I'll bet you say that to all the girls. What if there are people who just want to stand there and drink for free?"

"Well..." We reached the door of the cider house where I found Mom standing up without her crutches.

"Sit down already!" I barked. "Are you trying to make me crazy?"

Mom gave me a glare. "I can't *sit* all day. Who does that?"

"Plenty of people. I'd like to try it myself sometime. Would you please get off that ankle?"

Mom sat down and reached for Audrey's hand. "Nice to see you, sweetie. Thanks for helping out today."

"My pleasure." Audrey smiled. "I always wanted to run a lemonade stand, but my mother thought it was low class." She rolled her eyes. "This is even better!"

"I'm right out here if you need anything," Mom said. "Griff will probably tie me to this chair, so I won't be hard to find."

"Good to know!" Audrey said brightly. "Come on, Griff. Do I get a uniform?"

"A uniform?" I laughed, and my evil brain served up an image of Audrey dressed in a tiny French maid's costume. "Just your smile, baby. That's all you need. The cups are over here. There are two different sizes. I don't care which ones you use up first. But if you use the big ones, don't fill 'em to the top."

"Well, duh! I'm not going to give away the store." She picked up two different cups and examined them. "The wider mouth will make for a better bouquet. But filling the smaller one to the top might look more generous..."

I opened the cooler and took out four bottles—one of each of the current lineup. "You'll go through a bunch, but here's your first batch. Have fun. Chat 'em up. That's the whole job. And somebody will bring you lunch or relieve you so you can grab some."

She spread her hands on the countertop. "I got this. Go chop some wood or whatever it is Farmer Griff does on a Saturday."

"Run around like a crazy man," I said. "And chase people away from my cider apples. Doesn't matter how big I make the signs, some numbnut always tries to pick my heirlooms."

"Those *assholes*. Do you shoot 'em or just go all Grumpy Griff on their asses?"

Now she was just teasing me. "Hang tight, princess." I leaned over the counter and snuck another kiss, while she looked at me through wide, silver eyes. "Bye for now."

"Bye," she whispered.

I went outside whistling to myself.

All morning a steady stream of cars arrived at the farm. They parked everywhere along our driveway, and when those spaces were taken, they parked on the main road and walked up. Dylan and Daphne made dozens of trips with the cart into the orchard. And mom's cash register said "cha-ching" over and over as people cashed out their pickings.

Whenever I passed the cider house I could hear Audrey's laugh, and I wanted in on the joke. No—I wanted a lifetime of having that laugh nearby. Anyone who heard me say that aloud would probably be stunned. I wasn't exactly famous for long-lasting relationships. But Audrey was under my skin. And she had been since the first time I saw her wander into my frat house in Boston.

You just want me for the sex. Ever since she'd said that a week ago, it had bothered me. I'd started wondering what might have happened if I'd handled the situation differently way back at BU. I'd acted like a punk, or at least a dumb kid, which I had been at the time. If I'd tried to be a better friend instead of just taking her to bed, would we have started a real relationship?

She might have been mine for real.

I was busy thinking about this when I saw a woman in a suit marching up the drive. There were probably thirty customers in view at the moment, but this woman stood out. In the first place, nobody had worn high heels in our gravel driveway since May went to her senior prom five years ago. But the woman also looked grim. That was unfortunate for a sunny day in a gorgeous (if I do say so myself) orchard.

She also looked a lot like Audrey. She had the same shiny hair and beautiful cheekbones. But her expression was hard in a way that I'd never seen on Audrey's face.

I found myself following her toward the cider house door where my mother sat. I didn't hear their exchange, but my mother sat up straighter and pointed into the cider house.

By the time I got to the doorway, the woman was yelling. Loudly.

"—a week ago!" she was screeching. "They were waiting for your résumé, young lady. You made me look like a fool!"

"I did no such thing!" Audrey yelped. "I never asked you to put my name down for that job. Or *any* job. I don't want your help!"

Customers were scattering. I had to move out of their way before I could step inside. "Is there a problem here?" I asked, holding Audrey's eyes.

"I'm so sorry," she said, her voice low. "My mother drove all the way here to yell at me. But we can take it outside."

"No need," I said, getting closer, bracing my hip against the tasting counter. I faced her so-called mother. "Unless you came here to taste the cider, could you kindly knock it off? Audrey's busy right now."

Chapter Twenty-Two

Audrey

Griff's words were calm enough. You'd have to know him as well as I did to see the tense set of his burly shoulders as he studied my mother.

She looked equally explosive. Studying Griff, her lip curled. "Audrey, this is not a *job*. Someone with your talents should not be hawking cider in a *barn*." Her eyes cut my way. "Get in the car. You're coming home to Boston."

I had never been so embarrassed in my life.

"Oh my God," I gasped. "NO! I *have* a job, okay? A real one at BPG. I'm told you're familiar with the place?"

My mother's head jerked back in surprise.

But I kept on swinging. "This"—I spread my arms— "is something I'm doing for fun, and to help out people who are *good to me*. They're nice. They even *like* me. I know that's unfathomable to you, but it's true. And anyway, you're wasting your time. You can't make me take a job I don't want. And you just squandered your Saturday to drive up here and make me miserable. Great ROI, Mom. Well done. How will you write off those wasted hours on your spreadsheet, now?"

My mother opened her mouth and then closed it again. Apparently she'd imagined this discussion going quite differently. "Look. I'll give you back your credit card," she sputtered. "Just apply for this position at—"

"No. No. NO! You need to understand something."

Even as the words came out of my mouth, I think it was the first time I'd understood it, too. "I would rather wash dishes for a living and live in squalor than go back to letting you criticize my choices. I am *done* with that, mother. Just done! You can stop with the emails that remind me to have my teeth cleaned, or tell me to set my clocks ahead for daylight savings. You don't get to cut me off and also boss me around. *It doesn't work that way!*"

The shrieky sound of my voice echoed off the cider tanks, and silence fell again. I could see Griff's mother peering through the door and Jude, too. My heart was pounding and I was beginning to sweat. I never meant to have a knock-down-drag-out in front of the Shipley clan. But this little eruption had been a long time coming.

"W-well," my mother stammered, straightening her blazer. "That's foolish. You're foolish. But I obviously can't get that through your head."

"Then stop trying!" I said, lowering my voice. "Because I'm *happier* since the day I stopped wasting so much energy trying to please you." My mother's body gave a little jerk of shock. Another awful silence descended on the cider house.

That's when I ran out of steam. Telling my mother to fuck off really took it out of me.

I put a shaky hand on the growler in front of me and poured a serving. I was so stressed out I considered chugging the stuff. "Would you like a sample?" I asked my mother. "It's organic, and it's about to sweep Boston off its feet."

She eyed the cup as if it were a venomous snake. "No thank you." Giving me one last laser glare, she turned on her heel and stepped toward the door. She was leaving.

That's what I'd told her to do, of course. But if I were honest, the sight of her turning her back on me hurt. A lot.

"Nice to see you too, Mom," I whispered. I meant it as a zinger, but it came out sounding sad.

My mother put one hand on the doorjamb. I saw her hesitate.

I was sure of it.

But she walked outside and disappeared.

* * *

Mom's little visit was a major buzzkill. I was embarrassed and depressed, and everyone knew it.

That night Griffin took me out to the Whippi Dip, where we ate our weight in hot fudge sundaes. Then we went to the Goat, where Zara made me what she called "my Chase Your Blues Away Margarita."

"Want to talk about it?" Griff asked as we enjoyed our drinks from the same side of a booth.

"Nope," I said cheerfully. "There isn't much to say. She doesn't get me. She never will."

"I'm sorry, baby," he whispered in my ear. "The rest of us get you. You're not that tricky to understand."

Aw. I gave him a grateful kiss. "I know, right? I'm trying to make it as a chef, not a pornographer. Why can't she just be happy?"

He shook his ridiculously handsome head. I felt like climbing into his lap and rubbing my face all over his beard. But people would stare, and I'd already caused a scene today.

Damn my mother. She got under my skin. "You know what's stupid?" I asked suddenly.

"What's that, princess?"

"Sometimes I picture myself winning the Green

Light Project at BPG. And in my head, she's the first person I tell." Griff's eyes went all soft and sympathetic. "Today I said I'd stopped trying to please her. But it wasn't even true! I can't stop wishing for her approval even though I don't value it very highly. I mean—this is a woman who learned to play golf only so she could do business on the weekends, too."

"That way lies the dark side."

"*And* she orders wine spritzers un-ironically."

"Wow."

"I know." I put my head on his shoulder. The beard tickled my cheekbone. So I wiggled a little to feel more of it. It was only a little weird. I'm pretty sure.

"Do me a favor, princess?"

"Yeah?" I mumbled into his neck.

"If you win the competition in Boston, will you tell me first, instead of her?"

I raised my head and blinked at Griffin. "Okay?"

"Thank you." He palmed my head and put it down on his shoulder again. And it was the highlight of my shitty day.

Chapter Twenty-Three

Griffin

Aside from Audrey's mom showing up to be a jerkwad, it was a great season. Summer turned slowly into fall. The leaves colored on the trees. The twins went back to high school and May started law classes again. And when Mom's doctor said she could begin to put some weight on her ankle, I thought everything was looking up.

I was wrong, though, because the next day Audrey was recalled by the imperial forces to Boston.

As if this weren't bad enough, Audrey didn't seem to take it very hard. In fact, I only found out about it when I called to ask her out to dinner.

"I can't," she'd said quietly. "I'm on my way back to the city. They've given me a five a.m. shift on the line at Bostonian Bakery for tomorrow morning."

It took a second to make sense of that announcement. But no matter how I turned the words over in my head, I came up with the same conclusion. "You left Vermont? Already?"

"Yeah," she said softly.

Just like that, my happy vibe collapsed. "Thanks for the warning."

There was a silence on the phone between us, and I wished I could claw back those ornery words. It wasn't that I minded being a little short with her. But by saying that, I'd made it painfully obvious that her leave-taking was harder on me than it was on her.

I preferred to nurse my wounds in private. What man didn't?

"BPG didn't need to keep me in Vermont anymore," she pointed out. "I already bought everything your neighbors will sell me. And since your guys are doing the deliveries, they don't need to pay to keep me in Vermont anymore."

Well, fuck. I wouldn't have agreed to those deliveries if I'd known it would come to this. "I get it," was all I said.

"You knew I was leaving. I can't believe they let me stay as long as they did. Don't tell me you're surprised, Griff."

I *was* surprised, though. I'd gotten used to having her at my side. And she didn't sound nearly as broken up about it as I'd hoped she would.

So that stunk.

A lot.

I cleared my throat. "Take care of yourself."

"You, too. Really."

And then there was nothing more to say. We hung up. I shoved my phone in my pocket and thought of my never-ending to-do list. Just like every day.

But without the possibility of seeing Audrey later, everything suddenly seemed like more work.

The week that followed seemed to go all wrong. A freakish afternoon hailstorm damaged some of my fruit. What would have been perfect organic Honeycrisps were pockmarked. I wouldn't be getting top price at the farmers' market anymore. I told Smithy that I didn't want to renew my lease, and then I sold off a dozen Jerseys to Mom's acquaintance from our church. That should have been a good thing, but Dylan moped and spent a long time saying goodbye to the cows. So I felt like a jerk.

Then the dairy complained about my reduced production, saying that they didn't want to truck out to my farm for the smaller amount. So I spent valuable harvest time calling around looking for a buyer for the rest of that herd.

"Why the long face?" my mother asked me on Thursday night. We were hosting the Abrahams for dinner, as we often did.

"Where's your girlfriend?" Isaac Abraham asked as he helped himself to another slice of Mom's famous apple cranberry pie. A couple of years ago when Isaac and Leah bought the farm down the road, we'd begun this tradition of hosting alternate Thursday night dinners. They were good people. They'd run away from the same weird religious cult that had kicked out Zach.

"She's, uh, in Boston," I said, not even bothering to correct him that she wasn't really my girlfriend. It had sure seemed like she was for a while there. "She's been there ten days already."

"But when's she coming back?" my mother pried, forcing me to admit to myself that I didn't think she ever would.

I shrugged like an idiot. *Thanks, Mom.*

My mother crossed her arms and gave me a glare. "August Griffin Shipley the third, I thought you were smarter than this."

"Than what?"

She shook her head. "If you care about that girl, why are you sitting here like a big lump? Go tell her."

Well, this was awkward. Isaac didn't even help. He just sat there with a weird smirk on his face.

"What?"

He grinned. "I knew when you fell for some girl, you'd fall hard. You've been mopey all week. Like a little teething baby."

"Who's a baby?" my sister May asked, sweeping her finger through the whipped cream on Isaac's slice of pie.

251

He moved it out of her reach. "Get your own. And the baby is your lovesick brother."

"Ah." May snickered. "The one person that keeps him happy left the state. We're all in trouble now."

They were, too.

Over the next several days my temper got shorter and shorter.

I gave Kyle a hard time over his system for organizing the cider barrels. It was a perfectly good system, but it wasn't *my* system. And if I got confused over what was what, the result would be a real mess.

"Fine!" he huffed, throwing up his hands. "I'll change it back to your way. But you don't have to be so combative."

"I AM NOT COMBATIVE!" I yelled.

Everyone within the vicinity laughed. It didn't help my mood.

Dylan got the worst of it one morning after I discovered he'd left the chicken coop open overnight. An opportunistic raccoon had eaten one of our best layers. Not only were we down a bird, but there were feathers and gore all over the place.

My brother's face was red when I finished my angry sermon. Then I made him clean up the mess. His eyes were shiny by the time he'd buried the remains. The punishment was worse than my rant. The kid liked animals more than any of us, and knowing he was responsible for the bird's gory death was hard enough. Dylan would probably be a vegetarian if his large and still-growing body didn't require five thousand calories a day.

Later in the day I apologized for going off on him, but he gave me an angry stare and stomped off.

Hell. He reminded me of myself.

Friday, Kyle decided that I needed a night out at the

Goat. I didn't see how that would lift my spirits any. But neither would it hurt. And Kyle deserved some fun after putting up with me all week, so I drove the two of us over there. Zach stayed behind to watch a movie with Jude and the twins.

The place was unusually crowded. It was leaf-peeping season, and some tourists had found our local watering hole, so the tables were filled. Kyle and I found seats at the bar.

"What'll it be?" Zara asked me, holding my gaze for a beat longer than I expected.

"Uh, a Long Trail."

"'Kay. And your sidekick?" she turned her attention to Kyle.

"I am not his sidekick."

"Uh-huh. You're your own man. Got it. What do you want to drink?"

"Well..." He eyed the taps.

"While I'm young?"

"I guess I'll have a Long Trail, too."

Chuckling, Zara poured our two beers. She served mine with a warm smile. I don't know what I did to deserve it, but if she'd decided to stop hating me, I wasn't going to complain.

Kyle and I drank our beer and talked about the new football season. We decided the Pats were going to have another great year. Right after I'd given up on football, it had bothered me to follow the teams too closely. I'd met a lot of my idols, and I'd pictured myself playing alongside them.

But football season coincided with harvest season, anyway. I'd been too busy to watch much football. Sunday afternoons always found me in the orchard, surrounded by tourists, selling a few thousand dollars' worth of product.

"Want to get tickets to a game next month?" Kyle asked. "I'll look at the schedule. Sundays don't work for you, but if we're lucky there'll be a Thursday night or a Monday game we could hit."

"Sure. Take a look." The idea of a road trip to Boston only made me think about Audrey, though. I found myself scanning the room for her, which was pointless. But hope springs eternal.

She wasn't here, of course. And there was no reason she should be.

Zara paused in front of us when our glasses got low. "Another round?" she offered.

"Sure," I said. "Thanks."

Kyle leaned forward on his bar stool and gazed up at Zara. "Mind if I ask what you're doing later?"

"Not you," she said, pouring his beer.

"I, uh, appreciate your honesty," Kyle said.

"No you don't." She winked at him. "But those college girls at the dartboard keep looking in your direction."

"In *my* direction," I said just to be an ass. I hadn't even noticed any girls by the dartboard.

Zara snorted. "Glad to know your ego is even bigger that your freakishly large head."

"Excuse me," Kyle said, standing up and running a hand through his hair. "I feel an urge to play darts."

"Go get 'em, big guy." Zara waved him off. She watched him go, then she looked down at me. "Got a second?"

"Sure?" Something in her frown made me pay attention.

She worried the bar cloth between her fingers in a nervous way that didn't seem like Zara. "There's something I need to tell you before you hear it as gossip and get the wrong idea."

"Okay?" Even though I felt a prickle of unease, I was unprepared for what she said next.

"Well, I'm nine weeks pregnant."

After I heard those words, the soundtrack of the bar did something odd. The chattering, happy voices and the rock tune on the sound system seemed to recede. As I stared up at Zara's worried face, I could only hear the *glug-glug* of my own pulse in my ears. Everything sort of ceased to reach me. Except for the big, awful word she'd just used.

Then Zara slapped my hand. Hard. "Jesus, Griff. Breathe. It's not yours. That's what I'm trying to tell you."

I inhaled on command, and the oxygen helped the rest of the room come back into focus. "Not..." I hesitated to even say it.

"Not yours. Do the math. Are you listening?"

I was, but all I'd heard was *pregnant*. "Are you sure?"

"Yes. Whatever you're asking, I'm sure. You know how this works—even if all your reproductive smarts come from breeding cows. The doctor can tell the, uh, timing. From a sonogram. And besides..." She swallowed. "You and I were careful."

The shameful expression on her face was what finally reunited me with my wits. "Hell, Zara. Are you okay?"

Her lip trembled, but then she seemed to pull herself together. "Sure. And thanks for asking. It took my brothers a lot longer to get around to asking that question. There was a lot of yelling."

Shit. "At *you*? That's not right. Do you need somewhere to go?"

She rolled her eyes. "No, Griff. I'm good. Really. It's just been a rough couple of weeks. Mom keeps crying, wondering where she went wrong. My brothers and my uncles are pissed at me because I won't say, um, who the father is. "

"You won't?"

She shook her head.

"Why not?"

Zara sighed. "Griff, you and I aren't going to have this conversation, either. It's *private*, okay? I have my reasons. The end."

I picked up my beer and drained it, trying to wrap my head around the weirdest conversation I'd had in a very long time.

"Shot of whiskey?" she offered, smiling down at me. I must look like a guy who needed one. And it was seriously tempted.

"No. I can't. I'm driving."

Her smile softened. "Responsible Griff. Saving the world one sober driver at a time. I could call you a cab, you know."

"Just promise me one thing," I said, beckoning her toward me.

She put her elbows on the bar and leaned close. "It's not yours," she whispered. "I'd tell you. I swear."

"No, I know you would." But that wasn't what I wanted to ask. "If things get too heated at home, you'll come visit us. Just take care of yourself."

Her face softened. "I'm fine, I promise. You know my family—we yell a lot. But then we get over it." She reached over and squeezed my hand, then let go just as quickly. "I have a question for you, too."

"What is it?"

She stood up tall and crossed her arms, so of course my eyes went right to her still-flat belly. Nothing to see there. "Eyes up here, mister." I complied. "You've been watching the door all evening. And Audrey hasn't come through it."

"She's in Boston," I said quickly. I didn't need another woman in my life grilling me about Audrey.

"Uh-huh. But let me just hit you with a hypothetical. What if she had walked in here tonight. And what if she sat right there." Zara pointed at Kyle's vacant seat. "And she said, 'Griffin, I'm pregnant.' I'm just curious. Do you still turn gray and nearly pass out on my bar?"

"I *did not* almost pass out," I corrected. "That's a damn lie."

"Right, tough guy." Zara's eyes twinkled. "But you didn't answer the question."

I hadn't answered it. Because my answer made me uncomfortable. The truth was that if Audrey told me she was knocked up, I'd...be ecstatic. *Jesus*. Where did that come from?

Maybe I needed that shot of whiskey after all.

"Miss?" A customer waved to Zara from the other end of the bar and she hurried over to pour a beer.

It should have been a relief to be left alone with my thoughts. But I couldn't shake off Zara's odd query. It seemed like bad juju to think about a pregnant Audrey. But since Zara brought it up, my brain wouldn't let go of the idea. And I'm pretty sure that Audrey wouldn't like all the ideas it gave me. I'd have to move her to Vermont and keep her close. And I wouldn't even feel guilty about the convenient way she'd have to give up her dream. For the sake of the child, right?

I snorted into my empty glass. Right. Selfish much?

My happiness all came down to a war between Audrey's big plans and mine. The conflict was irreconcilable. And even if I had some crazy notion of giving up my plans to chase after her, I couldn't do it. My family depended on me.

"Here." Zara reappeared in front of me and pushed a

glass in my direction. It contained birch beer, my go-to soda. "To all the big questions," she said, raising another glass of birch beer.

I touched my glass to hers. "And to your health."

She smiled as we each took a sip of our non-alcoholic libations. "I miss beer."

"I'll bet. You feel okay?"

"Mostly. I'm tired, is all. But who isn't, right?"

I watched Zara lift her chin in that proud way she had, looking down her strong, aquiline nose at me. She was striking. Beautiful even. And I'd never felt about her or anyone else the way I felt about Audrey.

Damn, I was in so much trouble.

"I can practically hear your gears grinding," Zara said, sipping her soda.

"Lots to think about. All of it complicated."

"Like any other day," she pointed out. "When are you seeing Audrey again?"

"No idea."

Zara rolled her eyes. "Well that's just stupid of you. And unfortunate for the rest of us. She softens your edges. Makes you tolerable. She didn't move to *Mars*, right?"

"During harvest, it might as well be Mars."

"So send her a present. Make her understand that you're thinking about her. You never know how things will end up with her. Maybe in three months she's done with that job. Things change, you know."

"I guess."

"He *guesses*." She wiped the bar. "Or you can sit there and brood. You're good at it. I always fall for the broody ones." She gave me a sad grin.

I wondered which broody guy had accidentally become the father of her future child. But I held back the question. "Hey, by the way?"

"Yeah?"

"I'm sorry if I let you down."

Her rag paused on the wooden surface. She raised her big, dark eyes to mine. "I appreciate you saying that. But you never broke any promises to me."

"Sure, but..." I cleared my throat, uncomfortable. "I can be an uptight jerk."

The smile she gave me was a knowing one. "Saving the world takes a lot of your energy, Griff. I get it. I *was* pissed at you, too. I had this dumb idea that you looked down on me. That you were this football-playing chemist who wanted to fool around with the townie until he found somebody from the right social strata."

"Hey...!"

She held up a hand. "I know, okay? I get it now. You and I have known each other our whole lives, but I still had it all backward. The truth is that we're too much *alike*. When I saw you with Audrey, I got it. It wasn't about me. You two just *fit*. She's flighty and cute and silly, and you two balance each other out. Now I get to watch her make you crazy." Chuckling to herself, she moved down the bar to fill another order.

Zara, man. Who knew she could scramble my head two or three times in ninety minutes? I watched her down the bar, chatting up customers, doling out advice like only a bartender could.

That got me thinking about her advice to me. *Send Audrey a present*, she'd said. It was a gesture of the kind that I never really considered. Maybe I wasn't the world's most romantic guy. But a gesture was a neat idea. The trouble was that I didn't know what to give her. Audrey had told me in passing that chefs didn't wear jewelry. So that age-old gift wasn't going to work. Besides, I didn't trust my taste in bling. What did a chef need, anyway?

I sat there thinking up ideas and rejecting them just as quickly. As if I knew a thing about kitchen gear. And none of it was very romantic.

Except...

When the answer came to me, I yanked my phone out of my back pocket and started tapping on it like mad. "Hey Zara," I said as she passed by. "You still have a laptop back there?"

"Yeah. Why?"

"I need to do a little online shopping."

She handed over the laptop with a chuckle. "Good luck. Pick something nice."

"It will probably be used," I said, opening up the computer.

"That doesn't sound romantic."

"Trust me." I navigated to Ebay.

"Don't blow it, Griff," she said kindly. "Go big, you know? Do or die. There is no try."

I eyed her over the top of the screen. "You just butchered that quote. Yoda is rolling over in his grave."

Zara gave me a smirk. "Yoda would approve of the sentiment. Now make it happen."

I turned back to my work, humming to myself. The *Star Wars* theme, of course.

* * *

An hour later I left Kyle in the clutches of one of the college girls. One of his new female friends would drop him home later.

Either that or he'd text me in the morning begging a ride home from God knows where.

I drove home feeling more contemplative than usual. And when I got out of the truck alone, Jude was sitting on the stoop of the bunkhouse, his chin balanced on his fists.

"Everything okay?" I asked, sitting beside him.

"Sure. I still don't fall asleep very easily. But when I do sleep, it's better than it used to be."

"That sounds like progress."

He shrugged. "If my cravings went away, that would be progress. But tonight was all right."

"Was it? Good meeting?"

"They're never *good*. It's not like I walk out of there feeling like superman. But lately I feel...solid. Like I'm not going to wreck myself by morning. And—hey—have you been to that gelato shop in Hanover?"

"What? No."

"Now there's something to live for. I took May there to thank her for driving me tonight. The dark chocolate hazelnut flavor could make a guy believe in God."

I laughed, because I don't think I'd ever heard Jude talk so much at once. "I'll have to remember to try it. You can show me the place after the Hanover market sometime."

He fiddled with his hands. "How long are you going to keep me on, anyway? By my calculations you'll be all picked out in ten days. Maybe two weeks."

Shit, could that be right? Harvest season was such a crazy time for me that when it ended I was always a little taken aback. But he was right. By Halloween, the bulk of it was done. Although now things were going to be a little different. "This year I'm going to have to press and barrel everything twice as fast." When I wasn't trying to produce six thousand extra bottles, I took my time. "I'd feel better with an extra set of hands around, at least until the middle of November."

It's not like I'd figured an extra paycheck into my November budget. But I really could use the help.

"You know I'll stay as long as you let me," Jude said

gruffly. "Don't want to go back to Colebury. That place gives me the willies. But my dad owns an auto-body shop. If he hasn't run it into the ground these past three years, I can probably pick up some hours there. It's not like anyone else will hire me."

I couldn't even imagine the tough spot he was in. Life was hard enough without a criminal record. "You gonna be okay?"

"Do I have a choice?" He laughed, but it sounded bitter. "I dunno. Didn't think I could make it this far. I've been clean for sixty days. So that's something."

"You're tough," I said, and meant it. "And you must be feeling stronger now. All this extra muscle." I gave his shoulder a friendly shove.

"It's all the good food," he said. "My appetite is back, finally. Speaking of which... How are *your* withdrawal symptoms?"

I grunted. "What do you mean?"

"Audrey's been gone a while now. What's your strategy?"

"Don't exactly have one. I'd like to try to get her to consider making things permanent. But..."

"But what? Worst she could say is no."

I wasn't sure that was the worst thing that could happen. "When I was almost exactly her age, I was trying to make it in professional football."

"No shit? I knew you played, though. All those trophies in the TV room."

I snorted. "Mom won't let me throw 'em away. I got drafted. Snuck on to a practice squad, but just barely. I wasn't ready to throw in the towel, though. I had a plan. That's when my dad died from a heart attack."

"Sucks," Jude said. "So you didn't get your chance."

"Honestly, I don't know if I'm any worse off. I could have tried and failed. It's okay now. But Audrey might get her shot, you know? I don't want to fuck that up by tying her down to the same farm that's got me pinned here."

"Huh." Jude was quiet for a minute. "I used to have someone, too. I thought she and I were forever. But it turns out I loved drugs more than anyone. Even myself."

Ouch. "You don't love 'em so much as you used to. Maybe she's still out there."

He shook his head. "I killed her brother."

"Oh."

"Yeah. That ship has sailed. But they tell us at rehab that if you want to be happy again, you have to truly accept the things that aren't ever happening. Everybody has their shit to get over. Like, I'm never having parents that give a fuck about me. And I can't unkill the guy who died in my car. It doesn't matter how bad it is, you have to really accept it before it eats you up."

"So..." I rubbed the back of my neck. "I guess I have to get over Audrey."

"No, dude." Jude turned to face me in the dark. "Your shit is that you're saddled with this farm, and that it cost you some choices."

"I accepted that a long time ago. I love this place."

"Challenge," Jude argued. "If you were really over it, then you wouldn't feel guilty about asking Audrey to move up here. You're making the decision for her. Isn't that the same thing her bitch of a mom does?"

Fuck me, it was.

"If you don't offer her the choice, she won't know you care. And if you *do* ask, she might still say no. Maybe that's why you don't want to ask the question."

Jesus. He was the second person tonight to hint that I was gutless. It wasn't true, though. "Lots to think about. I'm going to bed," I said, standing up.

"You're not gonna fire me for saying that, right?"

"No, asshole," I nudged his ass with my boot. "Goodnight."

"'Night!"

I went to bed wondering how to talk to Audrey. And marveling at the fact that a recovering addict and felon was my second-best employee. And that a guy who hadn't had sex for three years just schooled me on my relationship woes.

Part Three

October

After a good dinner one can forgive anybody, even one's own relatives.

–Oscar Wilde

Chapter Twenty-Four

Audrey

Another Friday. Another long shift in another jerk's kitchen.

This chef didn't know my name, but he wasn't shy about ordering me around. "Prep girl! A dozen eggs. Separated."

Yes sir! Right away, sir! I got the eggs out of the walk-in and got to work.

When that was done, I brought him two bowls—one of yolks and one of whites—and he peered into each one with suspicion before ordering me to do something else. "First wipe down the salad sink. Then check everyone's station for herbs."

If I followed his commands in that order, I'd have to clean the salad sink twice. But I knew better than to point out his error. "Yes, chef."

I did it his way, because he signed the checks. But there was no joy in it.

This job, though, was exactly what I'd wanted from BPG since I'd signed on with them in May. So why were the days so freaking long?

At least they couldn't keep me here until late at night. Mosaic was a breakfast and lunch spot across the street from the contemporary art museum. It was the sort of place frequented by Ladies Who Lunch. The menu was high quality but a little boring. Or maybe that was just me. I'd already spent six hours sectioning blood oranges and mincing parsley. I trimmed scallions for quiche and rinsed baby lettuces for eighteen-dollar salads.

The pay was decent due to BPG's labor agreement with its workforce. They weren't allowed to stuff their kitchens with underpaid interns, which was good because I needed the money. All my travel expenses from my weeks in Vermont were on my credit card, and BPG had been slow to reimburse them. At least once a day I called the travel department to check up on them, and was always told that they were "in process."

Meanwhile, I still owed two hundred bucks to my pothead roommate, Jack. And since Jack worked at Mosaic, too, he reminded me. Hourly. So I picked up as many extra shifts as they'd give me, and I worked my tail off. And in the evenings I wrote out menus in my notebooks at home. The contest was one week away. I'd decided to pitch a tapas restaurant. I'd made sketches of the food and of the restaurant and taken notes about the neighborhood and its traffic patterns.

For once in my life, I was going to make a serious run at something. Whatever happened, they wouldn't be able to laugh me out of the room. If I lost, I'd lose knowing I'd done my absolute best.

One bright spot in the otherwise boring grind of my work-and-then-work-some-more existence was that BPG chefs all over town were praising the produce I'd purchased in Vermont. There had been a total of four weekly shipments now. My email address was on all of the packing slips. To my utter shock, I'd begun receiving gracious notes of thanks from the chefs who received this bounty. "Gorgeous zucchini flowers!" one of them had crowed. "I can use all you find of these. I'm stuffing them with fois gras."

Another chef—a Frenchman—wrote to say that he'd used sweet corn in a dish for the first time in his career.

"Maize is food for cattle in my country. But this is so sweet I made it into a roulade."

That felt damn good. And now there were several BPG chefs who knew my name. That and a couple of bucks would get me a ride on the T.

Today was Friday, so someone from the Shipley clan would be making another delivery. I spent every Friday feeling a little crazy, looking into the driver's seat of every passing truck. But the man I was looking for never appeared.

It had occurred to me that if I asked him to make the delivery himself and then meet me for dinner that he might be able to swing it. But then what? He'd get back in his truck and go back to Vermont. And in another few weeks the Friday deliveries would stop for the winter. Maybe forever.

Right. *Back to work, princess.*

I was sectioning yet another dozen blood oranges when the restaurant manager sidled up, smelling like an ashtray. "Want to work tomorrow morning?" he asked. "You're not on the schedule 'til Tuesday, but I'm a little short."

"Sure," I said automatically.

He went away without saying thank you. And then his spot was taken by Jack. "I need the zest of twenty lemons."

"Then you need to say please," I snapped.

"And also two hundred bucks."

"*God.* Save it. I know, okay? If BPG ever refunds my hotel bill, I'll give it to you."

"It's been *months*, Audrey."

"No kidding. But do you want me to pay it to you out of my rent money? I really don't think you do."

He chuckled. "If you win the Green Light project next week, I might have to raise your rent."

"You do that." *If I win next week, I will move out.* Duh.

"What are you entering? From your drawings it looks like tapas."

Fuck. "That's just a draft." I should have kept my notes better hidden.

He clicked his tongue. "You don't have to bullshit me. I'm too lazy to enter. But I know you're not lazy, so I'm sure you've been kissing ass in the C-suite all month. You probably have that shit locked up already. Everyone knows Burton always feeds the winner his entry."

"He..." I put down my knife. "What?"

Jack grabbed one of the orange wedges I'd prepped. After looking over both shoulders for management, he popped it in his mouth. "You know. The Burtons are like any boss, anywhere. They want their own bullshit fed back to them, so they can feel validated. Whatever idea they gave you, I'm sure you'll make it shine. But I'd wear a low-cut top just to be safe." He stole another orange wedge and walked away.

I stood there, weighed down by horror. Jack wasn't the sharpest knife in the block. But I didn't doubt he was right.

Why hadn't I realized the showdown would be rigged? Had I not lived twenty years under the roof of one of the most conniving businesspeople to ever grace the planet?

For one awful second I actually considered calling my mother. That's how badly I wanted to win the competition. It entered my mind that Mommy might know what Burton wanted to see on the design board next week.

But the urge fled as quickly as it had appeared. If she helped me, I'd regret it for the rest of my life. The whole point of entering was to open a restaurant without her help.

Not like she'd help me, anyway. We hadn't even spoken since the showdown in Griff's tasting room. I hated myself a little for noticing, too. I'd told her to get out of my life, and she'd finally done it.

But why did I mind so much?

I took my carefully trimmed orange slices to the salad guy and fetched two-dozen lemons. The job required a lot of concentration, because the zester loved nothing more than to remove a layer of my skin whenever I wasn't paying attention. I picked up the first lemon and began to work. Shave and turn. Shave and turn. Perfect curls of bright yellow peel landed on the clean cutting board. I tried to slip into my zen place, where efficient work with my hands could set the world to rights again.

The dishwashers were having an animated discussion of the Patriots' chances. The sous chef was dressing down a waiter over a mistimed order.

Just another day at the office.

So imagine my utter surprise when somebody barked, "Princess! You back here somewhere?"

My head snapped up, and I saw the most unlikely thing in the world. Griffin Shipley was standing in the doorway to the kitchen, his tanned face practically gleaming with health. He was wearing a nice button-down shirt and khakis. But even city clothes couldn't disguise the truth. People who spend their days outside are more beautiful than the pasty kitchen rats I spent my days with. I missed Vermont and the happy faces of his family and the scent of all that fresh air.

It took me a second to gather my wits and then say something brilliant. "Uh, hi?"

"You working? They told me at headquarters that

you'd be done about now."

I looked at the clock. I should be done now. Lemons be damned. "Right. Give me three minutes." I gathered up the lemons and brought my cutting board over to Jack. "I'm taking off on time today. Have fun with the zesting."

"What? Bitch, you cannot leave me hanging. What is this shit?"

I patted him on the shoulder. "Punching out. Catch you later."

When I reached Griffin, he bent down and put a soft kiss on my nose. "What if I took you to Vermont for the weekend?"

"Wow." The offer was unexpected. But there was no chance in hell I'd turn him down. "How would I get back?"

"I'd drive you. Monday, maybe?"

Could I just take off with Griff like that? "I'd need to stop by my place and grab a few things."

"Then let's go."

I yanked my hairnet off. Because those aren't sexy. And I took off my baggy chef's jacket.

"Don't do that," Griffin growled. "I'm having a French culinary fantasy right now. Later you can wear that with nothing underneath." I snorted, but he shook his head. "I'm not even joking."

I gave him a shove on the chest. "You've got it bad."

"Maybe I do."

My neck got hot all of a sudden. This conversation had veered in a strange direction. "Let me punch out."

"I'm right behind you."

In the back hall I got my purse out of my locker and dealt with my time card.

"See you tomorrow," the manager called from the end of the hallway.

"Wait!" I chased him down. I'd already forgotten about the shift tomorrow. "I can't fill in tomorrow. I made a mistake. Sorry."

His eyes protruded. "But you said you would! I'm in a jam here."

"We spoke a half hour ago. So I'm sure you'll find someone else. See you Tuesday morning."

"You can't...!"

I pulled Griff out the back door into the warm autumn afternoon. "God, it's nice out. I forget sometimes."

"There aren't any windows in there," Griff pointed out. "How can you stand it?"

Most commercial kitchens were windowless. "That's not even bad. You should see some of the dungeons I've worked in. You get used to it."

I expected him to argue, but he said, "The truck is over here."

* * *

An hour later we were leaving Boston on 93, my hastily packed duffel on the back seat.

In my dingy little room in Jack's apartment, Griff hadn't said much. But I could read the disapproval on his face. "It's ugly, but I don't spend much time here."

"I know you're saving up for your own place," he'd said, squeezing my shoulders. "How's that going?"

Badly. "Fine."

I'd brought my notebooks with me, just to keep them away from Jack. I didn't trust him.

The first part of the car ride was a bit too quiet, as I tried to figure out what to say. This excursion was a weekend booty call plain and simple. But I'd left Vermont rather abruptly, and it weighed between us.

"Hey," I said, reaching to cover his hand with mine on the steering wheel. "How did you know I'd be free to go out of town this weekend?"

"Didn't," he said. "Until I made the drop-off and called corporate headquarters asking for you. They pulled up some schedule on a computer and told me where you were working, and that if I needed to speak to you I'd better hurry, because you weren't on the schedule tomorrow. So I drove over there quick."

"I'm glad you did."

He stole a glance at me, as if trying to decide whether I meant it.

"Griff, I'm sorry I left last month without saying goodbye."

His eyes cut toward mine for a fractional second before returning to the road. "That wasn't nice, princess."

"I know." I cleared my throat. "It was the middle of a work day, and I *hate* big goodbyes."

"Don't we all." Silence fell again, and I thought it might swallow us whole. But then he began to tell me how well his mom's ankle was healing, and I listened as he went on with other farm gossip and trivia. Daphne and Dylan were at war over naming the new rooster. Jude had his mind blown by the new *Star Wars* movie, released while he was in prison. I laughed, and he reached over to give my knee a squeeze. And it felt so good that I forgot to be tense.

Two and a half hours after leaving the city limits, we bumped along the road toward his farm, the windows down. I felt like someone who'd been let out of jail. For the whole ride I'd been sneaking glances at Griff's face or watching his big hands on the steering wheel. After thinking about him so often for a couple of weeks, it was odd to finally sit beside him. My palms got sweaty and I felt as tongue-tied as a seventh-grader at her first middle school dance.

"So," I said as he turned onto the gravel drive. "What are your plans for this weekend?"

He turned to me with a look so hot that it could have been used to brown up the top of a creme brûlée. "We could go out to dinner, but that's more time on the road. I'd want to take you somewhere nice. I don't want to hit the Goat tonight."

I was afraid to know why. Had he started things up with Zara again?

Griff parked the truck, shut off the engine and turned to me. "Do you mind having dinner with the family?"

"No," I said quickly. "I love your family."

The word *love* slipped out a little too firmly. Maybe Griff noticed it, too. Because he gave me the sweetest smile. "Okay, princess. Then we'll eat out tomorrow night."

His laser gaze was doing things to me—filling my belly with nervous butterflies. So I opened the truck's door. "What shall we do before dinner, hot stuff? I think there's still enough light to butcher something."

He let out a bark of laughter and got out of the truck. "I really know how to impress the ladies, don't I?"

"Well, it was original."

Griff came around the truck and took my hand. "The cider apples are starting to ripen up. You want to see them?"

"Of course I do." I squeezed his hand. "Show me, Farmer Griff."

Chuckling, he walked me toward the line of trees that began beyond the tractor shed. "You know how I sometimes get all spun up over the price of produce?"

"How could I forget?"

"Right. I'm going to show you some apples that are actually priceless."

"So I shouldn't offer you a dollar a pound?"

He pinched my ass. "When I say priceless, I'm not kidding. These are apples you can't buy on the open market. They just aren't for sale."

"Why?"

"For decades nobody planted any of the old cider varieties. There were trees here and there in peoples' farmyards. But there was no commercial market for them, so everybody planted dessert apples. *Dessert* is what we call—"

"—the kind everybody eats."

"Right. And even with grafting, it takes a few years to get fruit. So although cider has made a big comeback in this country, there aren't enough bittersweet apples to go around. If I were willing to pay a hundred bucks a bushel, I still couldn't get bittersweets. So these trees are my babies."

"How many babies do you have?"

"About a thousand."

We passed a sign that made me laugh. DO NOT PICK. NON-EDIBLE FRUIT. "So you're using scare tactics? You should have Dylan draw you a picture of the evil queen offering an apple to Snow White."

He snorted. "It wouldn't even help. I'll bet you ten bucks I'm chasing people out of here tomorrow."

I paused after we'd walked a ways up the row. "What am I looking at?" In this part of the orchard every tree had a metal tag hanging from a low branch. Like an overgrown dog tag, with three digits. "What is tree number one-twelve?"

"One-twelve means an Ashmead's Kernel. That's a tasty apple. Want to try one?"

"I want to try the weirdest cider apple you've got."

He grinned. "Are you sure about that? Bittersweets can be pretty intense."

"Hit me." How weird could an apple be?

"You've been warned." He took my hand again and led me between the trees into the next row. After a couple minutes' walk, we arrived in front of a tree bearing the number forty-four. It was loaded down with pale yellow apples. "This variety is called White Norman. My dad planted them when he was my age, because he needed some tannic apples to fill out his blends. A good cider has between five and twenty percent bittersweet juice from something like this." He plucked one off the tree and handed it to me.

The twinkle in his eye should have been a warning. But I'd never had a cautious palate, so I took a big old bite and chewed. The texture was...

Fuck the texture. My mouth was suddenly full of the most bitter, vile flavor I'd ever known. *Oh my God.* I chewed faster, hoping to choke it down as fast as possible. But that only made it worse.

Griffin was chuckling now. "Just spit it out, baby. Everybody does."

I turned away from him and hawked the entire mouthful into the grass. Then I spit again just for good measure. The only other sound was Griff's laughter.

Turning around, I wiped my mouth in the crook of an elbow and struggled to regain my dignity while Griff's great body shook with hysteria. "Enough," I grumbled. "You had your fun." Even now I swallowed hard, still trying to scrape that stubborn flavor off my tongue. It wasn't working. "*Quick.* Give me a better apple."

But Griff solved the problem a different way. He stepped close and pulled me into his arms. Then, chuckling, he gave me his mouth. And all at once I was overwhelmed by a different set of sensations. The familiar brush of his beard against my face, and his firm, full lips pressing against mine. I relaxed instinctively, welcoming him in. His bossy tongue invaded my mouth, and the bitter apple was long forgotten. There was only the pull of his mouth and the soul-deep grunt that rose from his chest when I responded to his kiss.

My hands explored the unfamiliar crinkle of a dress shirt over his broad ribcage. I had to stand on tiptoe to get my arms around him properly. It had been way too long since we'd touched, and I wanted to scale him like a tree and reacquaint myself with the strength of his limbs.

With a groan, Griff cupped my ass and squeezed. He lifted me against his body, bringing my core into contact with the evidence of his enthusiasm for my visit to Vermont. I ground against him to get closer, and he moaned into my mouth.

Hell. We were going to end up naked beneath one of these trees in under a minute if things escalated any further.

Fine with me.

I wound my fingers into his hair and kissed him as hard as I could.

His hand wandered under the hem of my skirt and I whimpered like an eager puppy.

"Hey, Griff!" It was Zach's voice.

He tried to pull away to save my dignity. But I wasn't having it. One more kiss...

"Griff! I think we— *Shit*. Sorry. Never mind." Zachariah retreated in a hurry.

But the damage was done. Griff and I quit mauling each other. I was left panting, my face tucked against his shirt, his hand clutched possessively around the back of my neck. The hum of expectation still sizzled between us, but it would have to wait.

I made an effort at conversation. "What shall we do tomorrow?"

"More of that," he rumbled.

I gave him a little pinch. "Besides that. It's Saturday. You'll be slammed, right?"

He gave a little growl and kissed my forehead. "Hopefully in more ways than one."

"Can I help?"

"Who else?"

I slapped his ass. "You know what I mean."

"Sure." He chuckled. "This place is going to be overrun with customers. So either we work or we get the hell out of here."

"You can't just leave, right?"

"Not easily," he admitted, easing back to get a look at my face. "But I don't get many hours with you. So maybe it's time to call in some favors."

"We can sell apples and then go out somewhere together."

He caught my chin in his hand and smiled. "Deal. You angling to drive the horses?"

"Hell no. But I could pour cider for tourists. That sounds like fun. Who doesn't like pouring free drinks?"

He grabbed my hand. "Come see my new tanks."

"I'll bet you say that to all the girls."

"It's my best line," he promised. "Come on. Walk with me."

We strolled down along the hillside together, making a detour to look at the Green Mountain range in the distance.

When we finally arrived at the cider house, Griff's new toys did not disappoint. Along one wall of his cider house stood three gleaming metal fermentation tanks.

"Wow! You must have tripled your capacity here."

"Almost. Aren't they shiny? I'll never own a sports car; I figure this is as close as I'm going to get."

The metal felt warm under my hand. "This one is full, right?"

"Yeah."

"Did you turn in your contest entry?"

"Of course."

I turned to him. "Did you enter the sexy cider?"

"Of course I did." He grinned. "I got some other people to taste it first. And nobody mentioned sex, but everyone liked it. Hang on..." He crossed to a shelf crammed with notebooks and took down the second-to-last one. He flipped its pages until he found what he was looking for. "Here's what people said: *Complicated. Earthy and edgy. Volatile. Unpredictable. Notes of mushroom and salt...*" His eyes lifted to mine. "*Sweaty and euphoric.*"

I giggled. "Wow."

"Yeah. They came close but they couldn't quite place it." He winked.

"Where are you going to display the trophy?" I looked around.

He shrugged. "I'm doing this for bragging rights." The dinner bell rang, and Griff tipped his head toward the sound. "You ready to face the masses?"

"Always."

Griff crooked his elbow toward me. "Come on, then. You're my dinner date."

* * *

I'd wondered if Griff's family would find my appearance surprising. But as we walked into the kitchen door, May simply said, "Audrey, come 'ere.

We're having a debate about the cranberry sauce. Orange zest, or no?"

"I'm a purist," I admitted. "I like it plain. A little sugar and nothing else. Are these your own cranberries?" I took the handle of the spoon and gave the bright red sauce a stir. "Beautiful."

"Nothing else is that color, right?" Dylan agreed. "It's the reddest of reds."

"Hi honey," Griff's mother said, as if I popped in every night. "We're having turkey with our own potatoes. It's simple but..."

"Perfect," I said quickly. Sometimes being a chef meant that others justified their food choices to you. Chefs ate Pringles sometimes, too. Not every meal can be a culinary adventure.

The food turned out wonderfully, of course. Ruthie Shipley was a very competent cook. She stuck close to the classic flavors, but her turkey was moist and juicy, the potatoes creamy, the wilted spinach dancing in garlic and olive oil. I ate plenty. And, throughout the meal, Griff held my hand under the table whenever he could.

It was dreamy, really. And yet the whole experience made me feel a little heartsick. The World of Griffin Shipley was a place I could visit from time to time, though I was always faced with leaving again. I looked around the table at all the faces shining in the candlelight. The twins. Kyle. Jude, looking even broader and healthier than the last time I'd seen him. Zachariah, as golden and smiling as always. Griff's grandpa, gnawing on a giant turkey drumstick which he held in two greasy hands. Ruthie, laughing at her daughter May's impersonation of a farmers' market customer.

This is *why* people cooked food—to create the perfect

meal for a table like this—for people gathering together. In the kitchens where I worked, you couldn't see the results of the labor. It was hidden from view.

Culinary school had taught me to create the food for the food's sake. But that was never supposed to be the point.

"You okay, princess?" Griff gave my knee a squeeze under the table.

"Never better," I replied. And it was the truth.

"Do you mind if we dine and dash?" May, standing up at the end of the meal. "Jude's meeting starts in forty-five minutes."

Ruth waved her daughter on. "Drive safely."

Jude, quiet as usual, cleared his plate, too. The two of them disappeared.

The rest of us had pie. It was my first taste of Ruth's legendary apple and cranberry pie, and I loved it. "Wow. The whole-wheat crust is amazing."

"I do love a whole-wheat crust," the cook said shyly.

"It's...nutty," I agreed. "This is terrific. I'd ask you for the recipe but I've seen you cook."

Griff's mother laughed. "I haven't measured ingredients since 1980."

Eventually, Kyle and Zach headed out, too. Their destination—The Mountain Goat. We were all in the kitchen scraping plates and loading the two identical dishwashers when Kyle asked, "You two coming with us for beers?"

"You go ahead," Griff said quickly. "I have a present for Audrey."

"Is that what we're calling it these days?" Kyle teased.

Griff gave him a shove. "Get lost already."

After they departed, he topped off our wine glasses and picked them up. "Come with me, princess." He headed toward the back door.

"Night, Audrey!" Dylan called cheerfully.

"Uh, night." I felt heat crawl up my neck. I followed Griffin out the back door.

We were alone again. Pebbles crunched under our feet, and a half moon had just broken over the horizon, lighting the way. I followed Griffin in silence, enjoying the stillness of the night. We stopped beside his truck, where I pulled my duffel bag off the back seat. Griff traded me a glass of wine for my bag and carried it for me.

Even gruff farmers can be gentlemen.

When we got to the bunkhouse, he held open the door, then kicked off his shoes on the mat.

I copied him and followed him into his room, my pulse elevated by nervous anticipation. Was I going to sleep with Griffin, even if it made me wistful later?

Of course I was.

Griff set my bag on the floor. He took a sip of his wine, then sat down on the corner of his bed. "So, I got you a little something. It's just a silly thing, but I wanted you to have it." He nodded toward the window, where I saw a wrapped gift on his desk.

He'd called it a little thing. But this gift was bigger than a breadbox. I crossed the room and put a hand on the polka-dot wrapping paper. There was even a matching bow. "Nice wrapping job," I teased, but my voice came out a little shaky. Griff got me a *present?* What the hell?

"Well, my sisters helped me wrap it." His dark eyes held mine, and their expression was so serious that I didn't know what to say or do. It was as if I were being tested somehow, but I wasn't sure what for. "Open it already."

I set down my glass and tugged off the ribbon, which

fell in a satiny pile onto the old wooden desk. I tore the folded ends of the wrapping paper and removed it, revealing a plain cardboard box. With a fizz of nervous anticipation in my chest, I opened the top and looked down into the box. And what I saw there made my breath catch.

An Easy-Bake Oven—the old kind, like I'd had as a child. The little metal cake pan was tucked into the side of the box, too. I slid it out and balanced it on my hands. "Oh my God! Where did you find this?"

"Ebay." Griff gave me a shy grin. "It's the model they were selling in 2002. I hope it looks familiar."

"It's..." I lifted it out of the box and hugged it to my chest. "My God, it's perfect. This is *so cool*." I set it down on the desk and opened the little oven door. And it was like looking into my whole life. I remember learning how to unmold a cake so that it was centered on the plate. And how to decorate one with a paper cone and icing. Weirdly, I'd done those things in my bedroom to escape the wrath of the kitchen staff and the prying eyes of my babysitter.

Maybe it's pathetic, but I remembered those hours as the best of my childhood. For once in my life I'd been doing something that interested me and only me. Nobody had graded me. Nobody had cared if I succeeded. It was just *fun*.

I looked into the box one more time and found the cake lifting tool—like a spatula, sort of, but it fit around the edges of the pan. The way it felt in my hand was as familiar as breathing. "Griff," I said, my throat constricting. "If I've ever said that you're no fun, I was wrong."

And now my damn eyes were wet.

"Aw." He was there in an instant, hugging me.

With the spatula still in my hand, I wrapped my

arms around him. He felt so good. He *was* so good. Damn it. I *loved* this man.

How ridiculously inconvenient. My traitorous heart only wanted things it couldn't have. It had a perfect record.

Griffin kissed me on the head. "I'm glad you like it. I just wanted you to know something."

"What?" I gasped.

"That I get it. Becoming a chef—a real one—it's important to you. I wouldn't ever try to talk you out of it, or ask you to give it up. But I wish things were easier. Because I'd really like to have you here with me."

"You would?" I pulled out of his grasp, because I wasn't sure I'd heard correctly.

He looked down at me as if maybe I was a little slow. "Yeah, baby. I don't know if you noticed, but we're a good fit. I miss you. All the time."

"You…" I pointed the cake-lifter at the center of his chest, as if asking him to hold still. My brain would not wrap itself around this conversation. "You can't just *say* stuff like that," I sputtered. "It's confusing."

Griffin just grinned. "You want me to stop talking?"

"Yes, please."

"Suit yourself."

A split second later, he gripped my hips and lifted me. Startled, I dropped my cake-lifter onto the rug, where it made a soft thud. Griffin turned, depositing me in the middle of his big bed. Then he covered me with his body and began to kiss my neck.

I shivered immediately. Griff's mouth was alternately soft and demanding as he tongued and then sucked at my tender skin. When he'd said we were a good fit, he wasn't wrong. Whenever this man touched me, I always melted like a stick of butter in a warm saucepan—first softening slowly, and then puddling all at once under his touch. As he kissed his way into the neckline of my shirt, I relaxed beneath him. And when he nosed into the cup of my bra, I gave a whimper.

He chuckled. "Is it talking too much if I tell you I need this gone?" He tugged on my bra.

With shaky hands I fumbled with my bra strap. When it gave way, I sighed with relief.

Griffin lifted my top over my head, extracting me from it. "Fuck, yeah." He tossed my bra away, too. Dropping his head, he nosed across my bust, his beard tickling me. The roughened pad of one thumb caressed a nipple, and I moaned loudly.

With a happy grunt, he took one nipple into his mouth and sucked. It was so good that I arched my back for more.

This man would be the death of me. There was nothing he had that I didn't want more of.

Chapter Twenty-Five

Griffin

I'd never made love to anyone. Great sex was something I'd experienced many times. But as I methodically kissed away every one of Audrey's defenses, it occurred to me that this was the first time I'd ever tried to show someone how I really 'felt about her.

Words were not my strong suit. My whole life I'd been told I was too blunt. Too gruff. But I'd done well enough at telling Audrey how I felt.

Then she told me to shut up.

But that was okay, because I knew I'd gotten through. I saw it in her eyes and in the joy on her face when she'd opened that box. And now I had one more way to show her the way things really were between us.

I was right where I wanted to be—on top of my girl. Her eyes were heavy-lidded, her face flushed. Nobody else put that color on her cheeks. It was all my doing. Maybe words weren't my best tool, but I had others at my disposal.

Kissing my way down her body, she squirmed as I reached the top edge of her skirt's waistband. Teasing her now, I left a trail of kisses across her smooth tummy. I loved the sugar-salt taste of her skin.

But Audrey was impatient with me now. She sat up and reached for the buttons of my shirt, then let out a frustrated huff when she couldn't really get to them.

"What do you need, princess?" I whispered. I rose to

my hands and knees in front of her and began to remove my shirt. "Is this it?"

By the time I tossed my shirt aside, Audrey's sweet fingers had already begun to slide across my body. They measured me. They took stock. She must have liked what she found because she rose up tall on her knees and kissed me, her naughty fingers plunging down to pop the button on my trousers.

At the first brush of her fingers at my waist, I throbbed for her. And when she lowered my zipper, I actually had to grit my teeth against a sudden surge of anticipation.

The rest of our clothes came off at record speed. Then I was holding Audrey against me, skin to skin. She fit perfectly in my arms, and I had to take a deep breath and remind myself to go slow. So I eased her off my body for a moment and pulled down the covers on the bed.

Audrey cooperated, slipping underneath the quilt and sheet. I turned her on her side, facing away from me, and curled up around her body. Whenever I lay here alone in this bed, wishing for her, my fantasy looked just like this. Tonight it was real. I snaked an arm around her waist and held her close. My impatient dick was like a fencepost against her back, but it was going to have to wait a minute.

She relaxed her body, lifting her chin to give me a smile. "This is nice," she said.

"Mmm-hmm."

"Although," she said in a small voice. "I can think of some ways it could be even nicer."

I smiled into her silky hair. "Patience, princess."

"Just sayin'."

I laughed, and so did she. But then she reached around behind her body and gave my dick an eager stroke. The sudden contact made me curse under my breath. So much for patience.

She did it again, the little vixen.

I gave her sweet ass a friendly slap. "If that's how you want to play it, put your hands on my headboard."

She moved as fast as I'd ever seen her move, including in the kitchen. And now I had definitive proof that the view of Audrey Kidder's hands on the wooden frame of my bed was the finest sight in the world. Her hair hung down her bare back, so I wound it around my hand. When I gave it a gentle tug, she whimpered.

I fit my body behind hers. She pushed her hips back, but I just waited there, teasing her. I kissed the nape of her neck, and she shivered in my arms. "Fuck, do it," she begged.

With a push and a groan, I slid home. She was so wet and tight that I had to bury my face in her hair and take a deep breath.

"God," Audrey gasped. "I missed you."

"I know." I let go of her hair so that I could claim her hips. With a tug, I pulled her even further onto me, until I was seated to the hilt. "Feel that?"

"Y...yes."

"That's where you're supposed to be."

She gripped the headboard and moaned.

"Right there." I bumped my hips once, and her breath caught. In my arms, her small body trembled. Waiting for me to go on. I leaned forward and put my mouth on her neck. "Don't forget," I ordered between kisses. Then I began to rock my hips.

Gasping, she met me eagerly.

I picked up the pace, but only a little. It's not every day you make love to someone for the first time. Even so, I was *made* of pleasure. Whether it was convenient or not, Audrey and I just fit. We'd always been good together. It's just that I'd never allowed myself to imagine a future where we shared everything. A bed. A home.

A *name.*

Hell. That got me panting. I wanted everything. There was nobody else who got under my skin like she had. To think of her as mine seemed like an impossible luxury.

It's the only luxury I've ever been greedy for.

I put one hand on the headboard beside hers, the size of my big paw dwarfing hers. Audrey hooked my thumb with her pinky finger. I gave it to her nice and steady while I stared at her hand, putting a ring on it in my head.

The image did crazy things to my body. Now I was greedy everywhere.

Wrapping an arm around her chest, I pulled her even further onto my lap. Then I disconnected our bodies and rolled, laying her down on the mattress and climbing on top. She grabbed my face and tugged me down for a kiss that went molten right away.

When I pushed inside again, she moaned my name. And I couldn't hold back any longer—neither my desire nor my words. I let it all fly. With pistoning hips and murmured endearments, I chased what we both wanted. Audrey hung on tight and went along for the ride, throwing her head back as we both went under.

I never wanted to come back out.

* * *

We lay in the dark a long time, not speaking. Eventually Audrey got up to use the bathroom. While she did her thing I pondered the ridiculousness of telling a girl I wanted to make us official even though I lived in a bunkhouse.

I was shaking my head as she climbed into bed again.

"What?"

"I know I freaked you out earlier. But my plans are bigger than my current situation."

She curled up to my body and put her head on my shoulder. "Your current situation doesn't scare me at all. But if I left Boston right now..." She trailed off.

"Then you wouldn't have to work for assholes."

"Griff," she warned. "You run a farm and make an amazing product with your name on it. I've failed out of two colleges. Culinary school went a lot better, but I've almost been fired from my first job twice. Or three times. I've lost count. I just want to do something well for once. If I came up here I'm sure you'd find me something to do. Some task I couldn't fuck up too badly."

"That's not how I think of you," I insisted. "You do a lot of things well."

"Uh-huh." She sounded unconvinced. "But I know I'd be a great chef. I'd listen better than most of the ones I've worked with. My kitchen wouldn't be a battle zone. People would do good work there, because they'd want to."

I liked the way her voice sounded when she was thinking about it. "Tell me about your restaurant," I whispered into the dark. "What's it like?"

"The one I'm pitching in a week?"

"Sure. Wait—no. Tell me about the one you really want someday. When you're at the top of your game. What's that one like?"

She nestled a little closer to me. And I knew she was *my* endgame. "The restaurant seats maybe sixty people. That's pretty small, but it will keep the quality high."

"Go on." I stroked her hair. "What's it called?"

She lifted her face and smiled at me. "Audrey's."

"Clever."

She pinched my hip. "I want a simple name. My place won't be *Le Princesse Fantasie* or anything stuffy like that. And the dining room won't be frilly. I'd want to put it in a renovated mill or somewhere in the North End. Bricks. Maybe a few industrial steel beams. Vintage factory lamps. The furniture will be comfortable but unassuming."

"Good thing. I'm going to need a table reserved for me every Friday night. So what am I having for dinner?"

"During which month? The menu will change frequently to accommodate the season."

"Fine. October."

"Okay, I recommend the pork tenderloin medallions in a balsamic reduction."

"Are there cherries in the sauce?"

"Cherries are out of season. Duh. But you'll get whole-wheat couscous on the side, with cranberries and walnuts. And garlicky wilted spinach."

"Wow."

"But if you're not in the mood for pork, you might want the buttermilk fried chicken with Jerusalem artichoke chips on the side. I think I'll serve it with a garlic and roasted pepper aioli."

"What's aioli?"

"It's homemade, flavored mayo. I'm really good at making it. And if I call it aioli I can charge thirty-six dollars for the dish."

I laughed and cuddled her closer. "Who says you don't have a head for business?"

She continued with her menu. "The beef dish of the evening is probably a hangar steak. There will be a salmon burger for variety."

"Okay, stop," I insisted.

"Why?"

"I'm hungry now."

She rolled over to face me, her lively eyes shining in the moonlight. "But we haven't gotten to the desserts!"

"Fine. What's for dessert?"

Audrey rolled away again. "I'll have to consult my pastry chef. But there are probably apples in it."

"Because it's October?"

"Right. And if they're Blue Permains I'm charging double."

"Hey—is there cider on the menu?"

"Of course. There's an award-winning cider on the menu. From Vermont. Some grumpy farmer makes it. I forgot his name."

"Ouch." I gave her boob a squeeze. "You can't forget my name. I'll be a regular."

She grabbed my hand off her breast and kissed it. "I'm never forgetting your name, Griff. Geez."

I ran a hand down her body, my fingertips brushing her mound. "Gonna have to remind you if you forget."

She gave a little shiver and sighed. We rested in silence for a few minutes, and I wondered if Audrey had fallen asleep. "What's your plan?" she startled me by asking.

"What?"

"I just told you my five-year plan. What's yours?"

Easy question. "To get Daphne and Dylan through college."

"That's not what I mean. What's the beautiful part?"

I gathered her hair in my hand and smoothed it off her shoulder, because I couldn't stop touching her. "I'm holding it right here."

"Griffin," she warned.

Apparently I wasn't allowed to say things like that. "Fine. In five years I've won a dozen awards, and I'm exporting cider to eleven different countries. There are guys regrafting orchards all over Vermont to try to get in on the new wave of interest in handcrafted ciders. I've bought my neighbor's land across the street and built a new tasting room where the cow barn is now. And I've built a house, too. With awesome views of the Green Mountains and a chef's kitchen. Just in case any chefs stop by."

"Nice."

"If I haven't convinced any woman to take me on as a project, I guess I'll just live with Zachariah my whole life. People will start to whisper about us probably."

Audrey giggled, so I tickled her. Then I flipped her over and kissed her. She wrapped her arms around me immediately.

This right here was my five-year plan. I didn't know how it was going to work out yet. But I wasn't giving up.

Chapter Twenty-Six

Audrey

I woke in the early hours of the morning curled up on Griff's chest. It was so roomy and comfortable that in my sleepy haze it seemed possible that I could move here permanently. There was almost as much space on his pecs as in my skanky little rented room. And I'd never have to pay for heat...

Someone knocked on the bedroom door. "Griff, you milking today? Or should I tell the cows you're too *busy*." It was his mouthy cousin, Kyle.

"Start without me," Griff muttered.

Kyle laughed. "You're catching so much hell for this later."

"Tell someone who cares."

There was the sound of feet shuffling past, and then the bunkhouse got very still. Griff's arms encircled me, and he sighed. "I have to get up."

"I know."

He kissed my temple. "You should sleep more. The guys won't come back this way until after breakfast, so you can have a shower later in peace."

"Good tip." Grudgingly, I slid off his chest and onto my side of the bed.

Instead of getting up like I expected him to, Griff rolled over on top of me. "I like having you in my bed."

I smiled up at him. "I like being had in your bed."

He snorted. "You always make a joke."

"You like my jokes," I pointed out.

"Every one." He kissed my forehead. "But I'd keep you here if I could. And I'm going to keep saying it, just in case you forget."

Then he got up and began to get dressed, and I couldn't help but admire the show. You know you've got it bad for someone when watching him pull on his jeans makes you heartsick. Roughened hands tugged the fabric up over solid muscle. His was a body that knew things. A single slap from Griff on a cow's rear end would align it perfectly with the milking station. His sculpted arms could lift a bushel of apples into the cider press.

His full, generous mouth could coax such pleasure from my body that it made me speak in tongues.

Griff pulled a merino wool T-shirt down over his broad back, covered it with a flannel shirt, and then the show was over.

He turned around slowly. I didn't even bother disguising my interest. I wasn't afraid to show Griff that I loved him. Loving him wasn't the problem. But loving *myself* enough to return to Boston and make a go of my career was the hard part.

"You make it hard to walk out that door," he said.

Back atcha, babe. "See you at breakfast," I said aloud.

I dozed in Griff's bed for another hour. It was lovely. And every time I rolled over on his pillow, my traitorous brain teased me with impossible ideas. *You could just stay*, it suggested. *You could go and see Zara, and talk her into letting you start up a breakfast service at The Goat.*

But then what? I'd be shacked with Griff at the bunkhouse. That would only put more pressure on him. One more person to support. One more complication.

What if we didn't get along? What if he got sick of

me? People usually did.

Audrey's would never become real. Even worse—I'd never know if I might have succeeded.

I got up and showered. Everything in the bunkhouse bathroom screamed *MEN LIVE HERE*, from the razors on every surface to the industrial soap and the athlete's foot spray on the countertop.

Hysterical.

I got dressed, taking care to smooth the wrinkles out of my shirt and brush my hair. But even as I crossed the open lawn from the bunkhouse to the farmhouse, I felt my neck flush. It was hard to walk into Griff's kitchen in the morning and look his mother in the eye. My guilty conscience would start shouting at any second, *I had dirty, dirty sex with your son!*

The kitchen was too busy for my little insecurities, though. "Morning, Audrey!" Ruth said from the stove. She had a pancake on the spatula, but the stack of plates was out of reach. "Would you mind...?"

I lunged forward and moved the plates.

"Thank you! Someone stole the platter."

"Sorry!" yelled May from the dining room.

"What else can I do?" I asked. "I thought you had another forty-five minutes until breakfast?"

"We do everything earlier on the apple-picking weekends. Can you see if the coffee is done and then start another pot?"

And so I was happily sucked into the morning Shipley family mayhem. I drained the bacon and broke a dozen eggs into a bowl for scrambling. Nobody called me "prep girl" or ordered me around.

When I brought the eggs to Ruth, she gave me a smile and a little pat on the shoulder.

It was embarrassing how much I loved this family and how badly I wished it were mine. But wishing wouldn't make it so. And they had enough people to care for already.

When the men came inside, May and I were just putting everything on the dining table. I felt the same electric jump in my tummy when Griff stepped into the room. "Hi baby," he said in his growly voice.

"Hi," I squeaked.

He lifted his strong jaw toward the pot in the corner. "Can I pour you a cup of coffee?"

You can pour anything you want. "Thank you."

Grandpa Shipley wandered in with his newspaper and took a seat. Ruth brought him a cup of coffee. But when she opened her mouth to ask him something, he held up a silencing hand. "Nope. Not today."

She clamped her jaw together. "I was going to ask whether you wanted a soft-boiled egg."

He looked disgruntled. "Well, in that case I accept."

Ruth brought him an egg in a little egg cup. Then she took her own seat. It was Zach's turn to say grace, which he did with quiet dignity while Daphne stared at him with stars in her eyes.

Then we dug in.

Griff ate with one hand resting on my bare knee, and it was distracting and wonderful.

The first tourists' cars pulled in even before the breakfast dishes were dried and put away. "Here it comes." May sighed. "Mom? Should I take the cash box outside?"

"I've got it," Ruth said. "I'll go first. You can finish up here. Have another cup of coffee. Just come and relieve me by ten-thirty so I can work on lunch."

"Deal."

* * *

I poured cider for tourists on and off all day. This time I wrote down everything they said about the flavors. In cooking school we're taught a lot of fancy words for describing taste. But I wanted to know what random people said about each blend. By lunchtime the page on my clipboard was filled with words like "sparkly" and "mushroomy" and "sweet-tart."

When evening came, Griffin took me out to dinner in Norwich. We sat in the front room at a restaurant called Carpenter & Main, after its street corner. With its old farmhouse architecture and its creaky floorboards, the place fairly shouted New England. We ordered venison duck confit and two appetizers and shared *everything*.

Vermont was doing its best to woo me. Staring over the rim of my wine glass into Griff's big, dark eyes, I wanted to stay.

So I did what I always do when I need to get back on track. I thought about my own version of the perfect Vermont restaurant menu. "Maybe tapas wasn't the right choice for my pitch. I could open a Vermont-themed restaurant on the edge of Brookline."

Griff made the first ornery face I'd seen all weekend. "Why can't you open a Vermont-themed restaurant *in* Vermont?"

"I'm pretty sure they have that covered here, big guy." It wasn't impossible to open a real restaurant in a rural area. But you'd have to live there long enough to figure out where it could survive. Norwich was a fancy town right across the river from Dartmouth College. The clientele at this restaurant was probably made up of professors and visitors. Other parts of Vermont had tourist traffic, but it was seasonal. Griff had told me that his apple pickers were often from Connecticut, and after years at the orchard, he knew exactly when to expect them.

Opening a restaurant in Vermont was a lovely thought. But without a lot of study and without the backing of investors? Crazy.

Every time I wondered why I was still working at BPG, it always came back to this: I was smart enough to know what I didn't know.

Griff was still frowning, so I put my hand over his bigger one, smoothing the skin, warming his hand until his face softened again. "Can I ask you something?"

"Of course," I said, bracing myself for another question about restaurants.

"Why didn't we go out? In Boston."

"What? Yesterday?"

He shook his head slowly, those dark eyes boring into me. And I realized he meant *before*. At BU.

I hadn't thought about that in a long time. "You left me a message," I recalled out loud. "And I didn't call you back."

"That's right." He lifted his bearded chin a little defiantly.

"Sorry," I said quickly. "I didn't think you cared that much."

His bushy eyebrows rose. "Why would you say that? I called, I asked you out, didn't I? Twice, I think."

It had honestly never occurred to me that I would have had the power to hurt him. "Let's see. You were this big football star, and I was just some freshman that was doing badly in all my classes. And my boyfriend had just obliterated my self-esteem."

God, just remembering that month gave me a pang in the center of my chest. College was supposed to be fun. That's what everyone said. But I was a ship at sea. My prep school friends were all conquering the world and I just couldn't get anything right.

Griff picked my hand up off the table and stroked

my palm with one thumb. "I liked you a lot, princess. But I did a shitty job convincing you."

I put an admiring hand over his brawny wrist and squeezed. "That was April or May of your senior year, right? We would have gotten a few good dates in, maybe. Then you moved to Green Bay. Timing has never been our forte, Griffin."

He gave me a sad smile and then paid the check.

Then we went back to the bunkhouse and had sex in absolute silence, because the building has no insulation between rooms, and we weren't in the mood to be exhibitionists. What was passing between us this weekend was romantic and difficult and also *private*. I wanted him all to myself for just a few hours more.

I got my wish. Griffin bent me over his desk and gave it to me right there in front of a sky full of stars. Then he scooped me up and tucked me into the bed where we napped until we were ready to do it again.

The weekend was perfect. But eventually Monday arrived. It always does.

In the pre-dawn darkness I heard Griff's alarm go off. He stopped its beeping, then rolled over to hold me. "Gonna miss waking up with you in my bed," he whispered. "But I understand why you have to go."

Since I didn't know what to say to that, I just hugged his big, naked body a little more tightly.

"I'll take you back after breakfast," he said quietly. "And next week when you make your pitch to those assholes, I hope they give you every last thing you want. And if they don't, I hope you'll try again." He stroked my hair. "I never got the chance to find out if pro ball was going to happen for me. I didn't get to figure it out for myself. But you can have that chance." He kissed the top of my head. "But if you get discouraged...if you need a day off from trying, I'll be here where you can find me."

I squeezed my eyes shut against the heat brewing behind them. I don't know what I'd ever done to deserve this man's attention.

"Never expected you to run a car into the ditch beside my road," he said. "But I'm sure glad you did. Most fun I had in a really long time."

I buried my face in his neck and hugged him tightly.

We stayed there pressed against one another for a couple minutes until the sound of footsteps moving about the bunkhouse let us know that the day was beginning whether we liked it or not.

With a sigh, Griffin Shipley slid out of bed, tucking the covers around me again afterward. Then he got dressed.

After he went out to greet the day, I hugged his pillow like the damn fool that I was.

* * *

It was a quiet journey back to Boston. Griffin turned on the radio after a while, which was fine because neither of us felt much like talking. As the buildings grew taller, so did my sense of dread. Saying goodbye to Griffin was going to suck. Tonight I'd go to bed lonely on my hard little futon, wondering what the hell I'd done.

But tomorrow morning I'd be back at work, learning the ropes of the restaurant business. The days would pass in a haze of kitchen work and then the terror of trying to impress a panel of seasoned restaurateurs.

"Baby?" Griff's voice shook me out of my reverie.

We were almost to my little apartment house already. "Yeah?"

"Can you do me a favor? I haven't gotten any paperwork from your buyer, and this Friday I can get him the first thousand bottles. Would you nudge him again?"

"Sure!" I said, happy to have a task to do. "I'll call him right now." I took out my phone and thumbed for Burton's number.

While it rang in my ear, Griffin found a semi-legal parking spot a few buildings down from mine.

"This is Bob Burton."

"Hi, it's Audrey Kidder calling with a question."

"Hi Audrey. Shoot."

"Shipley Orchards is set to deliver forty cases this week, but they're still waiting for a contract. Could you nudge the contracts department for me? This is the biggest dollar amount of all our Vermont purchases, and the man needs a contract."

There was a silence on the line. But I didn't panic. I gave Griff a smile, and the one he returned to me was so handsome that I actually missed what Burton said in my ear.

"Could you repeat that?" I had to say.

"I said—there's not going to be a contract, Audrey. We found a better price."

"A...what?" I gasped. That didn't even make sense. "A better price? How?"

"You brought us the cider at six-seventy-five. But there's a New Hampshire cidermaker who will do six bucks. So we sent him a contract instead. Didn't anyone tell you?"

"No!" I yelled. No to all of it. "You can't do that."

Another pause. "Of course I can. Business is business."

"But...!" I couldn't even decide what to freak out about first. "They're labeling it for you. It's going on a truck in four days. You *agreed* to purchase two hundred and fifty cases at six-seventy-five a bottle. If you needed a six-dollar price, you should have said that weeks ago."

I heard a viscous thump. Like someone smacking the dashboard with two fists. I couldn't even look at Griffin.

This *had* to be fixable.

"Burton," I said. "Listen to me. A family business has changed its entire operation to accommodate your order. You can't just walk away from them."

"We don't have anything on paper," he said. "It's done, Audrey. We contracted with the folks in Lebanon already. They brought us our first cases last week."

"Then you'll have *two* ciders on your menus," I said through gritted teeth. "More is more."

"Not this time. I have to go into a meeting now."

The man hung up on me. I was still in shock, sitting there on the seat of Griff's truck, my phone against my ear.

"Oh my God," I whispered. Then I finally risked a look at Griff's face. His jaw was as tight as I'd ever seen it. His face was hard, as if carved from granite. "I'm going to go over his head," I said. "I'll go to headquarters today and talk to his father."

Griffin didn't look at me. His gaze was fixed straight ahead. "I should have gone with my gut. I never do business with people I don't trust. This one time I took a chance..." He reached for his steering wheel and gripped it in two angry hands. "Fuck."

"I'll..."

"It's not your fault," he said, but his voice was icy.

"I know, but..." But what? I'd set that price. Griff had been willing to sell at six bucks, and I'd negotiated a higher price. I'd thought I was so smart. "They can't do this. I won't let them. You invested a lot of money in those tanks."

Griffin gave an angry grunt. "My mistake. I make a lot of those, apparently."

That statement sent a chill running down my spine. I knew without any doubt that he also meant *me*. "I..." My first attempt to speak failed, because I choked on the word. Swallowing hard, I tried again. "I have to go. I'm going to fix this." I yanked my duffel bag off the floor and grabbed for the door handle.

He didn't stop me.

I jumped down and turned around to find Griffin still staring out the windshield, his jaw tight.

After slamming the truck's door, I hoofed it up the block. My hand shook as I unlocked the door to my building, and the jog upstairs was a blur.

Once inside the apartment, I ran through a fog of marijuana smoke and into my little room. I threw myself and my bag down on the bed and tried to think. The cider order was worth just over forty thousand dollars to the Shipley family budget. Every manager in the BPG C-suite was going to get a call from me.

So I unzipped my bag and got out my presentation notes. I'd put a BPG org chart in there as a cheat sheet—so during my presentation I'd always know the function of anyone who asked me a question or made me clarify a point.

Beginning at the top, I started dialing.

The president didn't take my call. But I left a message with his receptionist, claiming I had to speak to him on a matter of utmost ethical import. Hopefully breaking out the SAT words would help. Then I called the corporation's general counsel and told *his* assistant that I had knowledge of the buyer trying to break an oral contract, and that BPG could be sued.

Finally, I called the elder Burton.

"Audrey! I've been expecting your call."

"You have?" *Shit.* "Sir, we have a problem."

"My son let me know that you're disappointed."

"D-d-disappointed?" I almost couldn't say it I was so fiercely angry. "You sent me to Vermont to do a job, and I did it. I put my *own good name* on the line for your company. You can't just steam roll the good people who are trying to do business with you!"

"Calm down, sweetheart."

I let out a little shriek of rage. "Why should I? You're destroying my credibility. As well as your own."

"You watch your tone," he snapped. "It's my name on the annual report, and it's me who has to answer to shareholders. There is a better deal out there in the marketplace. That's how markets work."

My stomach rolled. Because I knew all too well how markets work. "He'll meet your six dollar price," I said quickly. "But you can't just yank the order."

There was a pause, during which I almost vomited from stress.

"Five dollars," Burton said. "I don't need the product now, but for the right price I would buy it."

Fuck. I closed my eyes and took a slow, calming breath. "No can do," I whispered. "No deal." That's what Griffin would say, anyway.

"Then I guess we don't have anything left to discuss."

Truer words had never been spoken. I took the phone from my ear and I tapped the screen to disconnect.

I looked around my little room, tidy except for my notebooks spread out on the bed. But inside I was all torn apart. Debris everywhere. My heart in tatters. I lifted the nearest notebook and opened it to a drawing of my tapas restaurant logo. I'd curved the words Small Plates into the top and bottom halves of a shining dish.

The page made a satisfyingly destructive sound when I yanked it out and tore it in half. I did the same thing to the rest of the pages. One by one I tore them down the center.

Next week I wouldn't be pitching for the competition. Griff always said he refused to do business with people he didn't trust. Now I understood why. I didn't want to breathe the same air as people who would do what they just did. So I sure as hell didn't want to be the face of their restaurant.

Fuck. Me. I just spent many months of my life trying to win their favor. What a waste of time.

Hello, square one? I'm back.

This realization was so exhausting that I lay down on my bed, in a nest of torn paper. I put my head on the pillow and tried not to think about Griffin's angry face. I'd just cost him forty thousand dollars. And because of me, his family was going to have to worry about cash flow every day for the foreseeable future. I pictured their worried faces around the dinner table as Griffin tried to explain what happened. I could see Ruth's patient frown so clearly in my mind. Dylan's scowl. May's frustration...

Lying there, hopelessness simmered inside me until it boiled over in the form of tears.

Chapter Twenty-Seven

Griffin

Anger was my primary reaction to BPG's fucking betrayal of our agreement. For a few minutes there I was so enraged I couldn't even speak.

Audrey disappeared in a frantic scramble toward her apartment building, and I'm ashamed to say I didn't even watch her go. I couldn't think about her just now. I was too upset to say anything comforting. And too pissed off at myself.

I *knew* those bastards couldn't be trusted. I'd told her that the second she showed up on my property. But instead of listening to my gut, I'd let my heart lead me astray. The cider business was my dream, so I'd let them convince me it was possible. I'd sunk a lot of money into equipment. And now my family would pay the price.

My overtired brain went right to damage control. I took out my phone and called home. My mother answered on the first ring.

"Griffin? Is everything okay?"

"I'm fine," I said carefully. "But I have a bit of a situation."

"Tell me."

"Don't let Dylan print any more of the BPG cider labels." That was the only thing I could save—a thousand pages of adhesive labels and the ink printed on them.

"Why?"

"The company is trying to cancel their order."

I heard my mother's gasp through the phone. "They can't do that!"

"I know," I said quietly. "But they are. It looks bad."

I had to give my mother credit. She was always solid in a crisis. The next thing she said was, "We'll be okay."

"Yeah," I agreed. Though the fallout was going to keep me up nights.

"Your father had almost the same thing happen to him once."

"What?"

"He had a handshake deal to sell milk to Kupper Cheeses. But they reneged. Your father also declined insurance on his outbuildings for a few years, then lost a barn in a fire. That cost us a fortune."

"Really?"

"Really. The man made a lot of mistakes, but they didn't make him a failure. You're going to make a few, too."

I shut my eyes, trying to wrap my head around Dad's fuckups. Logically, I understood that everyone made mistakes. But I hadn't allowed myself any room to make any.

"Audrey must be out of her mind," my mother said gently.

I flinched. If not for Audrey, I wouldn't be in this pickle.

"Griff," my mother pressed. "Is she okay?"

"I don't really know," I admitted. "At the moment, I have bigger problems."

"No, you really don't," she pressed. "Unless you think you can change the company's mind, I think Audrey is your only problem. Where is she?"

"Her apartment," I guessed.

"And where are you?"

"In the truck. I need to come home."

My mother's silence spoke volumes. She was not pleased. "Talk to her," she said. "Don't leave Boston angry."

"Then I'm gonna be here all year," I snapped.

"Honey, this isn't her fault."

I knew that. Mostly. But I'd let my guard down in a serious way. Ever since she'd waltzed into town I'd lost my mind a little. She'd made me think selfish thoughts, when I really hadn't been able to afford to think that way. "I gotta go, Mom. I'll see you in a few hours."

"Don't make a little mistake into a big one," she said.

"I don't even know what that means. Take care." I hung up.

Then I called Isaac Abraham and got his wife Leah. "Hey, lady. I got a little bad news." I told her what BPG had done. "So I'm not going to be trucking any produce to them next week. I'll tell the others, too. You all can make your own decision—either take the stuff into Boston together or bail on them. But I'm done with BPG."

"Man, Griffin, I'm sorry," Leah said. "I don't think Isaac will want to sell them anything now either."

"That's your choice," I said quickly. "But I wanted to let you know right away so you could plan ahead."

"I think we'll take a lot of product to the Norwich market tomorrow and try to move it locally instead."

"Sounds good," I said.

"Do you want me to make some calls for you? The baby is napping."

"Would you?" I gave her a list off the top of my head of farmers whose goods I'd hauled into town last week.

Then I just sat behind the wheel of my truck feeling lousy. I'd just undone Audrey's work for the second time. Many of those farmers were about to bail on BPG just on principle. Unless they couldn't afford to. And now transportation would be an issue.

But I couldn't really worry about that. It wouldn't be me hauling their shit after they backed out on forty large of cider.

That done, I needed to get home and think through my next few months' cash flow. If I sold off the rest of the herd across the street, I could use that money to get by. Though I'd need to find a buyer for all the cider I'd been pressing, and quickly.

I cranked the truck's engine and waited for it to warm up. Then I reached around to the back seat in search of the sandwich May had sent me for lunch.

But my hand collided with something else. An Easy-Bake oven in a box.

Hell.

Audrey had leapt from my truck like it was on fire. She'd forgotten the gift I'd given her. Maybe she didn't care about it after all.

Yes she does, my conscience complained. *She cares a great deal.*

She could get it later, though.

I started the engine and extracted myself from my parking spot. It took me twenty minutes to get out of Boston. I'd lived in this city for five years in college and the traffic pattern still confounded me. Finally I reached the highway and accelerated northward. I still felt like an utter heel. But there was work to be done.

My phone rang. The number was our landline at home.

I ignored it.

It rang again. Ever since my father died, I got a little weirded out whenever it seemed like my family needed to reach me. So I pulled off at the next exit and parked the truck.

"What?" I barked when my mother answered.

"Do you really want to take that tone?" my mother chided. "I called to give you a shred of good news."

"Really?" I couldn't think of anything that could make a dent in today's shit show.

"You won that contest—the pricey one—American Tasting Society. Best in Class and Best in Show. The letter says there's a trophy coming."

"I...Are you sure?" Fate had only kicked me in the ass today. I didn't trust it.

My mother snorted. "I can read a letter, Griffin. It begins with, *Congratulations, Shipley Ciders. It is our pleasure to announce that you've won top honors...*"

"Wait—which cider won?" I'd actually spent the extra cash to enter three of them.

"Hang on." I heard the sound of paper unfolding. "Entry number one-forty-seven, you called it...aw."

"What?"

"Audrey."

I laughed for the first time all day. "No shit?"

"Don't use foul language. But yes."

"Thanks for telling me, Mom. I have to get back on the road."

"Chin up, Griff. When the Lord closes a door, he opens a window."

That was nice and all, but I had a door to open myself. "See you in a few hours. Gotta run."

After disconnecting, I turned the truck around and got on the highway in the other direction. It took me even longer to get back through traffic to Audrey's street. But the same semi-legal parking spot still waited.

I got out and walked down the block to Audrey's door. There were no names on the buttons but I rung the one for number three and someone buzzed me in.

Hmm. That didn't seem safe. I carried the box up to

the third floor and knocked.

The door flew open to reveal a thin, red-eyed guy. "Who are you?"

"I'd ask the same," I growled. "I'm looking for Audrey Kidder." It was the right apartment. I spied the same dingy sofa I'd seen when we stopped here on Friday afternoon.

He nodded toward Audrey's room and lost interest in me, drifting back toward the sofa.

Her door was closed, so I knocked.

No answer.

I knocked again, and then listened. The only sound was a stifled sob.

Opening the door, the first thing I saw was Audrey, crying, curled up on a bed littered with torn pieces of paper. My cranky heart broke right in half, like one of the drawings on the bed. "Baby, don't cry," I insisted.

She raised her head, startled. "But...I..." She tried to take a deep breath, but she hiccuped instead. "Everything is wrecked."

I was over there in an instant, setting down the box and then scooping her up into my lap. "It sucks, what happened. But you and I will be fine." All it took was one look at her for me to understand that some things were more important than selling two hundred fifty cases of cider. I wiped tears off Audrey's face with my thumb.

"But my mother was right. I can't do anything without fucking it up."

"No! She's not right about a thing. You didn't fuck this up. Don't take the fall for their bullshit."

"But I told them you wouldn't go below six-seventy-five! I wanted you to make the extra money. So they found someone at"—she hiccuped again—"six bucks even."

Aw, hell. "You were trying to help me out, and I appreciate it. Why did you rip up your presentation?"

"Can't work for them. I won't do it."

I hugged her even more tightly. She smelled of my own shampoo. "That's your call. I can't sell them apples or truck their stuff into the city, baby. I'm sorry. I told the other farmers they were on their own."

"Okay." She sounded defeated.

"Come home with me?" I asked.

"And do what?" she squeaked. "Wreck something else?"

"No," I said softly, rocking her. "Just be with me. We have a whole lot of cider to make, sweetheart. You can help. And now we need to market it, too. Find another buyer. Get noticed by a big distributor. Enter more contests. Win some prizes. There's work to be done."

"You're just trying to be n-nice," she stammered.

"I'm not that nice. You said so yourself."

Now I had her laughing and crying at the same time.

"Baby, we need to regroup. I'd rather do that with you than without you."

She pushed her face into my shoulder. "I need a job, Griff. I'm never going to stop wanting my own restaurant."

"And I don't know how that gets done," I admitted. "But there has to be more than one way. In the meantime, you're very employable. I think Zara, for one, is going to need a lot of help in the next year."

"She is?"

"Yeah. I'll let her tell you all about it herself." I wrapped my arms around her and went in for the kill. "I think you'd make a hell of a cidermaker."

"That's *your* thing," she said.

"Apparently not, baby. Your sexy cider won the grand prize."

"Wait, really?"

"Swear to God. Mom just opened the letter. We have to make a whole lot more of it now, and jack up the price. You have to help me get the blend right."

"You blended it yourself."

"Yeah, after you told me it was a winner. As I remember, you *demanded* I enter it into the contest. And it worked. You got a whole panel of judges horny so they gave me Best in Show."

She jerked her tear-stained face away and looked up at me. "You swear you're not just trying to make me feel better?"

I crossed myself. "Swear to God and hope to die. Come home and read the letter yourself. Besides—you left your oven in my truck. Those little cakes are not going to bake themselves."

"Oh," Audrey moaned. "I was going to stop being impulsive. I was going to have a chef's career or die trying."

"As the saying goes, you're supposed to *do what you love*." I tapped my chest. "I'm it, baby."

She giggled through her tears. "I do kind of love you. A little bit."

My heart gave a squeeze. "Just a little bit? Because I'm falling for you big time."

The smile she gave me was teary. "Give me ten minutes to get over my shock at all the turns this day has taken."

"Fair enough." I set her onto the bed and stood up. I held out a hand. "Come on. Pack a big bag this time." I looked around the little room. She had clothes, a laptop computer and a collection of cookbooks in a milk crate. "Bring all of it. I'll tell your landlord you're moving out."

She pushed her hair out of her face. "I hope you don't regret this."

"Not a chance. I'm getting everything I want. I hope *you* don't regret it."

She stood up and took a deep breath. "I won't. I want to work in Vermont."

"Good!"

"You have a fun job. And I get to make cider donuts, damn it. They'll cost almost nothing, and people will pay up for a hot donut at an orchard. Maybe there should be dipping sauces. Like caramel apple flavored..."

"Oh, fuck. You're killing me. I'm hungry again."

"Figures. Let's get out of here. We could almost get back in time for dinner."

Chapter Twenty-Eight

Audrey

We stood up, and I was still a little stunned. I went over to my tiny closet and opened the door, but then I just stared at the clothing for a moment, still trying to make sense of this plan.

My mother had always accused me of being a wild girl who wasn't smart enough to stay the course. But she was wrong. I'd been single-mindedly pursuing my dream job for the past two years. Until an hour ago I'd been ready to wait as long as it took.

But, damn it, it was okay to want things. It was okay to change my mind and move to Vermont on a whim and skinny dip beside an organic apple orchard if I felt like it. I wanted that life, and I wanted this man.

I wasn't giving up. I was trading up.

Feeling giddy, I hastily packed up my things. I didn't have any boxes, but almost everything fit into my luggage. I stole one of roommate's garbage bags for a place to stash my bedding.

The futon I left for the next poor slob who needed it.

As we tossed my stuff into the back of Griff's truck, I felt like I was making some kind of unlawful getaway from my troubles. Mom would say I was being flighty again. She'd accuse me of quitting before I'd accomplished anything.

And maybe I was. But I was so freaking *happy* to climb into that truck beside Griff. That had to mean something important. It was possible to run *toward* something instead of running away, right?

"Griffin?" I said as he pealed down my street. Good riddance to it.

"Yeah, baby?"

"I was just thinking about my mother. I need to call her."

He winced. "Why?"

I yanked my phone out of my bag. "Just an idea I have. You'd still sell to BPG at six-seventy-five, right?"

He tapped the steering wheel. "I suppose I would. Not like I love the idea anymore. But I do need the cash."

My mother's receptionist answered on the first ring, as always. I think Mom docked their pay if they didn't. "Karen Kidder's office. How may I direct your call?"

"Hi," I said carefully. "This is Audrey. Allison's daughter."

There was a beat of silence on the phone. The new receptionist—they were always new, because my mother rode them like rodeo bulls—clearly didn't know her boss *had* a daughter. Either Mom removed my picture from the silver frame on her desk, or else this girl was too timid to ask about the photos. "Let me see if she's available. One moment please."

I held my breath while the assistant verified my identity. My mom picked up only a few seconds later. "Audrey? Is anything wrong?"

That greeting was unexpected. If I weren't crazy, I detected a note of concern. Then again, I hadn't called her office in two years. We'd only spoken on a few occasions when I'd answered the phone without looking at the caller ID. And then there was that awful time in Vermont...

"I'm...I have a problem. And I need your help."

"Are you in jail?"

That brought out a nervous snort of laughter. "No, Mom. Still haven't been locked up yet. It's a business problem. At BPG. I'm still an intern there. Or I was until an hour ago."

"What happened?"

"Well, they broke their word on a purchase from a farmer, and it's a make or break kind of thing for him. As an investor in BPG, I thought you should know how they operate."

My mother listened quietly while I wove the tale. "They made a deal, and then they broke it. We have emails telling us the contract is coming. That has to count as proof! And maybe forty thousand dollars isn't a big sum to them, but it could sink a small farm."

"And you're involved with this farmer, aren't you?"

"That shouldn't matter," I said quickly. "A deal is a deal."

She sighed. "I know that, and you know that. But the rules are different for women. I'm going to call Burton now and ask why the hell he's done this."

"You are?" I couldn't even hide my shock.

"Isn't that what you wanted me to do?"

I opened my mouth but for a second nothing came out. "Yes," I managed eventually. "Yes, *please*. It's just *wrong* to..."

"I *know*, Audrey. I get it. Let me see what I can find out." She hung up on me then. My mother never had that extra half-second you needed to say goodbye.

Griffin stole a glance at me. "I didn't hear any shouting."

"Yeah... That didn't go how I expected. She's actually going to investigate." A few miles went by in silence. "I almost didn't call her. I didn't think she'd care."

He reached over and squeezed my knee. "Maybe

your mom wised up a little. You want to reconsider pitching for the contest? I'll drive you there on the big day. You could still give it a shot."

I turned to study Griff's strong profile as he drove. That was a face I wanted to see every day. If by some miracle I beat the stacked deck and launched a restaurant with BPG, there'd be no way for me to spend any time with Griff. I'd be looking at sixteen-hour days in a windowless Boston kitchen, trying to make sure the top brass at BPG didn't screw with every product source and price tag on my menu.

It would be a *big* life. But it wouldn't be a good life.

"I'm done with them," I admitted. "They made every day a trial. If I were spearheading an expensive project, they'd only be more awful. I'd rather fight with you than fight with them. Because, make-up sex."

Griff tipped his head back and laughed. "What are we fighting about?"

"I'm not sure yet. But you get cranky sometimes when there's stress."

He rubbed his chin. "People tell me I'm nicer when you're around. You know what that means, right?"

"That you need to be getting it on the regular or you're a grumpy bear?"

He shook his head. "That sure doesn't hurt. But come here."

I unbuckled my seatbelt and slid across the bench seat. Then I buckled myself into the center spot because we were doing seventy-five on highway 93. "What?"

Griffin put an arm around me. "That's better."

It was. Truly.

"At the risk of freaking you out, because you don't like it when I say these things..." He stole a glance at me and then returned his eyes to the road. "I love you, princess. You're the sweet that balances out my natural tannins."

My face flushed as I replayed those words in my head. *I love you.* I'd learned to avoid these words from men who'd let me down. But it sounded entirely different coming from Griffin Shipley. "Wow."

"I know, right? Everything good in life can be explained by cider."

I put my hand on his cheek, letting his beard tickle my palm. "I love you, too, Griff. All two-hundred stubborn pounds of you."

He tilted his head into my palm. "That's all that matters. The rest will work out," he promised. "Somehow."

* * *

We got to Vermont just before six. I'd left it less than eight hours earlier, but I still looked around carefully when I got out of the truck. The rooster came around the side of the house, on patrol. Dylan was reading a history textbook in the hammock on the porch, while Daphne sat catty-corner in one of the wicker rockers. I saw her stick out one leg and kick her brother in the thigh.

His hammock wobbled. But he didn't even look up.

"Damn, I love it here," I admitted. "Can we pour a glass of tea and sit on the porch later?"

Griff opened the back door of his truck and took out my Easy-Bake oven. "I guess so. Sitting down is something I never do when there are apples hanging on my trees."

"So you'll sit down in, say, November?"

"Sometimes. Other times I split wood while other people sit down."

Huh. Watching Griffin split wood sounded like a

good time. I was looking forward to November.

We took a load of my stuff into Griff's room, where it seemed to clutter up the place immediately. I felt a little guilty just leaving it there in the corner, but Griff put a hand on my back and said, "Let's not be late for dinner. Mom won't like it."

So we crossed the yard one more time, and I began to feel self-conscious. I hoped she'd just say, "Hello, Audrey, dear. Could you hand me those napkins?"

But that's not what happened.

A little cheer went up from May, Jude and Ruth when we stepped into the kitchen.

"Oh, thank heavens," Ruthie said, tossing down a basket of rolls to come around and kiss my cheek. "I thought my son had lost his mind. I'm happy to see he's found it." She grabbed an envelope from beside the telephone. "Here, honey. Look what Griffin won."

"I heard," I said, removing the letter from the envelope. I skimmed the congratulatory bits at the top until I reached the prize statement at the bottom. BEST IN CLASS, BEST IN SHOW: *AUDREY* by Shipley Farms. "Omigod!" I squeaked. "You named it after me?"

Griffin made a serious face, but I think I saw his neck turning pink. "How else was I supposed to remember which one was your pick?"

"I'm on your prize!" I shrieked. "I've never won a prize."

"Everybody wins something," May said.

"Not me!" I stared down at the letter, reading it again. "There's going to be a trophy. It might say *Audrey* on it."

Griffin chuckled. "Maybe? Hell, if it doesn't I'll have it engraved on there just for you."

I jumped into his arms. "Thank you!"

"For what?" he said, his voice muffled by my clumsy

enthusiasm.

"For entering. For everything."

He gave me a big, sloppy kiss on the neck. In front of everyone. "You're my prize, princess. Now let's celebrate." He set me down, then rubbed his stomach. "With some dinner."

* * *

Fifteen minutes later we were all sitting around the table, waiting for Grandpa. His tires could be heard in the driveway just as Ruth took her seat, frowning up a storm over his tardiness.

"You're late," she said as he entered the room.

"Apologies," he said, shuffling around to take the last available seat next to his granddaughter. He kissed May on the cheek and then shook out his napkin.

"Griffin, it's your turn to say grace."

He shot me a warm look and then took my hand. "Dear Lord, thank you for these blessings we are about to receive. Thank you for watching over the cidery today while Kyle was in charge of the press. This time he didn't clog the grinder and I thank you."

Kyle rolled his eyes across the table.

"And thank you for bringing Audrey to her senses and back to Vermont, the most beautiful state in the union, to be part of a loud and sometimes uncooperative family who already loves her."

There was a small cheer at that, and I'm not ashamed to say that it brought tears to my eyes.

"Poor girl has to put up with *you*, though," somebody muttered.

"Amen."

The moment the prayer ended, the passing of dishes commenced. There was turkey with stuffing, yams and cranberry sauce. After filling his plate, Griffin got up and disappeared. I heard the kitchen door open and shut, then I heard it again after five minutes. He reappeared in the dining room with a growler in his hand.

"What's that?" May asked as he set it on the sideboard and counted out wine glasses.

"What do you think it is? An award-winning cider." He began to pour and then to ferry filled glasses to everyone at the table (except for Jude.) He even put glasses in front of the twins. "Special occasion," he muttered.

Then he put the growler in the middle of the table. AUDREY was scrawled on the label in Sharpie.

Standing behind his chair, he raised his glass. "To more greatness!"

There were cheers and taunts. "Yeah!" "Congrats!" "Ego, much?"

I drank, and the wonderful, musky strangeness of the cider hit me just as hard the second time. "Wow." I took another sip. "It's so...dangerously good."

"It's..." His mother paused, then tasted it again. She swirled the cider in her glass. "Remarkable, honey. It's really unique. What *is* that flavor?"

My eyes met Griff's over the rim of his glass. But looking at him was a mistake, because he was struggling not to laugh. So now I was struggling not to laugh.

I jerked my eyes elsewhere, watching the faces around the table as everyone tasted the sex cider. At least Griffin hadn't scrawled *that* on the growler. Amusement bubbled up inside me again and threatened to spill out.

Jude picked up May's glass beside him and gave it a deep sniff. "Fascinating," he said slowly. Then he winked at me.

I might have lost it completely if Griffin hadn't distracted me. "Grandpa," he said. "How does tomorrow sound for moving into the farmhouse?"

His grandfather—a fork in one hand and Griffin's excellent brew in the other—only grunted.

"I can't persuade Audrey to stay in Vermont if I've got her shacked up in a bunkhouse. We could use a little more space, and you could use better access to the dining room table."

I saw Ruth hold her breath. Grandpa said nothing for a moment. He shoveled in a bite of stuffing and chewed. Then he sipped his cider. "Coconut rice," he said eventually.

"Come again?" Griffin said.

"I'll move in here tomorrow if Audrey makes that coconut rice. And the spicy veggies." A little groan of recognition rose up from others at the table.

"Anytime," I said quickly.

He nodded at his grandson. "You are a smart kid, you know that? Finding the right girl, treating her right."

"I'm trying," Griff said, his voice low.

"You can bring me over some empty boxes tonight. After pie, of course."

"I'll do it," Griff promised.

Ruth squeezed her hands together. "All right! I'll get your room ready tomorrow, first thing. We'll set up your TV, and I think Griff could even wrestle your recliner in there, if you want. Or I'll make a space for it in the den."

"Whichever," Grandpa said as if he couldn't be bothered to care. He reached for an additional slice of turkey from the platter.

I hardly said a word after that. I ate my meal and listened to the Shipley family squabble over whose turn it was tonight to control the TV remote. (Monday night football versus Daphne's show. It didn't go Daphne's way.) I sipped my namesake cider and marveled at my own good fortune.

* * *

"You okay?" Griff asked me an hour later. We were driving slowly down the dirt road in his truck. When he made a sharp right-hand turn, it was onto a little track that I hadn't even known was a driveway.

"I'm fine," I said. "Just thinking about your grandfather. I hope we're not shoving him out of his house."

Griff chuckled. "Not a chance. Mom's been working on him for months. But the guy has been stubborn."

"Sounds like somebody else I know. Can't think of who."

"I know, right?" Griff touched me on the knee. "Grandpa feels a little weird having his daughter-in-law take care of him, that's all. He already shows up for every meal, though. And Dylan shovels the snow off his steps. May shops for the coffee and cookies in his cabinets. My mother drives him to doctors' appointments and fills his car with gas so he can make the trips to our house. He's dependent on us, but he doesn't want to be. You and I just gave him the excuse he needed to move in. That's all."

"Okay." I just wasn't used to a big family where everybody helped out. I didn't know how it worked.

"Here we are. It isn't much, but..." Griffin's headlights illuminated a cute little cape cod with wood shingles and red shutters. Two dormers popped out from the peaked roof like eyes, and a stone chimney rose up toward the sky in the center.

"It's *adorable*. Now I really feel guilty."

"Don't. Really." He leaned in and kissed my cheekbone. "He needs a main-floor shower, which this house doesn't have. And mom will feed him all the pie he wants, because she won't be lying in bed at night wondering if he's slipped on the stairs. Come on."

We carried the boxes Ruth had found inside. "Those can go in the bedroom," Grandpa said from the recliner. "Or just drop 'em. I'm watching the game."

"Who's winning?" Griff asked, stopping to check the score.

I decided to carry a few boxes upstairs myself. Because it was either that or get caught staring. The house was at least as cute inside as outside. There were gorgeous oak floors, and a stone fireplace with a mantel just begging for Christmas stockings. I climbed the polished wooden stair treads carefully. The staircase *was* a little steep. I'd have to rein in my clumsy ways.

When I got to the top I found two bedrooms—one of them obviously unused. It smelled dusty. But the other was gorgeous, with a peaked ceiling with oak beams and walls painted a buttercream color. The generous bathroom had a claw-foot tub set over antique black and white tiles.

"Hey." A few minutes later Griffin caught me standing there, mentally adding cute towels and a fluffy bath mat to the picture. "It's not the Plaza..."

"Stop. I want to live here with you. Shower sex is out. But that's the only negative I can find."

"There's still the outdoor shower, so we're covered." He set the boxes down and kissed me. "This place needs a new kitchen," he said between kisses. "I can't renovate until the cash flow improves. Sometime in the next millennium."

"I don't care."

"You haven't seen those ugly 1960s countertops." *Kiss.* "But we can do some simple things." *Kiss.* "We can paint." *Kiss.* "You can choose the colors."

I gave him a long, slow kiss. The idea of making a home with Griffin was wonderful and so unexpected. I felt giddy just picturing it. "We're gonna christen every room," I breathed.

"Damn straight." He growled into my mouth. "I'll get work done twice as fast if I have that to come home to."

Breaking off our kiss, I wrapped my arms around him. When I tucked my head against his chest, I saw the Green Mountains out the window. "This place is so beautiful. I don't know if I deserve this."

"Really?" He gave me a squeeze. "I'm pretty sure I do. So why wouldn't you?"

My phone rang in my back pocket. It took me a moment to care, but when I realized that I was expecting a call from my mother, I let go of Griff and answered it. "Hello?"

"Hi, Audrey. I have some news."

"Wow. Okay?"

"I had it out with Burton. I told him we're not going to do business that way. But when he pulled out the contract he has with the other cider producer, it had an exclusivity clause."

"What?"

"The other cidermaker's lawyers put into the contract that theirs would be the only cider on the menu at BPG this year."

I groaned. "So you're saying that the other guy was smarter than I am."

My mother sighed. "More experienced, maybe. Or just *jaded.* Audrey, you're not a stupid girl. I'm sorry if I ever made you feel that you were."

It took a moment for that to sink in. My mother

never apologized to me. "Um...thank you?"

"I got a call from Ruth Shipley a few minutes ago."

"You *did?*" I squeaked.

"She's lovely. And she has a lot of nice things to say about you."

Oh, boy. "Did she want to talk about cider?"

"No. She just wanted me to know that you'd arrived in Vermont again, and that you'd been a big help to her when she was injured over the summer. And that she'd look after you." My mother cleared her throat uncomfortably. "They sound like a lovely family."

"They are," I gushed. "That's why it kills me to see them cheated."

"I get it. And this wasn't your fault. Burton sent you to negotiate without telling you any of the rules of the jungle. But I know you're not incapable. Putting yourself through culinary school was a big deal. I want you to know that I'm proud of you."

My head was about to explode. "That's...thank you, Mom. But Griffin is still forty grand poorer than he was this morning."

She groaned. "I know. If he sues, he can probably win. But a lawsuit—"

"—costs a lot of money," I finished.

"It does," she agreed.

"Okay." I took a deep breath. "Thanks for trying to help. We really appreciate it."

"If you have any other questions about it, or want to ask me anything about BPG, I'm happy to talk."

Again I was floored by the humble tone of her voice. "Thank you. But I'm finished with BPG."

"I understand. Maybe you could come and have lunch with me whenever you're in town again."

I was so surprised that I didn't respond.

"Audrey?"

"Sorry. Sure. Maybe after I get settled here."

"Good," she said quickly. "Until then, take care."

"You too," I said softly.

I hung up the phone, uncertain of which of today's events was the more shocking—me moving in with Griff or having a civil telephone conversation with Mom?

"She couldn't fix it," Griff whispered. "But she tried."

I leaned into him, shaking my head. "I'm sorry."

"Not your fault. I'm still going to make a hell of a lot of cider. We just have to sell it to someone else. Got any thirsty friends?" He wrapped his arms around me.

"We were outmaneuvered."

"*This* time," he said firmly. Then he kissed the top of my head. "Let's go turn in early. We have a lot to do tomorrow."

"Is that the only reason you want to turn in early?" I asked as he steered us toward the stairs.

"What do you think?"

Smiling, I followed him downstairs.

Chapter Twenty-Nine

November

Audrey

I was sealing up a paint can, kneeling on the tarp covering our living room floor when the phone rang. The number had a 617 Boston area code, so I got a little excited. I'd been trying to convince a couple of beverage distribution companies to take a chance on Shipley Ciders, and if one of them was calling me back, that was definitely a call I wanted to take. "Hello?"

"Hi, this is Sarah from Beantown Restaurant group. I have a call for Miss Audrey Kidder from Raphael Asher. Have I reached Audrey?"

"Uh, yes?"

"Hold please."

I searched my brain for anyone I might know at the Beantown Restaurant Group and came up empty.

"Audrey! This is Raphael Asher. I'm the buyer and local forager for twenty-seven Boston restaurants. How are you today?"

"I'm well, thanks. How can I help you?" Did he say *forager? What the...?*

"Ah, well we've just hired Chef Michael Quigley, formerly of North End Kitchens. Do you know him?"

My mind whirled, trying to place that name. I'd met Chef Quigley once for fifteen minutes. He was one of BPG's rising stars. "We've met," I hedged. "He left BPG?"

"He did. We lured him away." This man on the phone—Raphael—laughed. "Anyway—Chef Quigley and I had a long talk about farm-to-table operations last week, and he gave me your name. He told me you sourced some beautiful organic pears for him in September. And some squashes, I think. You ran the farm-to-table program for BPG?"

"Well..." Should I tell the truth? If I said I ran a *program*, that would be a terrible exaggeration. "I spent the summer doing laps around Vermont, finding farmers with product to sell. But BPG's program was too loosely formed to be very effective." I took a breath, hoping that I'd been diplomatic enough in my description. A girl didn't trash her ex-employer, even if they deserved it.

"I heard that place is a *wreck* right now," Raphael said, his voice low. "But I also heard that you did good work. In fact, I'd love to sit down with you to chat about the new program I'm starting here. I could use someone like you on my team. Someone experienced."

What does a girl say to that? "I'd love to talk," I said cautiously. "But you should know that I'm not based in Boston right now. I've moved to Vermont."

"That's all right," he said quickly. "Could you drive into the city for a chat? You can pick the day. The job I have for you works better if you're stationed in Vermont. I have big plans, Audrey. I want to build our farm-to-table program the *right* way—I want to hire buyers like you to form a real partnership with farmers. It would be a year-round gig, but only part time."

"Wow." It wasn't the most sophisticated response, but the job sounded awfully neat. "So you're looking for boots on the ground to coordinate between farmers and restaurants? If it was year round we could actually direct the crops we want before they go into the ground."

"Yes! Exactly. I'd love to hear your thoughts about how best to execute it."

"Okay." My heart fluttered. "I'd love to have the discussion. Farmers start ordering their seed right after New Years..." I'd heard Isaac Abraham talking about it at Thursday Dinner last night. "BPG didn't understand how much lead time matters. They thought they could just roll up for a day or two and farms would just hurl their best produce at the truck. But it doesn't work that way."

"I know it. So meet with me. Later this month, maybe? You can work it out with my assistant."

The front door of our little house opened, and Griffin walked in with the mail in his hand. He gave me a wave.

I gave him the universal sign for *just a second*. "All right, Raphael. I'll do that. By any chance would you like to meet an award-winning Vermont cidermaker, too?"

"Hmm," he said. "Why not?"

"I'll bring him," I said quickly.

"Can't wait! Thanks, Audrey!"

Click.

I stared at the phone in my hand.

"Princess!" Griffin kicked off his boots and then came over to kiss me on the forehead. "Who called? Tell me some good news."

"It *could* be good news," I said carefully. When I met with Raphael from Beantown Group, my eyes would be wide open, that was for damn sure. I explained to Griff what the man had asked for.

"Huh," he said, stroking his beard. "If this guy is smarter than those tools at BPG, it might be a decent job for you. If you're interested."

"I'm interested," I said quickly. In the past eight

weeks I'd begun helping Zara by taking over her morning hours at the Goat, and getting her breakfast and coffee service started. I'd helped Griffin make a whole lot of cider. But a decent job for a restaurant company could come in handy. "Maybe we can sell some cider, too."

Griff smiled. "We'll try."

"And if he has a part-time job for me that I could do here—"

"—that's pretty much perfect," Griff finished.

"It is. And the money would come in handy."

"Speaking of money." Griff sifted through the mail in his hand. He handed me an envelope.

I turned it over to find the seal for my mother's bank. "What's this?" I slit it with my thumb, and pulled out a folded piece of paper. No—a check. For forty thousand dollars. "Oh my god."

"Hey," Griff said as something fluttered out of the envelope. He bent to pick it up. "There's a note."

It was in my mother's hand, on her prim, embossed notepaper. *Audrey— I'm proud of you for completing culinary school. Here is the tuition money I owe you.*

"Holy crap," I whispered. My throat got tight and my eyes hot. That was *twice* my mother said she was proud of me. Maybe she even meant it.

"That's a lot of money, baby. Want to buy some cider?"

I looked up into Griff's teasing eyes, and started to laugh. "Sure. Four dollars a bottle."

"Aw, fuck." He grabbed me into a hug. "No deal, my little corporate raider." He lifted me off the floor and squeezed me.

I buried my face in his beard. "The money is going to come in handy, though. Maybe you won't worry so much."

He set me down, then stepped back, both big hands on my shoulders. "We are going to be fine, princess. The cider will sell—just not all at once like I wanted. Put that money in the bank. Someday you'll have a big plan of your own to carry out. You'll see a building for sale and realize that it ought to become a restaurant called Audrey's. I still want that for you."

"I like how you think, Griff." I stood up on my tiptoes and kissed him.

"Mmm," he said against my lips. "I like how you think, too. But we can't do this right now. I came home to get you so you could say goodbye to Jude."

Oh. "It's time?"

"Yeah. He and Zach tuned up that heap he just bought. And he's loading the trunk now."

"Okay. I'm coming." I tucked my mom's check—and her note, which was even more precious—into my purse. Our living room furniture had been shoved to one side and covered by a tarp while I painted. The little house was pure chaos right now, but I'd been enjoying every moment of making it ours. Our living room walls were becoming a warm cream color, and I'd painted a bookcase sage green. Ruth was going to help me re-upholster the sofa and make throw pillows.

I ducked into the kitchen—which really did need a renovation, but wasn't going to get one anytime soon—to get the cookies I'd made for Jude. They were gingersnaps, his favorite kind.

Grabbing a coat, I followed Griff to his truck. It was a windy November day. The scarecrow Dylan had made to guard the mailbox waved its tattered sleeves in the breeze as we rolled past and up the driveway to the farmhouse. I was going to get to watch all the seasons change. The Green Mountains looked more purple than they had a month ago. Soon they'd be covered in white.

Griff killed the engine beside the ugly old car that Jude had bought for a few hundred dollars cash. My boyfriend gave his head a little shake just looking at it.

"Jude will fix it up," I said, unbuckling my seatbelt.

"Some things can't be fixed," Griff said, his face grave. "I hope he's okay at his dad's in Colebury."

I poked Griff in the ribs. "Look who's a softie."

He turned his rugged face toward me, brown eyes gentle. "Never said I wasn't. Especially for you."

"Aw. Just for that you get a kiss." I scooted closer and put my hands on the sides of his face. Then I planted one on him. He leaned into the kiss, teasing my lip with his tongue. Thank God for our own private little house down the road because we'd both been insatiable since the day I arrived.

Most every night we went to bed early, and not because we were sleepy.

A loud horn blast startled us apart. I looked out the window to see Jude leaning into his car, a hand on the horn, grinning up at us.

Griff opened his door. "All right. Jeez."

"Well I'm waiting for you here, boss. And it's rude to go at it in front of the guy who's gone three years without any."

Beside him, Zachariah blushed, as he often did when sex came up in conversation.

I hopped down from the truck and handed Jude the cookies. "I didn't let Griff eat even one," I promised. "The whole batch is for you."

"I'm still bitter about that," Griff muttered.

"You're the bomb, Audrey." Jude pecked me on the cheek, and I hugged him.

"Take care of yourself, okay?"

"I will."

"You'd better," Ruth said, coming across the lawn,

her arms around a box. "Here's something for breakfast tomorrow. And some wool socks, because it's getting cold."

Jude put a hand up to the back of his neck and stared at his shoes. "Thanks, Mrs. S. I really appreciate it."

"I know you do, dear." She patted his chest. "Keep eating. You look healthier than you did back in July."

He really did. She wasn't wrong.

"Don't forget Thursday Dinner," Ruth said as Jude tucked her offerings onto the backseat of his awful car. "We expect to see you."

"Thank you," he said quietly. But it wasn't the same as saying, *I'll be there.* "Really, thanks for everything." He offered his hand to Griff. "I don't know what I would have done without this job to get me on my feet."

"I don't know what I would have done without the extra set of hands," Griff returned.

Jude shook hands with Zach and accepted a hug from Ruth. The other Shipley siblings were at school today. Kyle had gone back to his parents' place a week ago.

Jude got behind the wheel, wincing when the engine roared to life.

"Needs a muffler," Zach said to no one in particular.

"Needs a lot of things," Jude said out the open window. He smiled, but there was no joy in it.

"Bye honey!" Ruth said, waving. "See you Thursday!"

Jude waved, but made no promises. Then he drove down the drive and disappeared.

We all stood there for a moment, feeling sad. "Zach will be all alone in the bunkhouse," I pointed out.

"S'okay," Zach said. "Are we going to barrel tank number three this afternoon?"

"Yep," Griff said. "Give me two minutes."

Ruth went into the farmhouse and Zach walked away to the cider house. That left Griff and I beside his truck. "You can drive 'er back. We'll have dinner here tonight, okay? Mom made a pot roast."

I could smell it. "Sounds great." Sometimes I cooked for Griff, and sometimes I cooked or merely ate at the farmhouse with the whole family. I couldn't decide which arrangement I liked more. On the one hand, a private meal with Griff occasionally led to kitchen-counter sex. But meals with his big, crazy family were awesome, too. "Do you think we'll see Jude again?" I asked suddenly.

Griff winced. "Hard to say. I think he wants to try to go it alone, you know? He needs to know if he can do it."

My eyes cut over to the driveway, as if Jude were still visible there. "I hope he's going to be all right."

"We all do." Griffin pushed me up against the truck and kissed my neck. "See you in a few hours? I might need you to taste a couple of blends with me tonight."

"Twist my arm," I said, loving the feel of his beard against my cheek.

He skimmed his lips down my neck. "Gotta see if I can balance my bittersweets with the right amount of acid."

"I love it when you want a tasting, baby."

Griff snorted. Then he stepped back. "Get in the truck before I jump you right here in the driveway."

"Fine." I pulled open the door. "But only because it would traumatize your mother and Zach."

He waved as I drove away. And I drove the half mile home to make another batch of gingersnaps for my man.

The End

Don't miss the next books in the

True North Series

Steadfast (Jude's book)

Keepsake (Zach's book)

Also by Sarina Bowen:

The Ivy Years Series

The Gravity Series

The Brooklyn Bruisers Series

86169023R00191

Made in the USA
Columbia, SC
30 December 2017